BULLET BEACH

*PI Deets Shanahan takes on the search
of his lifetime*

When seventy-one-year-old private investigator
Deets Shanahan learns from a snippet of news
on the Internet that his brother (who disappeared when they were kids) could be somewhere
in Thailand, he immediately sets out, accom-
panied by his lover, Maureen, to find his errant
sibling. But it turns out that this is much more
than finding a missing person who wants to stay
missing, and treasure, deceit and murder soon
interrupt their search on the streets of Bangkok
and on the beaches of Phuket...

The Deets Shanahan Mysteries

THE STONE VEIL
THE STEEL WEB
THE IRON GLOVE
THE CONCRETE PILLOW
NICKEL-PLATED SOUL *
PLATINUM CANARY *
GLASS CHAMELEON *
ASPHALT MOON *
BLOODY PALMS *
BULLET BEACH*

*The Carly Paladino and Noah Lang
San Francisco Mysteries*

DEATH IN PACIFIC HEIGHTS *
DEATH IN NORTH BEACH *

*available from Severn House

BULLET BEACH

A Deets Shanahan Mystery

Ronald Tierney

Severn House Large Print
London & New York

This first large print edition published 2014
in Great Britain and the USA by
SEVERN HOUSE PUBLISHERS LTD of
19 Cedar Road, Sutton, Surrey, England, SM2 5DA.
First world regular print edition published 2011 by
Severn House Publishers Ltd., London and New York.

British Library Cataloguing in Publication Data

Tierney, Ronald. author.
  Bullet beach.
  1. Shanahan, Deets (Fictitious character)--Fiction.
  2. Private investigators--Indiana--Indianapolis--
  Fiction. 3. Missing persons--Investigation--Thailand--
  Fiction. 4. Serial murder investigation--Indiana--
  Indianapolis--Fiction. 5. Detective and mystery stories.
  6. Large type books.
  I. Title
  813.5'4-dc23

ISBN-13: 9780727897084

Severn House Publishers support the Forest Stewardship Council™
[FSC™], the leading international forest certification organisation. All
our titles that are printed on FSC certified paper carry the FSC logo.

MIX
Paper from
responsible sources
FSC® C013056

Printed and bound in Great Britain by
T J International, Padstow, Cornwall.

ACKNOWLEDGEMENTS

Sincere appreciation for the contributions from my brothers Richard and Ryan and from David Anderson, Jovanne Reilly and Karen Watt.

Dedicated to Lost Brothers

'I live my life as if every moment precedes my death by seconds.'

Fritz Shanahan

ONE

If Dietrich Shanahan didn't make the trip now, odds were diminishing that he ever would. For a man of seventy-two, he was in pretty fair condition. His organs worked – most of them, most of the time. He was agile enough to putter in the garden and had enough endurance to take his dog Casey on long, brisk walks. He could make the overseas trip pretty easily, but who knows how much longer that would be the case. True, his mind was slipping a bit. That particular facet of aging seemed to accelerate after a bullet made its way through his thick skull not that long ago.

The incident had him clinging to life, something he hadn't had that much affection for until, in his late sixties, he met Maureen and living became meaningful. Though he would never tell anyone this – he wasn't given to sentimentality – she made life worthwhile. Only she. If she were gone there would be no point.

Maureen, a couple of decades younger, was beautiful, smart, fearless, funny and hungry. Almost always hungry. Hagan Daz Swiss

Almond Vanilla was a better gift than diamonds. Dinner at a nice restaurant and she was happy for a week. He had no idea what she was doing with him. While he considered himself unfairly fortunate, he wasn't about to ask her why. That would only screw it up.

From the bathroom, even with the door closed, he could hear her doing her morning routine, slippered feet padding about the hallway's hardwood floor, then hushing away in the distance as she went to the kitchen. He'd been up for a while, long before she climbed out of bed. He had his own routine. He'd fed the ancient, bony cat, Einstein, and let his sixty-pound, spotted and speckled Catahoula hound out the back for his morning constitutional. A little breakfast and coffee as he read the morning paper.

He dropped his razor and in his search noticed the cap of the toothpaste further over by the bathtub. He kicked the razor toward the cap so that he'd have to bend over just once. What laziness he thought. He noticed his embarrassment as he glanced at his own image in the mirror.

Shanahan was feeling a little self-conscious, a new and foreign feeling. He'd decided to grow a beard for the first time in his long life. He'd always thought them pretentious, but he was going where no one knew him – another continent altogether. And in some way he didn't quite understand he wanted to see without being seen.

Maureen was coming with him on the trip. He knew the reason she was coming with him. She wanted to make sure he was all right. She wouldn't admit it because if she did he wouldn't allow her to come along. And he wouldn't ask her if that was the reason because he didn't like the idea of her lying. It was one of those compromises he learned to make late in life.

On the other hand, she was the one who suggested he go. It was her idea to exorcise – out of the many he had been forced to confront – the remaining ghost in his life.

'Did you sleep well?' Shanahan asked Maureen as he came into the kitchen. She washed some blueberries to put into her yogurt.

'I always sleep well,' she said, grinning. 'A guiltless conscience.'

'That's telling.'

'Telling what?' She had that look.

Perhaps he could pull it back.

'That you are an angel.'

'Ah,' she smiled, 'very good.' She wore tan slacks and one of Shanahan's old, white shirts, open two buttons at the collar. Her auburn hair caught a bit of morning light that angled through the window. 'You are much more agile in the word department than you were when I first met you,' she said.

That was true. And to further show what he'd learned, he kept quiet.

9

She looked down, stepped over the sleeping cat, and headed toward the coffee maker. Einstein had found the sunlight as well and sprawled in the warm spot it made on the floor. If cat years were the same as dog years, Einstein was one hundred and twenty-six. The vet called him an 'elderly gentleman.' Though he moved slowly and his bones sometimes made him look like a walking tent, there was an enduring elegance to the old tom.

'We should get to the airport by ten thirty. The plane leaves at midnight,' she said.

Shanahan went outside. In a few hours, the air would thicken and the temperature would climb. It was best to get the watering in early. Otherwise, he'd have to wait until evening. August was to summer as March was to spring – ugly months. Were there the Ides of August? It wasn't all that much better in Thailand in August. He and Maureen could expect hot, humid days in between the monsoons, he thought.

He unwound the hose and pulled it toward the big beds of lilies and iris. Both the irises and the peonies, down a slight embankment, were on their last legs. The growing season for most of the plants in the garden was over. Maintenance seemed to be the challenge – prolonging life, he thought as his thumb on the nozzle produced a fine spray that danced a bit in the air before falling toward the ground.

No dreams of Fritz last night. But his brother permeated his thoughts. Sometimes it was hard to tell which thoughts came from actual memories and which were dreams. Could be both, entangled somewhere in the complex circuits of the brain. But the dreams of Fritz vexed him, resurrected a tremendous guilt. He wasn't one, he thought, to dwell in the past. But here it was. Whatever madness possessed him to find out about his brother after sixty years was intensifying. And there was a race now – to find Fritz Shanahan before one of them died.

He moved the spray, the low sun creating various rainbows in the mist. The air was heavy and made the morning quiet and still. The quiet was eventually breached. A wife shouted something to her husband. Shanahan looked down the slope of the slight hill his home rested upon, through a break in the scraggly trees and across the creek to the street on the other side. A man in a gray suit climbed into a late model Hyundai. The man yelled back. Casey, nearly as old as Einstein, was awakened by the noise and noticed a trespasser. He made a half-hearted effort to catch the squirrel, turning the event into more of a scolding than a murder attempt. Quiet, still again except for the sound of the water coming out of the hose.

It was a long shot, Shanahan believed, trying to find his brother. The news article in an English-language Thai newspaper was two years old. Maureen found it on the Internet. The para-

11

graph was just one item in a compilation of recent crimes.

American expatriate Fritz Shanahan, 68, was released yesterday when witnesses failed to show up for a trial. Shanahan, under investigation for smuggling, had been arrested for assault and battery in January.

Two years ago. That would make this seventy-year-old Fritz Shanahan the right age. Could there be two seventy-year-old Fritz Shanahans in the world? After days of searching Maureen could find nothing more of old Fritz. Yet it was enough for a plan. A silly plan Shanahan was inclined to think. Even if Fritz was still alive and still in Bangkok, finding him wouldn't be easy.

Maureen tapped the horn lightly as she backed her Toyota down the driveway. He turned, waved. She was off to pick up some things for the trip and she would stop by the realtor's office to make sure her clients were being covered in her absence. She was gone for the day. He was on his own.

The bar was empty. Harry, the owner, sat at the far end, face in his hands. He looked up as Shanahan approached. He shook his head and was quiet for a moment.

'Growin' a soup catcher, Jesus Christ, Deets, what in the hell is wrong with you?'

'Thought I'd see what it looks like.'

'Looks like hell, that's what it looks like. You get yourself a grocery cart too? I got a razor around here somewhere. You can shave it off in the men's room.'

'Now that I've got your opinion, I guess I'll keep it.'

'You know, you've been actin' strange for awhile now. Sixty years drinkin' the same beer and then you just change to Guinness. Just like that.'

'Sixty years?'

'What?'

'You saying I started drinking at twelve?'

Harry laughed. 'Look at this, will you? Just look around. You know what happened to my customers?'

Shanahan shook his head 'no', pulled up a stool a couple down from Harry. Harry got up, ducked under the bar and found a bottle of Guinness for Shanahan.

'Dead,' Harry said. 'That's what happened.'

'You kill 'em?' Shanahan asked.

Harry set the bottle in front of Shanahan and went to the back bar to pour him a shot of J.W. Dant bourbon.

'No, I didn't kill 'em,' he said.

'I was thinking the stew did it. You never got it right.'

'No,' Harry said, suppressing a grin. 'My stew didn't kill anybody. Might have made 'em wish they were dead, but it didn't kill 'em.

13

What I'm sayin' is that they're all dying off, or moving some place where the sun takes the chill off their bones or where people look after them. Nobody left in the neighborhood. Not even much of a neighborhood left.'

Harry was right, though he wouldn't tell him that. It wasn't the same neighborhood and it wasn't the same times. People didn't go to neighborhood bars and drink the afternoon away anymore. Not like they used to, anyway. It had been happening little by little, year by year. And finally, Harry noticed.

'It's the end of an era,' Harry said. 'I can't make it here anymore.'

He couldn't. Used to be that there'd be three shifts of men coming into the bar each day. An old, early crowd – sometimes a few women with them. They went home just about the time the younger blue-collar workers came in after work. And there'd be the late night guys. Guys. Mostly guys – many of them like Shanahan was at the time, drinking a few beers to while away time they didn't know how else to fill. Shanahan thought of it as God's waiting room.

'The lease is up first of the year.' Harry shrugged and it seemed to say that to continue was futile.

'Oh crap, Harry.' There wasn't anything Shanahan could say. He'd like to say something a little more sympathetic, but he couldn't get it out and even if he could Harry would be uncomfortable. They'd known each other for

14

decades and never said anything nice to each other, nothing consoling certainly.

'Well enough of the schmaltzy stuff,' Harry said, poking at Shanahan's beard. 'What's with you and your friend there?'

'Going to go look for my brother.'

'Your brother?'

'Yep.'

'Didn't know you had one.'

'Practically speaking, I guess I don't.'

'You're not making sense again.'

'One night when I was young some people came and took my brother away. Never saw him again.'

'And you're just now getting' around to lookin' for him?' Harry asked, suddenly animated with frustration. Shanahan would call Harry 'excitable.'

'Slipped my mind,' Shanahan said. There was no point going into it. It was hard enough for Shanahan to understand. Why had he waited so long? Why was his mind dredging it all up? Why was it so important now? 'How about another shot?'

'Where are you looking?'

'Start in Bangkok?'

'Thailand?' Harry looked shocked.

Shanahan nodded.

'When?'

'Tonight,' Shanahan said.

'And just when were you plannin' on tellin' me?' Harry asked, wide-eyed.

15

'About now.'

Harry shook his head.

'And Maureen?' he asked.

'She's going too.'

'Why on earth would she go on that kind of trip with you?'

'Brand new menu.'

Shanahan looked down the empty bar, shook his head. While things were slowing down for Harry, they were speeding up for Shanahan. He had a lot to do before the search for Fritz actually began.

After they switched planes in Chicago, Maureen and Shanahan would be off on a quiet, five-hour flight to San Francisco. The plan was to freshen up at a cheap hotel in San Francisco, spend a little time with Shanahan's son, daughter in-law, and a grandson for brunch and catch another late night flight to Hong Kong. From Hong Kong to Bangkok, last known address for a Fritz Shanahan.

TWO

Howie Cross never thought of himself as having a Good Samaritan-type personality. He tried to do the right thing, if he knew what it was, in any given situation; but he hadn't spent his life doing good things for people as a matter of course. True, he'd been thrown off the police force because he had trouble putting people away for possession of marijuana and he disliked the idea of hassling prostitutes who had entered that life willingly. Unfortunately these weren't the qualities the Indianapolis Metropolitan Police Department wanted in a vice cop. On the other hand he wasn't volunteering at a soup kitchen or carrying a protest sign.

Lately, though, he was drawn in to these sorts of things. He had decided to take care of an orphan, originally thought to be his. Even though she wasn't he had grown to love her and felt the need to protect her. He spent weekends with her at his parents', where the young girl lived now, and where he began to repair his folks' aging, teetering farmhouse. Now he was taking his friend – and in some ways mentor – Deets Shanahan and his companion Maureen to the airport. He had also volunteered to take care of Shanahan's dog and cat. They weren't happy about the change in scenery, but they were familiar with it and would adapt.

Was there a Saint Howie, he wondered, hidden under his Peter Pan complex? He laughed in his empty car. After dropping the animals at his house and Maureen and Shanahan at the airport, he headed toward the Eastside where he would pick up Slurpy. The two of them would drive a little further east and then north to pick up a repo Lincoln near 21st and Drexel. No Saint Howie, he concluded. If there was some sort of post-life justice system, his worries were simply about which rung of hell he'd occupy for eternity.

It wasn't quite midnight, when Cross found Slurpy at Slurpy's home away from home. He was sitting on the steps at the bar's rear exit staring out into the parking lot.

'Hey Slurp,' Cross said as the huge guy climbed into the passenger seat. Cross could feel the car dip to that side. Slurpy slammed the door shut. It wasn't an angry gesture. It was just the way he did things. Slurpy wasn't a bad guy. He was a little slow, seemed to have to be told everything twice and tended to behave as if all problems had physical solutions. This unfortunate set of characteristics and his – Cross guessed – three hundred and forty-five pound body made him unpredictable and extremely formidable.

'Hey,' he said solemnly. 'You said there's fifty in it.'

'Yep.' Cross said, putting his Audi loaner in gear and getting back on the street. 'And all you got to do is follow me to the car lot and I'll drop you back here.'

'You doing the jackin'?'

'Yep. Only, it's called repossessing.'

'Whatever.'

This would be easy. Cross had already picked up a duplicate set of keys, keys kept by Irving Edelman, owner of the car lot from which the Lincoln was bought. Edelman was clever; he always kept a set of keys when he financed the loan. This allowed quick and easy entry, a quick getaway and best of all, no car alarm. It was to be an evening of surprises starting when Cross picked up the keys. He had caught Edelman pulling a bottle of vodka from behind a huge sailfish mounted on the wall over a tattered sofa. Cross had stepped too lightly into the darkened office. His sudden presence startled Edelman, who quickly shut his now not so secret compartment.

Cross didn't find the next surprise nearly as funny. The night was faintly lit by a half moon and there was a little light spill from a street-lamp on 21st Street. Cross could identify the silver Lincoln Town Car. He parked the Audi down the street, told Slurpy to get in the driver's seat and wait until Cross pulled out.

Slurpy would follow.

One might think that it was cooler outside during evening hours. But it was like turning the light out in the oven. Perspiration gathered on Cross's neck.

He looked up and down the street lined with two-bedroom, post-World War Two bungalows. A few lights were on, but shades were drawn. No one was out walking and there was the steady hum of air conditioners to muffle any sounds on the street.

Cross had no sooner slipped into the leather seats and put the key in the ignition than he sensed a presence. At first he thought it must be Slurpy and some silly question. But it wasn't Slurpy. It was a slender figure, face hidden in the darkness, the light from the Lincoln's interior glancing off the shotgun.

'It's the Cartier Edition,' the man said. His voice was both light and full of gravel. It had almost a breathless quality. 'The Lincoln, a special edition. Lived all my life to have a car like this. It's not new, but it's really sweet. Nothing has made me happier.'

'It's beautiful,' Cross said.

'And you can't have it. It's mine,' the man said.

'You know, I'm just doing my job. Seems as if you've missed a few payments. I'm sure you can work this out, but in the meantime...'

'In the meantime, get outta my car.' The man had a shotgun.

'I can do that.' As nice as it was, Cross wasn't going to put his life on the line for a Lincoln Town Car.

A third voice entered the conversation, this one behind the man with the shotgun.

'Fair warning, fool. I'm gonna snap your neck you don't put down that piece.'

'I don't think you've got the picture just right,' the man said. 'You make one move, your friend doesn't have a head.'

'Listen Slurpy, we can...' Coming back the next day with the sheriff wasn't a big deal. Dying was. Cross's attempt at pacification was about to fail.

'Hey,' Slurpy said, interrupting, 'my friend here? We ain't that close.'

Slurpy reached around and took the shotgun from the man's hands. He turned the slender man around and gave him a shove. The man fell back on his butt in the street. The guy was in a suit. In the dim light, Cross couldn't tell whether he was a light-skinned black or a dark-skinned white. He was between forty and sixty. Maybe.

Shotgun in hand, Slurpy walked back to the Audi.

Cross climbed in the driver's seat of the Lincoln.

'Look at it this way. You could have been arrested,' Cross told the man.

The guy got up and Cross drove off. He checked the rearview mirror to see the Audi headlights. Slurpy was moving in behind him.

Things turned out all right. But Cross wasn't happy with Slurpy's intervention. It worked this time. But the danger was unnecessary especially when the stakes were so low.

Cross hit the interstate off Emerson and exited on Washington where Edelman had his car lot. The car was a dream. Unfortunately it wasn't a smart car for a private investigator. It stood out. Better for a lawyer. Or a pimp.

Even on this short little multi-lane jaunt, hitting a cruising speed and riding for a distance without stoplights relaxed him, let him gather his thoughts. And what were his thoughts tonight, he asked himself. The thoughts he had were about himself. They were the same as they often were: about how his life was a continuous loop, a short loop because he was going no-where. He was marking time. He wasn't getting wealthier. He wasn't falling in love. He wasn't having fun, particularly. He was in the same place he was ten years ago and it was the same place he'd be ten years from now. Cross felt no sadness. It was a cold assessment of his life. And after reviewing the situation he did what he always did. He shrugged. Better than being dead. Better than being in prison.

He pulled into the lot and then behind the buildings. The instructions were to leave it in the locked garage behind the office. The previous owner might return to reclaim his car, so keeping it off the lot and behind locked doors was advisable. He'd collect from Edelman tomorrow or take it out in trade – another loaner off the lot when the time was right. The deal prevented all those complicated tax calculations.

The light from the Audi caught him and illuminated the garage door. Slurpy remained in the car. Cross opened the garage door and got back in the Lincoln. He was about to pull it in the garage when he saw the red and blue flashing lights coming in behind the Audi. Cross wasn't worried until the sirens began and there were more lights. Cross got out of the car and – being familiar with how jumpy cops can be, especially at night – raised his hands immediately and waited for instructions, which he was inclined to follow to the letter. But his stomach sank as he realized Slurpy was in the Audi. Worse, Slurpy was in there with a shotgun.

'Get down on your knees,' said the voice behind the lights now aiming at him. Cross did. 'Now lay down on your belly.' Cross did. He was tempted as anyone would be to ask for some sort of explanation or to tell them who he was. But he knew better than most that this wasn't the time for anything other than doing what you were told. He'd have time to show them his license and explain their presence on the car lot past midnight. He understood. They had to secure the scene. 'Now put your hands behind your head and keep them there. Make no moves.' Cross followed instructions.

'You!' came the voice. 'You in the car.'

Cross couldn't see what was happening.

'Get out of the car slowly, keep your hands where we can see them.'

'I want a lawyer.'

Cross recognized Slurpy's voice.

'Jesus,' Cross said to himself. He had a bad feeling.

'Get out of the car slowly, keep your hands where we can see them.'

This was going down by the book.

'Go fuck yourself,' Slurpy said.

'Do as you're told, Slurpy,' Cross yelled.

'This is the last time we will tell you. Get out of the car slowly, keep your hands where we can see them.'

Cross heard the car door open.

'Now get down on your knees,' the same voice said.

'We didn't do nothing,' Slurpy said.

'Get down on your knees.'

'Do as you're told,' Cross repeated.

'We didn't do nothing, Cross.'

He heard the dogs now. The barking was louder, angrier, it seemed. What followed was serious gunfire. Cross couldn't count the shots. He was sure some were simultaneous.

After several minutes – it seemed like hours to Cross – he was searched and pulled to his feet. He saw Slurpy's body on the ground, face up. One of the cops was holding the shotgun.

Cross figured it out. Slurpy had pulled the gun out, maybe in response to the onslaught of the police dogs.

Could the night get any worse? 'That was so unnecessary,' Cross said to the cop standing beside him.

The cop didn't respond.

There must have been two dozen uniforms on the scene. They were searching the Audi and a couple of them had moved to the Lincoln Town Car. The trunk was popped from the inside.

'Over here,' a uniform said.

Cross was close enough to see what the cop wanted the others to see. A body. Probably dead, Cross thought. It could get worse. It just did.

He was led to the back of a police cruiser and put in the back seat. His hands were cuffed behind him so he couldn't scratch the inevitable itch above his right eye and he couldn't get comfortable. Not all the cops were busy now. Most of them were standing around, but no one was talking to him. No one asked him questions. He thought they ought to be full of questions.

From the back window, Cross had a view of the action when it came. The medical examiner's team arrived and passed by him, red, white and blue lines flashing on the white clothing. So many times, too many times crime scenes looked like carnivals or celebrations.

Then, in time, Cross knew why no one asked

him anything. A late model, shiny, black Ford Victoria pulled up. From a rear door a tall, black man stepped out with the demeanor and the look of a celebrity. Cross knew him. The man's grandmother would have called him Maurice Collins. But others would refer to him as Lieutenant Collins, perhaps Ace if they were truly close to him. He was the hotshot on the homicide team.

Collins talked with a couple of uniforms, was taken to the body in the trunk. He took a look around the Town Car and then the body. He talked to someone with the medical team. He did all this patiently, it seemed to Cross – taking his time, taking it all in.

Finally, he turned to look in Cross's direction. He walked slowly toward him and as he closed in Cross saw his impeccably white and starched shirt, open at the collar and his expensive dark suit. The man wasn't smiling. But he wasn't angry either. His face was blank, uncommitted.

The lieutenant opened the door and motioned for Cross to get out. Cross did, awkwardly because of the cuffs. Collins grabbed an arm to steady him. Collins unlocked the cuffs and motioned again, this time for Cross to follow.

They went to the back of the Town Car. It wasn't just one corpse, but two, one of each gender. As the flashlight danced over the bodies, it was clear that they were wet from roughly the waist down, higher on her.

'You know them?'

26

Cross saw what appeared to be a young man and woman – maybe in their twenties.

'No. You?'

Collins smiled.

'I will. What in the hell are you doing hanging out with Slurpy Thurman?' It was said calmly.

'I needed a hand,' Cross said.

'What kind of hand?'

'I needed a driver. I pick up a repo. Slurpy follows in my car.'

Collins nodded, guided Cross back to the un-marked Crown Victoria.

'I didn't think I'd see you so soon.'

'That was the plan,' Cross said. 'How'd the police know to come here?'

'Someone saw you guys in the lot in the mid-dle of the night. Thought it was suspicious.'

'Not true,' Cross said. 'You sent half the police force.'

'All right, anonymous tip. Said we'd find bodies in the back of a silver luxury car. Killers were at the car lot.'

That made sense to Cross. He nodded in the direction of Slurpy's corpse.

'That didn't have to happen.'

Collins gave him a sharp look.

'Is that why you're being nice to me?' Cross continued.

'Am I?'

'Seems like it.'

'You complaining?'

'Worried,' Cross said. 'I always worry when a

cop is nice to me.'

'About Slurpy, he was living on borrowed time. If he didn't have a massive heart attack some gang banger would kill him in a bar fight. You have any idea how many times he was arrested?'

Cross didn't answer. He knew the police didn't want any trouble with the police shooting. Collins nodded toward the back seat. Cross climbed in. Collins followed.

'What happened tonight? Tell me everything.'

Cross did, and when he was done, Collins leaned forward and told the uniformed driver something and they drove off. The driver also said something into his mic.

'We're going to have to keep you overnight,' Collins said. 'Otherwise it looks like I'm soft on you. You should go ahead and call a lawyer. You still run around with that biker? Kowalski?'

'I know him. He'd be my pick.'

'You're a funny guy,' Collins said.

'Is that a compliment?'

'No, funny as in odd. What are you doing with your life?'

'I'm getting by.'

Collins shrugged, shook his head. 'You hang out with strange people, that's all.'

Cross knew what he was getting at. Cross had fallen in love or lust or obsession, whatever it was, with an exotic dancer who turned out to be a murderer. Cross was friends with what the police thought was a trouble-making old private eye. And in the thick of it was a trouble-making, Harley-riding defense attorney. 'Why don't you like normal people?'

'You want to do dinner and catch a movie later?'

Collins laughed. 'I think you'd be going from bad to worse.'

There were about ten minutes of silence, Collins sitting in the back of the car with seeming immense patience. The car pulled up in front of a house on Drexel. The same house. Two cop cars pulled up beside them. Four uniformed police officers in flak jackets with serious weapons approached the house, two in front, two toward the back. In moments, a short, chubby black man was on the front lawn. An equally chubby black woman was outside on the porch. The porch light and the shadows might have exaggerated the look of horror on her face.

Collins and Cross remained in the car.

'That him?' Collins asked.

'No,' Cross said.

'That was quick.'

'Couldn't be more different.'

Collins looked down, rubbed his hands together.

'Wait here,' he said and went out to talk with the stunned man in a sleeveless tee shirt and boxer shorts.

THREE

Shanahan was not superstitious. The only signs he accepted as true were the literal ones – dead end, sharp turn, no parking. So he was surprised at the softening of the walls of his rules of reality. The dreams about Fritz took him to new places, places perhaps opened when a bullet traumatized his brain, making new pathways. Just as Maureen had come along and brought new life, the bullet came along to remind him the world was still a mysterious and dangerous place. And it was clear he was being driven on this venture by something that was altogether unclear.

Here he was now in the cool and cramped interior of a silver tube sliding through space to another world. Maureen was asleep beside him. A couple of rum and tonics and she was blissfully unaware of anything in the conscious world. He pulled the blanket up over her shoulder and around her neck. He sat back and closed his eyes. He would recount what led to this trip, this moment, until he fell asleep.

It began when he rummaged through old photographs. He came upon several small black and white photographs of his childhood. There was one of a young Dietrich Shanahan. The boy was looking at something off camera. But it wasn't entirely off. There was part of a leg showing in the lower right hand corner of the picture – a leg kicked up behind. Someone running, as if trying to escape. It was his brother Fritz.

And it was true in some fashion. Fritz had suddenly disappeared when he was maybe eight years old. And the boy was not an acceptable topic of conversation. Before he disappeared, Shanahan had hazy memories of the boy being shut in a room, of a doctor coming and going, sad faces in shadowy light. And he remembered a somber evening when a big, black Hudson pulled up in front of the house. That was an event in itself. And Fritz was taken out to the car. Shanahan remembered Fritz taking one last look back. That was the end of it. It was truly the end of it. Fritz had been purged from Shanahan's mind until he saw the photograph. His parents had missed it, this little piece of Fritz, proving his existence.

About a year ago, perhaps a little longer, the dreams came – Fritz running through hallways, hiding, going up stairways, teasing Shanahan. It was hide and seek with a sinister edge. If it was a game, it wasn't fun.

Shanahan opened his eyes. He looked around the coach. So quiet. It was pleasantly dark, except for a scattering of lights for those trying to read and a bluish light that came from TV sets mounted on the back of seats. There were those who could not sleep and didn't want to think. He thought about turning on the set in front of him, but decided against it. Perhaps he should try to remember his brother, his personality. Maybe something like that would provide some insight into what he was like now. What he could remember.

His brother dove into the slick surface of the night water. The skinny kid screamed with happiness until he penetrated the glass-like sheet of water. Shanahan waited on the dirt ridge that surrounded the pond. He waited to see if it was all right, whether or not some monster resided there, gobbling up boys who swam at night. Given his druthers, Shanahan would prefer to poke around the water with a stick before getting in.

The air was sweltering hot as it can be on only a few midsummer evenings in Wisconsin.

His brother, in the moonlight, was pale as the porcelain on the bathroom sink as he climbed from the water, up the dirt mound toward Shanahan.

'C'mon, Dietrich. You gotta do more than look in this life,' Fritz said, shaking off the water. 'You got to live.' He laughed. 'There are no sharks in there. Anyway that's why I'm here. To protect you. And you to protect me. OK?'

Shanahan said nothing.

'We gotta protect each other,' Fritz said.

32

Shanahan felt as if he was diving into a pool now. He sensed the danger.

'Your son was sure happy to see you,' Maureen said, eyes opening as a few streams of light came through windows where shades had not been completely drawn. Morning was coming.

The word 'son' had an odd sound to Shanahan.

'I didn't have much to say.'

'You never have much to say. They don't mind.'

The lunch had gone well. Son, son's wife, son's son were there. Wine was sipped. The five of them walked across the Great Highway to Ocean Beach. They weathered the wind, the blowing sand that bit at them, watched the kite flyers who ran around with boundless energy, who were undaunted by the treacherous drafts of air.

His grandson, now a young man, was bright and warm. He encouraged them to come spend some time with them in wine country. Shanahan remembered how Maureen's eyes brightened at the suggestion.

'I'm glad we stayed over a day,' Maureen said.

'Me too,' Shanahan said. The stay-over broke up the dreary, prison-like hours in the plane. The airlines, it seemed to Shanahan who remembered when flying was something elegant, were doing their best to make their trips unpleasant.

Cross didn't get out the next morning. He spent an additional night. Lieutenant Collins backed off his initial offer when it was clear that the man who lived in the house on Drexel and who owned the Lincoln Town Car wasn't the man who supposedly came upon them with a shotgun. This, said Collins, destroyed the time line. This meant Cross and Slurpy had hours to set all this up – find the victims, shoot them, and attempt to hide them in a locked garage on East Washington.

'One lie,' Collins said, 'that's all it takes for me.'

James Fenimore Kowalski finally got him out by threatening to sue for wrongful death on behalf of Slurpy Thurman, which he thought he might do anyway. Slurpy, Kowalksi contended, had a well-below average IQ, and, not knowing there was a body in the trunk, was merely retrieving the shotgun, which was probably true.

The police were edgy. On one hand, they had to stand behind the shooting no matter what. Deny, deny, deny that firing was premature and that they were not really threatened. It was likely that most of the likely interest groups would support the police. On the other hand, the police weren't eager to make it a public debate and Collins didn't believe that Cross shot a couple of young people and threw them in a trunk.

Kowalski made bail for Cross and stopped by Cross's place to take care of Shanahan's dog and cat as he had done the night before.

'You know a five-year-old could pick that lock,' Kowalksi said.

'Have to be that old, you think?' Cross asked. They went to Harry's bar on Tenth and sat in a booth at the back.

'Where's Shanahan?' Kowalski asked.

'In Thailand. Either fried or drowned.'

'Sounds like boiled to me.' Kowalski wasn't as big as he looked. He was probably just six-foot, and no more than 200 pounds. But he had a large head and it looked like it was cut from granite. He had jagged features, long black hair with silver streaks, swept back. He looked like he was moving when he wasn't. He always wore a black suit, a white shirt, no tie, and motorcycle boots. It was the same whether he was riding his Harley or arguing in court.

'So he went, after all?'

'You knew?' Cross said.

'I know he wanted the name of a guide, but I didn't know when – or what it was all about, for that matter.'

Though Shanahan probably wouldn't have minded Kowalski knowing, the younger detective knew the older one kept things to himself.

'What do we do now?' Kowalski asked, sipping a glass of bourbon.

'Find out who set me up.'

'Is that what you think happened?'

Cross nodded. 'I don't know if it was personal. I mean I don't know if someone wanted to set *me* up. But that someone wanted to set someone up. It was good.'

Kowalski sat back, looked up to catch Harry's attention. He lifted his glass, indicating another. Cross still had half a beer.

'Think about it. They steal a car. Kill people. Put them in a car and park in the same spot they stole it from.'

'How often do people check the trunk of their car unless there's an emergency?'

'Until it smells,' Cross said. 'Even then time has passed.'

Kowalksi nodded again, thanked Harry for the refill.

'You coming along when you did was just a coincidence?' Kowalksi continued.

'Was it?' Cross shrugged. 'I don't know. But if it was part of a plan, then they are even smarter. In addition to the clever plan to abandon the bodies, they set up a murder suspect. It forces the police in a direction other than the killer's. If nothing else, it complicates the case.'

'Is anybody that good?'

One of the bodies had been identified, Cross told Kowalksi. A Marshall Talbot, 26. He lived in Woodruff Place. The body of a young woman was not identified or just not revealed. The only other thing Cross knew was that the man whose car was repossessed was Wilbert Morgan. He worked as a bank guard and was one of several laid off after various buy-outs, consolidations, and bankruptcies. Because he lost his job, he was about to lose his car. And he wasn't the man who came upon Cross with the shotgun.

'Let me know if I can help,' Kowalksi said. 'In fact, just let me help.'

'I can't afford you.'

'Oh I'm in it for the satisfaction, mostly. I'd like to find the bastards who killed a couple of kids.'

'You said "mostly."'

'Yeah, well I got to keep you out of trouble. You could become expensive and you don't offer any fringe benefits.'

Cross took a sip of beer, surveyed the dark, empty bar. He needed to get out of there, get someplace cheerful or at least distracting. The thought he was about to share came out of the blue and he was ashamed that it took him so long to figure it out.

'James?' Cross said.

'Yes, dear.'

'They knew it was me.'

'What?'

'The guy was there. Waiting. Ready to set me up. He had to know I was coming.'

'Maybe he just knew someone was coming.'

'I'm the only one Edelman sends on repos.'

'Why is that?'

'He doesn't have that much work that he needs a posse. And we have a deal to keep it off the books. I don't report it as tax income. He

37

doesn't have to go through all that reporting. I get some cash to pay someone like Thurman. I get a car off the lot. Works out well. So Edelman knew who was going to pick up the Town Car.'

There were things to do, but it was too late to do them. Tomorrow Cross would pay a visit to Edelman and to the man who owned the Town Car.

Shanahan thought there was something antiseptic about such trips – from the narrow impersonal space of the plane to the vast impersonal space of the airports. That set up the shock of the real, teeming world outside – the sudden overwhelming heat, the buzzing swarms of motor scooters, the toxic smell of exhaust. He could see the air. That couldn't be good.

'We're here,' Maureen said cheerfully after a moment registering the impact of reality.

'We are,' Shanahan said. He had arranged for a guide to meet them at the hotel and was told that he should take a taxi from the airport. 'The tuk-tuks are fun if you are twelve,' the man said. 'The taxis are air conditioned.'

A small orange Toyota with a Buddha dangling from the rearview mirror made itself available. Baggage was stuffed in the front and in the trunk and Maureen and Shanahan were stuffed in the back seat. Off they went, eventually entering an even greater density of humanity.

* * *

In maybe half an hour, Maureen and Shanahan were checking into a pleasant, very inexpensive hotel. A slender, well but comfortably dressed, fortyish man, who had lingered about the desk, introduced himself.

As Shanahan struggled with the name, the man smiled. 'Use Channarong.'

'Deets,' Maureen said, pointing to Shanahan. Then to herself, 'Maureen.'

'Maureen and Deets, nice to meet you. I am your guide if you like.'

'Let me find someone to get the bags upstairs and then we'll talk,' Shanahan said.

'You going to tell the little lady to go sit by the pool,' Maureen said, 'while you go do guy stuff?'

'I'm sorry, I thought you might like to freshen up?'

'Do I need to?'

'Just a question. Trying to be thoughtful.'

Maureen's eyes half shut and she grinned just a little. She nodded.

'I've just been played,' she said to Channarong.

He nodded, face giving away nothing.

'We're going to grab a drink...' Shanahan looked at Channarong.

'Trolley's. Outside to the right. A couple of doors down.'

'That the name of the bar or are you suggesting I go for a ride?' Maureen asked.

'Name of the bar.'

A young man had put the baggage on a cart and he and Maureen headed for the elevator.

Shanahan followed Channarong back out into the heavy hot air. The noise of the city kept them from speaking until they were inside a bar – one that looked as if it could be back in Indianapolis. Clean, lots of wood, a wide-screen TV over the bar. Shanahan ordered a beer and got something in a green bottle with an elephant logo. Channarong drank water. Shanahan was perspiring, even after that short walk. Channarong wasn't.

'Mr Kowalski speaks highly of you.'

'He is a very interesting man,' Channarong said. 'Very good to people. Getting someone out of a jail here is not so easy unless you know how to talk to people. Your friend picked up on local customs very quickly.'

'I take it you know the city.'

'All my life.'

'The rest of the country?'

'Some places better than others.'

'What is your relationship with the police?' Shanahan asked.

'I was an officer at one time.'

'No longer.'

'No.'

'Why?' Shanahan asked.

'Political.'

'They don't like you?'

'I have many friends as well as enemies. If I

40

may ask, what are you doing here that you are worried about the police?'

Shanahan shook his head. 'Probably no worries. Missing person.'

'Daughter, son?'

'Brother.'

Channarong nodded. 'He did something bad to you?'

'No. Just trying to find him.'

'Pardon me, but does he owe you money?'

'You have good questions. No.'

'You have a picture?'

'No. Haven't seen him in sixty years. I have no idea what he looks like. Probably a little like me – maybe heavier, maybe not, maybe taller, maybe shorter.'

The guide smiled a mischievous smile.

'I know. We all look alike anyway.'

'I wouldn't have said that,' Channarong said.

'No, I suspect you wouldn't have said it out loud.' Shanahan took a sip of his beer. The lighter Thai beer was perfect for the hot weather. 'One more thing, would you consider looking into something before tomorrow. Begin today, is what I'm saying. Can you?'

Channarong nodded.

Shanahan reached into his pants pocket, pulled out a folded piece of paper. He unfolded it, handed it to the guide. As he read it, Shanahan continued.

'I need to know what my brother was accused of smuggling and any other details you can find

41

out about the case. Who did he hit? Who arrested him? Has he been brought up on charges
since then? Is there a home address in there
anywhere?'

Channarong nodded again, looked at his
watch. 'Yes, I can probably find that out. I need
to get started right away.' He took another sip of
water and bowed slightly to Maureen who had
arrived as he prepared to leave.

'I hope I didn't frighten him away,' Maureen
smiled.

'He couldn't withstand the power of your
beauty.'

'That must be it. I can barely stand it myself.'

FOUR

Howie Cross was a problem for the police. That was how James Fenimore Kowalski explained it to Cross as they headed for breakfast at Dufour's in Irvington. There wasn't enough to hold Cross, the attorney told him, but it was 'plenty bad enough.' Not only were there bodies in the trunk of a car he was driving, it appeared he and his dead accomplice were trying to hide the victims in a garage at the back of a used car lot in the middle of the night. What the police really needed was to have a wall of evidence or a witness to the shooting or at least a clear motive to hold him because if he were found not guilty then Slurpy's sloppy death would be a dark cloud.

'So,' Kowalksi said, 'you are under suspicion, deep suspicion, but are free to go.'

'At the moment.'

'Very much at the moment. Did you know you're eating at an historic spot?' Kowalski said, reading the menu. 'Used to be a drugstore and it was robbed by John Dillinger in 1933 says here. Cross and Dillinger. This place is a real magnet for tough guys, it seems.'

Cross tried to smile, but the only thing that was about to brighten his day was the pancakes, eggs and sausage coming his way. Kowalksi ordered Mama Dufour's French Toast.

'What are you planning to do?' Kowalski asked.

'Talk to the guy who owned the Town Car, find out who was in the trunk and, I hope, what they'd done to get there.'

'Where to?' Kowalski asked as they stepped out on to Washington Street.

'I need to get to a car. Can you drop me at the car lot?'

It was a straight shot east on Washington, the main east/west thoroughfare crossing dead center Indianapolis and a demarcation some saw as the real Mason-Dixon line. Though it didn't take long, and as exhilarating as it was, Cross was glad to be off the Harley. His legs were a little shaky. It was a little like riding a horse except for the weird buzz between his legs. And it was just a little too intimate for Cross.

Edelman was outside talking to a uniformed cop who stood by the area where the Town Car had been parked and where Slurpy met his end. There was yellow crime tape around an empty space. Someone was playing by the rules even if the rules made no sense, which was one of the reasons Cross was no longer a cop. Edelman glanced up, his face, below a strongly receding hairline, gave nothing away. If he was worried, or scared, or happy, or pissed, you'd have to deduce the mood from very subtle changes in his voice.

When Edelman turned toward Cross, the cop meandered away and eventually into a row of cars.

'What went down last night?' Edelman asked, his eyes following Kowalksi's loud Harley departure.

'You tell me,' Cross said.

'Don't know. You were there.'

'I went where you sent me. So tell me, how did I end up driving a car with two dead people in the trunk?'

Edelman lit a cigarette and began walking toward an area in back of the office, maybe, Cross thought, to distance them further from the cop.

'Look, I call Wilbert Morgan about the payments. He says he can't. Says as soon as he gets back from Memphis or Chattanooga or something in a couple of weeks, he'll have something for me. I ask him when he's leaving. He says 'tomorrow,' which was the next day. I want the car back before it gets lost in some fucking bayou somewhere. So I call you.'

Edelman took a hit off his cigarette, stared at Cross and continued.

'Now I stop knowing what happened and now you start knowing what I don't know.'

Edelman shook his head, flipped the burning ash with a finger and rubbed the end on the bottom of his shoe. He held the stub in his hand, no doubt to dispose of it in a proper receptacle.

'I need a car,' Cross said.

'Use the one you were using. The Audi.'

'The police have it.'

'Why?' Edelman asked, curtly.

'Maybe I shot two kids, put them in the Audi before transferring them to the Lincoln.'

'So now,' Edelman said, 'I don't have the Town Car. I don't have the Audi. And you want another car. That's three cars because of you. What's going to be left on the lot, sport?'

'You have to be kidding,' Cross said.

'Our deal was one car at a time,' he said, as he turned to leave.

Cross grabbed Edelman's shoulder.

'Don't fuck with me,' Cross said, almost surprised at the harshness in his voice.

Edelman turned back. He looked a little taken, then wary.

'You threatening me?' Edelman asked.

'Look, if it weren't for you I wouldn't be facing murder charges.'

Edelman's smile was bitter, but he said nothing.

'You think I'm not serious? I'm facing two murder charges. What's one more?'

Edelman relented. 'Look around. No Hondas. Take something nobody wants.' Edelman walked away, stopped and turned back squarely. 'When this is all settled, you and me don't have any business anymore.'

* * *

Before leaving the east side in a battered old blue Trooper, Cross drove by Wilbert Morgan's place on Drexel. Wilbert wasn't home. Neither was anyone else. He slipped his business card in the door after writing 'call me' on the front above his name. Maybe the man found a way to go south without his car.

Cross stopped by the market on 56th and Illinois to pick up some food as he headed home. He was cautious walking up the steps and on the path that eventually led to a ramshackle gate and the fenced inner yard of his strange home. It was a place built in 1929 as a chauffeur's quarters. The large two-car garage was now a living room. The middle room was Cross's office and someone, over the years added a bedroom. The walls of the original structure were thick clay tiles. The roof was tile as well. It stayed surprisingly cool in the summer.

Casey, the dog, and Einstein the cat had made themselves comfortable and were surprisingly nonchalant about getting fed. Casey went out in the yard, sniffed around, did his business and came back in where it was cooler. Einstein nibbled at his food and found a sunny spot on the sofa in the middle room.

Cross used his landline to call his folks.

'Hello Mom,' he said, feeling like he was twelve again.

'Howie, everything all right?'

47

'Sure. How are you guys?'

'Nothing changes here, you know,' she said.

'Is Maya there?'

'She's napping. Should I wake her?'

'No. She probably needs the rest.'

'You OK?' she pressed.

'Of course, just touching base.'

'See you this weekend,' she said.

'Yes. Give Maya my love and you and dad.'

'If you need anything let me know.'

Cross hung up, realizing he'd called not to give them reassurance but to get it for himself. It had been a rough couple of years and now any thought that the bad times were over had to be dismissed. Even so, he was a little ashamed. His mother and dad had their own problems. What was left of their farm seemed to be crumbling around them.

As he took his long, hot shower, he vowed he would work harder putting things back in shape during his weekend visits. This afternoon, after catching a few hours of sleep stolen from him by the sounds of jail, he'd do his best to find out what he could about the young victims.

The night was long. Time was screwed up. Shanahan seemed to be battling with sleep and unsure of which side he was on. Twice it was the rain that awakened him. Even over the hum of a rattling air conditioner, he heard the sometimes steady beat of heavy rain and then a sudden tumult, wind whipping, so that the drops

48

smacked against the glass doors.

And there was Maureen in her guiltless sleep, no doubt basking in the scents of turmeric, garlic, coriander, chilies, garlic and lime leaves.

The third time he was thrust back into consciousness it was the quiet that did it. The rain stopped. He got out of bed, looked out of the window, but saw nothing, just darkness. Not a handwringer by nature, Shanahan second-guessed little. Maybe it was the idea that when he had only his life on the line his world was balanced. Now, not only must he protect Maureen and not lose her, he must also protect himself. Losing his life would lose her as well. It was all part of second-guessing the wisdom of this potential misadventure. All of that weighed upon him in a night that had finally grown silent.

When the light came and Maureen gave up her luxurious sleep, Shanahan's mood lightened considerably. He had already showered, leaving the bathroom to her. While she prepared for the day, he brought coffee up from the restaurant several floors below. He waited on the balcony, looking at the foreign view – rooftops of older buildings, some with gardens, some with clothing out on lines, and some bare. High rises randomly popped up on the landscape.

Maureen came out of the bath, the hotel's white terrycloth robe wrapped around her. It couldn't hide her voluptuousness.

'I feel better,' she said, toweling her auburn

hair. 'What's the plan?'

'We'll know soon. Channarong will meet us in the restaurant. He'll tell us what he knows and we'll go on from there.'

The restaurant, on the mezzanine above the busy lobby, was sunny and cheerful. There were three stations in the dining area where food was served. A slender young man was behind one station, willing to make you an omelet or pancakes. Another station provided a selection of fruit, juices and coffee or tea. Another had shelves of various pastries. If one were seeking the mysteries of the orient, the exotic food from ancient Siam, this wasn't the place. All of this could have taken place in Kokomo, Indiana. But it was the complimentary breakfast that came with the room – all too reasonable.

Channarong showed up half way through the scrambled eggs and coffee. He gave a slight, almost prayerful bow to Maureen.

'Would you like something?' Maureen asked him.

'I had some food with the family earlier,' he said, putting a manila folder on the table and sitting down.

'How did you sleep?'

'Very well,' Maureen said.

'It will take a day or two to adjust to the time and the temperature,' Channarong said.

'You found something?' Shanahan asked.

'The last thing the police and the courts have

on Fritz Shanahan is what you pulled from the Internet story. He is wanted for questioning, but it isn't something they are likely to spend time on.'

'The arrest? What was that about?'

'Rubies.'

'Rubies?' Maureen's eyes widened. 'Well, thank God it's not drugs.'

Channarong nodded. 'That would be worse from a police perspective. However, it can be dangerous. From what I understand – and I am not an expert in these matters – the money in ruby smuggling is getting the rubies out of Burma, or Myanmar if you prefer. This does not make the officials in Burma happy and they are not kind people.'

'How do we get the scent?' Shanahan said, but it was as much a question to himself as it was to anyone else.

'Ruby dealers, perhaps,' Maureen said.

'And how do we find them? You know any ruby dealers?' Shanahan asked Channarong.

'I know where they are. They are near Chinatown. Rubies can be found in stores on Mahesak Road.'

'Rubies have their own street?' Maureen asked.

'More or less,' Channarong smiled. 'You find gold on Yaowarat Road, diamonds on Silom, silver on Charoen Krung and the colored stones on Mahesak. They are all near each other.'

'Handy,' Shanahan said.

'Thailand is a center for expensive gems,' Channarong said.

'So Fritz is in the heart of it,' Shanahan said, wondering what his sibling had become.

'Let's go shopping,' Maureen said.

The taxi provided some sane relief – cooler, quieter. The driver appeared sane too, driving civilly on busy, clattering streets, past beehive crowded sidewalks. Buses, taxis, tuk-tuks, cars, scooters, motorcycles kept the air full of sound and carbon monoxide. At first it was difficult to see how the neighborhoods changed as they drove along. They all seemed alike, which made it difficult for Shanahan to get his bearings. Chinatown presented some difference. Many of the signs were in Chinese, very different from the more script-like Thai.

Passing through on a wide thoroughfare, he could look down the shady narrow streets and alleys that branched off and see activity. The driver and Channarong spoke to each other in pleasant sing-song tones. The weather? Politics? He looked at Maureen. Her eyes focused outside on the world she was passing through. She had never really traveled, Shanahan recalled. What travel she had done was with him – Hawaii, California and one year a daring trip to Italy. Nothing like this.

She seemed to sense his looking at her, thinking about her. She turned and smiled. She was happy. He was not surprised. She was not worried or afraid. She was brave and curious.

Mahesak Road turned out to be a bust. The jewelers in the top shops either knew nothing or pretended to know nothing of any Fritz Shanahan and certainly their business was above board. The smaller jewelers, located in an area known as the Gem Center, seemed a little frightened at the questions. They knew nothing about anything. And they quickly excused themselves to take care of other business. At Shanahan's urging, he and Channarong spoke to everyone who worked there.

'You are dogged,' Channarong said. 'Is that a correct way of saying?'

'Oh yes,' Maureen said. 'He is dogged.' She smiled at Shanahan. 'Personally, I think it's charming. I'm fond of dogs.'

'I didn't expect anyone to have any information,' Shanahan said.

'Why did we do this?' Channarong was taking his measure of the old detective.

'To let them know someone is here. Someone is asking about him and about the dirty side of the business.'

'Some one who knows something will find you.' Channarong said.

Shanahan nodded.

'What is the schedule, Mr Shanahan?'

'Temples. Let's go look at temples.'

Channarong nodded. 'I never tire of it,' he said without a song in his voice.

'Food,' Maureen said. 'Let's not forget lunch.'

53

FIVE

Cross slept until darkness. The length and depth of his sleeping surprised him. And it was only the knock on his door that awakened him. He slipped on his jeans and flicked on lights as he headed for the front door. The light on the front porch illuminated the handsome face of Lieutenant Ace Collins.

'We've had somebody waiting out there to tail you,' Collins said, stepping in. 'But you never came out. I thought you had slipped out through a secret passage.'

'Who said I didn't?' Cross said, slipping into his bedroom to retrieve a shirt. Casey, who had met Collins before, sniffed the policeman's hand and went away satisfied. 'I could have come and gone several times through a tunnel I have to the liquor store.'

'I expected you to be more proactive.'

'Proactive,' Cross shook his head.

'I know. I use words like 'proactive,' and 'synergetic,' as well as 'my team.' It makes me the professional I am. Anyway, I am glad but surprised you're not out there stirring things up. You are still a suspect. Is it because you know

54

who did it?'

'I fell asleep.'

'As simple as that?'

'As simple as that. Have you identified the victims?'

'The male is Marshall Talbot. The female? We don't know yet.'

'It was a fancy shotgun,' Cross said.

'It was. A Merkel 303E. Real silver engraving. Worth five thousand to ten thousand dollars, I'm told.'

It didn't make sense to Cross. It was all set up for the repo guy to take the fall and that seemed to mean losing the shotgun was part of the plan. That was an expensive throwaway.

'And it was empty, right?'

'Yep,' Collins said.

'Is that why you're being so nice to me?'

'You've got some friends downtown. Swann says you're a smartass but honest. Pretty much the same thing from Rafferty. Says he owes you one, whatever that means.'

'I've got some enemies too.'

'Even higher up. You are not universally loved. You and your pal Shanahan seem to have a problem with authority.'

'I'd be happy to have that on my gravestone.'

'I'll make a note of it,' Collins said. He sat, minding the creases in his expensive pants, in the only seat available other than the one behind the desk. 'So, if we assume you are innocent, then somebody either wanted to set

55

someone up for the fall or they wanted to set *you* up for the fall. You have enemies who have it in for you that much?'

Cross thought for a moment. 'I don't think anybody hates me so much they would kill two people just for me to take a fall. But if someone had to kill someone and needed someone to take the fall, maybe they'd remember me.'

'I could do with a list.'

'I think they're all dead.'

'You that tough?'

Cross didn't answer.

'Could be an accident of timing,' Collins continued. 'But how would they know someone was set to pick up the Lincoln and when?'

'Wilbert who owned the Lincoln maybe. And Edelman who wanted it back,' Cross sat on the edge of the desk.

'But it wasn't about the Lincoln,' Collins said.

'No. You wouldn't think so.'

'What about Slurpy?'

'Slurpy didn't know where we were going until we got there. What kind of pressure you under?'

Collins smiled.

'Does it show?'

'Top city homicide cop,' Cross said, looking at his watch, 'working late and pretending he's not in a hurry. The victim is a VIP?'

Collins nodded. 'Marshall Talbot is the son-in-law of Raymond Taupin.'

'Chief asshole in city politics, business bloodsucker,' Cross said, 'Or so I've heard.'

Collins nodded again.

'And the girl in the trunk is not Mrs Talbot.' Cross said.

Collins nodded still again, this time with a big smile.

'You are in for it,' Cross said.

'No, *we're* in for it. You and me. Mr Taupin wants your ass.'

Before Collins left, he gave Cross both a blessing and a caution. The lieutenant was willing to look the other way if Cross wanted to do a little investigating on his own. That would make it easier for Cross to do what he intended to do anyway. The caution itself was two-fold. Don't embarrass the police and be very, very careful of Raymond Taupin. Very powerful people would do his bidding because if they didn't they would lose their power.

Cross left his four-legged charges – fed and watered – to head into the night. He wasn't sure why he was leaving and had no idea where he was going. But he was compelled to do something. He was not only suddenly claustrophobic, he also felt too closely contained by someone who seemed to hold power over him. Worse, it was an unknown someone. He couldn't just sit in a chair and wait.

The thing was Cross didn't know whether this was personal or not. If it wasn't, what could he do? Whoever it was had taken a shot already. It was too early to know if it worked; but it was likely the person wouldn't strike again – at least not strike him. If it was personal, it meant he had an enemy. Having an enemy wasn't a problem. He'd had enemies before. He wasn't frightened. The problem was that he didn't know who the enemy was. He had no clue, other than he – or she – was capable of murder.

He drove by Wilbert's place on Drexel in the beat-up Isuzu Trooper that Edelman let him take. The lights were out. He pulled in front, sat back, sighed. What next. He could go to a bar. Harry would have shut down by now. The whole idea was boring. He could drink at home and he didn't want to do that either. He could go to a strip bar – at least there was something to look at while he sipped tequila. But those places seemed to get him into trouble. That's how he met Maya's mom. That didn't go so well.

Cross closed his eyes. He replayed the previous night. Something troubled him. The guy was waiting for them. If the murderer had stuffed bodies in the trunk of a random car why would he wait around? The guy waited because he knew someone was coming and he – and this was the thing Cross figured out at that moment – wanted the shotgun to be in their hands. It was an excellent set-up. The bodies and the weapon that were used to kill them, were all tied to Cross and Slurpy.

Cross tried to see the guy. It was dark enough that all he could make out was the man's build.

Maybe a little taller than average – six foot something maybe. Fit. Skin not dark, but not light either. Baseball cap. Cross recreated the moment the man aimed the shotgun at him. The man held it at his waist. The man's hands were lighter than his face. Could be he was wearing gloves. That would make sense.

The man knew someone was coming to pick up the Lincoln. Cross could now be sure of that. The only person who could have known someone was picking up the car was Edelman.

'I know where you live,' Cross said as he sat forward and put the old SUV in gear and headed north. Edelman lived not far from Cross – on 50th between Central and Washington Boulevard. The city was quiet as he took 21st to Sherman Drive then north to 38th and then up Central. He had gone from the small, quality-built, post-World War Two bungalow neighborhood through some tough areas and then gradually up to upper-middle class homes.

The lights were on in Edelman's house. In the back of Cross's mind, he knew what he was doing was not a good idea. But he'd never rest until he had some resolution to the nagging doubts about his own future. A knock on the door. Then again. No one came. Cross remembered Edelman's wife spent most of her time, even in the middle of summer, in Florida. It was an informal separation. He knocked again, this time harder and the door opened.

'Edelman!' Cross called out. He stepped in

calling out again and again, slowly checking each of the rooms. It wasn't one of the giant homes in the area so it didn't take long. The door in the kitchen that went out back was open. Cross stepped out cautiously. The darkness was sudden. He walked around the yard, this time calling out Edelman's name softly. He came to the garage door. He could hear the car running. It was one of those older garages that have two side-by-side doors.

Cross opened it and was swept back by the heat and, while there was no smell, he felt something evil invade his lungs. He stepped out, took some breaths and then held a deep breath, moving in, opening the door on the passenger side. The open door triggered the interior light. No Edelman. He switched off the engine and turned on the headlights. Still holding a hand over his nose and mouth, he saw the body, strung up by rope on the rafters.

Cross backed out quickly, getting far enough away from the garage to breathe fresh air. He pulled the cell phone from his pocket and started to punch in 911. Instead he called James Fenimore Kowalski.

'Usually when you call you interrupt a carefully prepared, long anticipated dinner,' Kowalski said not allowing Cross to speak. 'It's past midnight. I wasn't dining. I was doing the only thing that's better than a fine meal.'

'Sleeping?' Cross gave in.

'You live a petty, unimaginative life.'

'Not really. But you were having sex, I take it.'

'And you've destroyed it,' Kowalski said. 'How do you do that?'

'It's a gift. Please apologize to her. It is a her, isn't it?' Cross had completely given in to the silliness of the universe and played along.

'I was just about to find out when you rang,' Kowalski said. 'Now it's your turn to talk.'

'OK,' Cross said with mock-enthusiasm. 'I'm standing outside of Edelman's garage ... at his home. He is hanging from a rafter inside and if the hanging didn't kill him he would likely have asphyxiated on the carbon monoxide from the running engine of his automobile. If anything, the man was thorough.'

'And you discovered the body?'

'Yes.'

'And you are alone?'

'Yes, depending on whether or not Edelman's soul has left his body.'

'Have you called the police?'

'No.'

'Call them. I'm on my way.'

After Cross called and failed to get connected to Collins, he provided the dispatcher with the information, after which he went around to the front of the home and sat on the stoop. He took out his handkerchief and wiped his face and neck. It was still pretty warm out. Then there was the stress. This wasn't a happy ending for poor Edelman. It wasn't likely to have a happy

61

ending for him either, Cross thought.

The lights on the neighborhood porches started coming on when the fire truck arrived. The firefighters arrived before the police and Cross directed them to the garage. A couple of undercover cops arrived shortly after and two marked cars followed in moments. What was once a quiet, dark street was now bustling with flashing lights and various vehicles.

One of the uniformed cops told Cross he'd have to hang around, that someone from the homicide section was on the way. Someone from the coroner's office entered the area behind the garage. Cross went back around front to get out of the way. He could hear the growling engine of Kowalski's Harley several blocks away. The lawyer pulled in at the same time as the big black Crowne Victoria parked across the street.

He had hoped for Collins. Instead he got Lieutenants Swann and Rafferty. Swann was an older cop with a not quite shaved head and Wal-Mart suit. He was what cops were supposed to be in an ideal world – by the book. Rafferty was a con artist. He was bigger and softer than Swann, but like Collins he dressed a bit too well.

'Who's this?' Rafferty asked when Kowalski stepped between Cross and the arriving officers.

'My attorney.'

Rafferty laughed.

'What are you doing here, Cross?' Swann asked.

'We have to talk first,' Kowalski said.

'It's all right,' Cross said to Kowalski, then turned to Swann, 'I wanted to talk to him.'

'To Edelman?' Swann was taking notes.

'Yes. He was the only who knew that the Lincoln was being repo'd.'

'The one with the bodies in the trunk?' Swann asked.

'That one, yes.'

'Why is that?' Rafferty looked bored. He glanced around.

'He wanted the car picked up that night and he wanted me to do it.'

'So you were upset?' Swann asked.

'Of course.'

'You were not just upset, you were pissed.' Rafferty said. 'You were so pissed you might have killed him.'

'I didn't get the chance,' Cross said.

'Why don't we make arrangements to talk in the morning?' Kowalski said.

'We need to get some facts now,' Swann said in even tones. 'Maybe he's the perp. Maybe not. But he's a witness and I am going to get a statement, attorney or not.'

'Tell them exactly what happened here tonight,' Kowalski said to Cross, 'and not a dime's worth more.'

Cross told them how he came to find Edelman in the garage. Swann took notes dutifully.

63

'Come by tomorrow morning,' Swann said. 'You can bring your lawyer if you want. Nine, OK?'

'Where's Collins?' Cross asked.

'Your place,' Rafferty said, 'having a look around.'

SIX

After a visit to the Gem Center and a few other places known for what was referred to as 'colored stones,' and Shanahan's business card with his Thai contact information written on the back had been appropriately distributed, he and Maureen went sightseeing. Channarong, after guiding them to some of Bangkok's most exotic landmarks, would take the late afternoon and evening off and return to the hotel in the morning.

Shanahan was pleased to see Maureen enjoying herself. Maybe not just Maureen. In Indianapolis, where he'd spent the last couple of decades, people drove to parking lots and then went inside a building, whether they were searching for food or movies or merely a place to wander. No one walked, not even, it seemed, to bus stops. Bangkok's streets were alive at all times. People walked, rode bikes and scooters, boarded and rode tuk-tuks, taxis and buses and hopped on the Skytrain for long trips or on to boats to travel the city on the canals. People spilled out everywhere.

When Thais were hungry they stopped for a

moment at one of the thousands of outdoor food vendors to pick up something to eat. These were mobile kitchens, fueled by charcoal, sometimes under small awnings, where the richest and poorest of Thais dined side-by-side, eating crepes or satays, coconut rice pancakes, grilled fishcakes, hot and sour noodles and many items that Shanahan could not identify. The sizzling of the grills and the aroma of the food added to the sounds and scents of the city.

Maureen was a curious and adventurous tourist. She nibbled her way back to the hotel. By late afternoon she had taken a short nap and a quick shower. She swam a few laps in the pool on the top floor, the city spread out three hundred and sixty degrees below her. Shanahan climbed up a few flights of stairs from their room to check on her and noticed that there was a guard posted on the stairwell of each floor, where he could also monitor people arriving by elevator. They did not stop him or even seem to notice. Was it for safety? Probably not, Shanahan thought. It was more likely the uniformed guards were there to keep freelance masseuses from taking the action away from those employed by the hotel.

Maureen, in her one-piece black swimming suit and white swimming cap moved effortlessly, parting the otherwise still water. Back and forth, again and again. When she had completed the last lap, she climbed out of the pool, took off her cap and shook her auburn hair free.

The two of them went downstairs, showered and dressed. Maureen was already looking forward to a nice meal at a restaurant of Channarong's recommendation.

The guide also suggested the two of them go to the Patpong night market with the admonition not to buy anything.

'Lots of fakes and even if you find something you like, you can get it cheaper at other night markets.'

They arrived early, and while initially disappointed, Maureen was enthralled watching the transformation of a busy street into a lively, magically lit marketplace. Dozens of shirtless, muscular young men hauled out trunks, tents, poles, tables and electric lights. The construction seemed choreographed, but no doubt the extraordinary coordination came from repetition. Night after night they would do this, eventually turning an empty street into a marketplace, back-to-back stalls of fabrics, carved wood, metal Buddhas and jewelry. On the sides were the regular businesses – many of them sex clubs, judging by their names. The music poured out from their doors.

It was Shanahan's nature to always be prepared for the worst. He looked around, realizing the futility of noticing anyone following them. Not only was it crowded, it was also dark.

Afterward, they strolled past stalls where vendors hawked the best names in designs – Rolex, Louis Vuitton and Gucci.

'Last chance for a real Georgio Armani,' Shanahan said to Maureen.

'It's probably Georgio's shady cousin Antonio.'

The two grabbed a tuk-tuk that took them down to the river.

'I want you to step into Thai culture slowly,' Channarong told them earlier, explaining that the market and the restaurant were both favored by tourists. 'You will see the real Thailand, I promise you.'

A teak-paneled boat picked them up and took them to the Supatra River House, which was across from the Grand Palace and where they dined on fresh, steamed fish. They sat outside, looking down at the reflection of the lights on the Chao Phraya River. Maureen was relaxed, happy, welcoming all the new sensations with the joy of a child at an amusement park. For him, underlying the calm he very much wanted to portray was impatience. He had come to do what he had come to do. He felt he was frittering away the time. It took him until the taxi-ride to the hotel to come to terms with reality. He had only set things in motion. *Tried* to set things in motion. Nothing may come of it. Something may come of it. But at the moment he could do very little. He relaxed. After all, wasn't he in an exciting city with the most beautiful woman in the world?

In the morning, Channarong met with them at breakfast. At one point he sensed Shanahan's renewed restlessness.

'This may strike you as foolish,' Channarong said, 'but the more you understand the ways of this little world, the less you will be at the mercy of them.'

Shanahan nodded. It was true.

Channarong offered to take 'the Americans' on a trip through the city. It began at the legendary Oriental Hotel, then on to a boat that took them along a canal to the Jim Thompson house. This was another of the 'tourist' trips, but rewarding. Thompson was a former military intelligence officer – Shanahan knew of him – who, after his service was done, helped revive Thailand's silk industry. After he built a spectacular home, where he kept his collection of Southeast Asian art, he mysteriously disappeared.

As Channarong told the story, his eyes engaged Shanahan, more than would be usual, suggesting, maybe, that the old detective, whose own background was in military intelligence, might find the story especially meaningful. It also meant that Channarong might have learned more about Shanahan than Shanahan thought.

'Is that a warning?'

'I believed the story might interest you. Many people find it fascinating.'

'It is fascinating,' Maureen said. 'Do these disappearances happen often?'

Channarong grinned. 'Many people come

here to get lost,' he said, 'sometimes voluntarily. It is all part of Thailand's charm.'

'There's charm and then there's charm,' Maureen said.

The guide smiled, his face nodded in a subtle bow.

Shanahan liked Channarong. And he liked the Thai people. From what he could gauge from taxi drivers, the hotel staff, and restaurant waiters and waitresses is that unlike many of their counterparts in other countries they were neither resentful nor subservient. They weren't disengaged either. Mutual respect was the atmosphere created between the server and the served. There was a pleasant civility here – at least on the surface.

Certainly last night's trip on the river with the fairy-tale lights glistening on the water was enhanced by the magic of the evening. In the harsh, yet gray light of the day, the water in the canal, or *klong* as they call it, was a pea soup green. It was dense and impenetrable. The water was as polluted as the air.

Jim Thompson's house, or houses – it was more like a compound – was simple and elegant. Doorways acted as frames for art or something artful that reflected the beauty of nature. Maureen was taken with it and wondered what kind of man would be able to create such a beautiful and peaceful atmosphere.

The afternoon unfolded with a further exploration of the canals lined with homes ranging from the dilapidated to the ornate. There were other boats on the canals, some filled with tourists and others filled with Thais going about their daily business. The boat passed through a floating market – small flat boats loaded with melons, long beans, bananas, coconuts, lychees, strawberries and other goods.

'Everything is available here,' Channarong said. 'Not all of it is so publicly presented.'

Maureen bought some lychees. She remarked at how beautiful they were. Slightly larger than a walnut, the surface was delicately patterned in rose and tan as if carved by an artist. Channarong showed her how to peel them. Her eyes widened as she tasted one.

'So sweet,' she said, 'it's almost painful.'

There were also floating restaurants. Channarong, Maureen and Shanahan dined on crab as their boat slid through the maze of canals. Temples rose to the left with orange-robed monks going somewhere. Half-naked children played along the canal, happily taunting the tourist boats.

Shanahan thought that Thailand had only partially given in to the great Western influence.

'Did you know,' Channarong said, seemingly picking up on Shanahan's thoughts. 'Thailand is the only country in this part of the world that has never been colonized, never been occupied by a foreign culture?'

'I did,' Shanahan said. 'They're still holding the rest of the world at bay.' It was an admirable trait, he thought.

Thailand was different from his decades old memories of Japan, China and Korea. He could see how someone could be seduced by how beauty nestled up against ugliness in Thailand.

Back at the hotel, Maureen and Shanahan showered, swam a few exhilarating laps in the rooftop pool. Shanahan had two bottles of beer, green bottles with an elephant logo and he too napped until Maureen woke him up, afraid she might miss dinner.

It was at dinner – a place not far from the hotel they took a chance on – that Shanahan began to believe his message had been delivered, that he was being watched. He couldn't be sure. There might be other reasons for a skinny man to be glancing at the old detective nervously. When Shanahan looked back, the man looked away. When Shanahan's gaze steadied, the man disappeared.

Rain came at night. Again. It was torrential as it was the night before. Shanahan fell asleep under nature's violent nurture.

SEVEN

If fate ruled the world, then fate had it in for him. If the world were ruled by chance, then he had been enduring a particularly malicious run of bad luck. Cross fought the self-pitying cloud that hovered over him, but he had just come through a hellish period and here it was again; unless he had another and quite evil personality he knew nothing about. Karma was ignoring fairness, he thought. He was being set up to take the fall for two murders he didn't commit. And fate or chance was piling it on.

Cross was back downtown. No doubt the cops were more than a little upset to be on duty and in the office that time of night. But things were going worse for Cross. The search that Lieutenant Collins performed at Cross's place uncovered a man's Cartier watch and an engagement ring, both belonging to Marshall Talbot, one of two victims of the shotgun murder found in the trunk of the car Cross was driving.

The two lieutenants had gone home. Cross had been brought into Collins's office to wait, guarded by a uniform. Kowalski was there, sitting in a chair beside Cross at Collins's desk.

The lieutenant was purportedly on his way back to talk with Cross.

Cross was numb.

'Why did Collins conduct the search?' Kowalski asked. 'One of the lesser mugs could have done it.'

'Yeah, one of the lesser mugs might have shot Shanahan's dog,' Collins said coming through the door.

'That happen a lot?' Kowalski asked.

'Too many times.'

The lieutenant sat on the edge of his desk. He held plastic bags containing the evidence in his hand. The expression on his face said: Explain this.

'If they are willing to plant bodies,' Kowalski said, 'it wouldn't stretch the imagination for them to plant some jewelry.'

'And by "them" you mean?' Collins asked.

'I believe you call them perps, don't you?' Kowalski said.

'Oh Kowalski, stop watching TV.'

'That's where the cops are the good guys,' Kowalski said.

'Maybe you don't watch TV.'

'I'm engaged in real life.'

'Cross!' Collins shouted to pull Cross from wherever he was. 'What are we going to do? Swann thinks you need to be put away. Rafferty is spinning the idea that you should be referred to as a "person of interest" or "valuable witness," rather than a suspect. But there's only so much we can do when the evidence that keeps rolling in says it's you.'

'I know,' Cross said. 'We're not looking for an idiot.'

'That supposed to disqualify you?' Collins said, smiling. 'All right. We've been through this already, but let's look at it again. Who has a hard-on so bad they'd go to all this trouble?'

Cross shook his head in bewilderment. Then he looked up. 'Edelman was the link between me and the trunk full of bodies. The only person who knew where I was going and when I was going, besides me, was Edelman.'

'So Edelman had to go,' Collins said. He shook his head and made a face. Disbelief.

'Sure. The murderer is tidying it up,' Cross said.

'Was Edelman murdered?' Kowalski asked. 'Do we know that?'

'Why would he kill himself?' Collins shrugged. 'I don't know what to tell you,' he said. 'I'm gonna make the call. You can go home. I'll have to deal with the DA in the morning. Who knows what will happen after that? In the meantime, keep your lawyer close. Right, Kowalski?'

Cross sat up for hours, sipping on tequila. What he wanted was to sort out all of the details, make sense of them. He was – and he knew it – sabotaging the effort with each sip. It was his nature.

He went outside, sat at the table under some pine trees. Casey followed him out and plopped down beside Cross's chair.

'Thanks,' Cross said. 'I need a friend.'

Cross wasn't a sad, self-pitying drunk. Or an angry or mean one. He was a what-the-hell drunk. And he only got drunk alone. He'd let no one see him drunk, except for Casey. And Casey would keep his secrets.

'It wasn't me they wanted to set up. They just wanted someone and I was handy. And really,' he spoke into the darkness, 'I was perfect. A low-life repo guy who has a track history of being involved in dirty business. Prostitutes, crooks, questionable deaths.'

It was refreshing in a way because, despite the tequila, he was looking at himself clearly, at least in the way the cops would, as a jury would, as the general public would depending on media spin. He looked good for all three murders. It wasn't a stretch.

He had his work cut out for him.

Shanahan woke earlier than Maureen. He pulled the drapery aside. Outside was an eerie gray; but the light was coming. She was enjoying her sleep. He was restless. He left a note in the unlikely event she would be awake before he returned. He went in search of a cup of coffee and an English-language newspaper. Outside the air was a vast steam room. The streets were flooded ankle-high in some places from the

76

night rain. Soon the sun would bring it to a boil. He dodged the water that would soak his socks, zigzagged on sidewalks and streets eventually making it to a news-stand and then with a little luck to a diner. The streets were bustling. He watched as well-dressed women boarded dilapidated and very crowded buses. In the short, narrow alleys vendors were bringing wares out to the street. Motorbikes weaved around waiting automobiles to get pole position at the stop light. When the light changed they swarmed off in a deafening buzz.

He ordered a cup of coffee at a table in a drab, colorless restaurant and spread out the colorful *Bangkok Post*. A few moments later a young Thai man in a baseball cap, olive tee shirt and jeans came in. Shanahan wouldn't have noticed except that the kid seemed to make a special point of not looking around. He was trying very hard not to be noticed. When the waiter came, Shanahan saw the young man steal a glimpse before his gaze too quickly retreated.

Shanahan looked down at his paper and paid no attention to the kid. He asked the waiter for two cups 'to go' and walked past the kid and out the door. He thought about trying to lose him, but he didn't want to. If he was right about the tail, this was the only connection he had made so far. He'd have to figure out what to do about it.

Maureen was awake and up when he got back to the hotel.

'Channarong called. Wants to know if you have plans for him.'

'I do.' Shanahan went to the phone and punched in the numbers.

'What's on our agenda?' she asked, while Shanahan waited for Channarong to answer.

'Breakfast and a long walk,' Shanahan said just as Channarong answered. 'Can you meet us at ten here at the hotel?'

'Yes.'

'Come on up to the room.'

Shanahan didn't want to discuss things in the lobby.

Maureen stood out on the balcony and sipped her coffee.

'Are we going to have breakfast out?' she asked.

'Can you wait until ten thirty?'

'No.'

'We'll go downstairs. It is part of our rate, I guess,' Shanahan said.

She was a little disappointed. The breakfast buffet was OK – for what it was – a breakfast buffet. And it was a food adventure she had already experienced.

Channarong stepped out on to the balcony. Shanahan followed.

Looking down, Channarong said, 'All that used to be a Chinese cemetery. On a morning like this morning the tombstones would look like sunken bathtubs in muddy water as if

78

someone forgot and left the faucet running.'

'I'm reminding you,' Shanahan said to Maureen who stood in the doorway. 'I want to be cremated and my ashes thrown on a mountain.'

She said nothing.

'What happened to the cemetery?' Shanahan asked.

'They've taken it all away,' Channarong said. 'Progress. I suspect no one liked the idea of soggy corpses.'

'Are you up for a little intelligence work?'

Channarong nodded.

'We need three people for this,' Shanahan said, counting each one of them. 'I will go for a long walk, perhaps to a park somewhere,' Shanahan said. 'You and Maureen will follow at a distance in order to see if we're being followed.'

Channarong nodded.

Shanahan described the young man who was at the restaurant.

'It could be someone else now. Anyway I'll go sit at a park bench somewhere. If I am followed, Maureen will come sit beside me. We will chat for a while. I'll see her to a cab and she will go back to the hotel.'

Maureen raised one eyebrow.

'Then I'll begin walking again and I will lose him.'

'You don't want to confront him? You want to lose him?' Channarong said.

'But I don't want you to lose him.'

'I see. You want to know where he goes.'

'Yes. You OK with this? It's beyond the call of duty.'

Channarong smiled and nodded. 'Our temples are beautiful, but I can miss a day of explaining the reclining Buddha.'

They stepped out of the heat and into the room.

'I have to come back to the hotel?' Maureen asked, a little bit of warning in her voice.

'No, of course not. You can go anywhere you want,' Shanahan said. 'A temple maybe. There are thirty-two of them, I believe.'

'Just not with you,' Maureen said.

'It's easier for one person to disappear than two. It's just playing the odds.'

Though the stretch from the hotel to Lumpini Park was walkable, perhaps even pleasant on a seventy-degree day, this was a ninety-six-degree day. The heat and heaviness of the air made it a bad idea. Shanahan boarded one tuk-tuk and Channarong and Maureen caught another.

Shanahan's motorized rickshaw sounded like a lawnmower and only went a little faster than one running on the power of human legs. At the entrance to the park, a statue of Rama IV stood at the front gate to welcome visitors. Just inside was a political demonstration. Banners flew, people on megaphones spoke.

Shanahan continued until he was further into

80

the park. He found a bench and sat, pulling out his now tattered newspaper and began to read as pigeons gathered around his feet. With the exception of the heat, it was very much like any city park. Strollers and bicyclists whisked along the wide walkways.

He read for about ten minutes looking for Maureen's arrival to signal that the tail had been identified. But she did not come. Instead a man in a light suit, not Thai, not Asian, sat beside him though there were empty benches nearby.

Perhaps the man just liked this bench. In a few moments the man reached in the jacket pocket and pulled out a number ten manila envelope, folded it in half, and put it between Shanahan and himself.

That's when Shanahan noticed Maureen maybe 75 feet away. Shanahan gave her the slightest head shake in the negative. She stopped and pretended to examine her shoe. The man sitting next to Shanahan got up, leaving the envelope, and headed further into the park. Maureen was walking again. She pretended she didn't know Shanahan and continued on in the same direction as the man. Once past him, she waved her arms behind her, letting him know he was *not* to follow.

Shanahan put the envelope in the newspaper, folded it up and walked back toward the entrance. He was worried about Maureen, but if he interceded he'd likely screw everything up and Maureen would be upset that he didn't trust her.

As he passed back through the gate Shanahan caught Channarong out of the corner of his eye. Neither acknowledged the other. Shanahan headed back into the business district. In the midst of a gathering of food vendors, Shanahan moved about as if he were interested in what they were selling. He doubled back a couple of times and noticed Channarong, which meant that he was being followed. But so far, he was unable to make out who it was and therefore he wasn't sure how to shake him, which was the point of the exercise.

Then again, Shanahan thought, who was the man in the park? Were there two, separate people interested in his comings and goings? He stepped into a multi-floor mall, glad to be in the cool air, if not thrilled about the choice of goods. He looked around for some other way out and couldn't find one. He went into a luggage shop and pretended to look at the wares. He came out again into the overwhelming heat. He thought about the Skytrain, which would whisk him out to the suburbs, but if he managed to dodge his tail, the timing might make it difficult for Channarong to follow the culprit. He was, he thought, a bit rusty at the spy game – though some things never change. The clandestine exchange on a park bench, for example. Only this time, it wasn't prearranged.

Shanahan wanted two things. To be cool

again and to read what was in the envelope. He did not want the person tailing him to know that someone else had contacted him. If neither knew about the other, he wanted to keep it that way until he could sort out the situation. He found a bar and went inside. The cool air hit the layer of perspiration on his face and it was instantly chilling. He pulled a handkerchief from his back pocket and wiped at his forehead before going to the bar where he would, as he understood already, be regarded as a typical sweaty westerner, a *farang*.

Shanahan sat at the bar, put the newspaper upon its smooth, worn wooden surface. He ordered the elephant brew, put enough baht on the bar to cover the beer, and relished the first, long drink of it, brought to him from an indifferent bartender. The bar had no particular sense of place. It was culturally neutral. He glanced around. No one had followed him in. He slipped the envelope from the folds of the newspaper and put it in his front pocket. He took another sip of beer and looked for the men's room. He spotted the little hallway, the only hallway and deduced that the bathrooms had to be in that direction.

The men's room was small and very clean. It was also well-lit. Light not only came from the fluorescent bulb above him, but through the window, which was open about half an inch. Shanahan locked the door and opened the envelope.

Come alone to the Kitty Club on Soi *Cowboy tonight at eleven. Walk straight through the bar to the back wall. Enter through the red, swinging door. Ask for Moran.*

That was it. No signature. No threats, but no explanation.

Shanahan put the letter back in his pocket and examined the window. The window was on a chain and could be opened halfway. He did and looked out. It was a short drop into what seemed to be a stairwell. No exit. He debated. There was a stairway that went up the side of another building. He decided to do it. He pulled himself through the window. For a moment his body was a seesaw, half in the bar, half out. He inched his way forward, putting his hands down to break the inevitable, but hopefully short fall.

He shook his head. He wasn't twenty years old, or thirty, or forty. He was seventy and breaking a hip was a distinct likelihood. Nonetheless, he managed the maneuver without much trouble. He went to the ladder – a fire escape of sorts – and climbed up past a second story to the rooftop. He moved over the roof to the front of the building and looked down.

Shanahan wasn't sure if it was the same or a different young man in the baseball cap. The kid stood across the street, smoking. He had donned sunglasses. Channarong was a block away, standing near a food vendor, nibbling on something on a stick. OK, he knew who he had to lose.

84

Shanahan looked to the left. Another building, but three stories. To the right there was another rooftop adjacent to the roof where he stood. He had only to climb over a three-foot wall. He went across easily and then to another where there were clothes hanging on a line. The colorful shirts and undergarments were leaden in the unmoving, heavy air. Behind the clothing was a small structure with a door. The door led to a stairway and the stairway to a landing and another stairway, which led to a lobby of sorts, and to the street. He waited until it was clear, waiting until his tail looked the other way. Instead the young man simply lowered his head. Tired, bored. Shanahan, who believed the young man was resting his eyes as well, took the moment to scurry the few feet to the corner and disappear around it.

Out of sight he stopped for a moment to take stock of his bones and organs. He was exhausted, sweaty, but all the vital parts seemed to be where they were supposed to be and functioning. He had no idea where he was, but he knew where he was going. Shanahan walked the small street until he found a busier one. He waved for a cab. He could count on the driver knowing the way back.

EIGHT

Cross told himself that if he could be calm and collected, cool might follow. This he said only in his mind as he cracked three eggs into a bowl. The oil was heating in a small skillet. He continued the internal monologue. 'You remember the good, old days when you were paid to get *other* people out of trouble.' He chopped up some onion and two slices of bologna.

The intended omelet turned out to be scrambled eggs.

'Same same,' he told Casey, who had just meandered in, no doubt picking up the scent of breakfast.

'All right, all right,' he said to the universe, 'I'm going to get on it.'

What was on the plate didn't look like an omelet or scrambled eggs.

'A scramlet,' he said, putting some of it in a bowl he put down for Casey and a tablespoonful of it for Einstein.

He took his plate into his office where he sat on a chair, putting the plate in his lap and the coffee on a side table. He flicked on the television. He glanced at his watch as the screen

86

gained life.

Five minutes until the news. He pushed the 'mute' button. There had to be something about the case. He nibbled on his eggs, sipped his coffee, thought about what it was that he knew. Marshall Talbot was the son-in-law of a powerful citizen, Raymond Taupin. The identity of the woman had yet to be disclosed. The relationship between them was also unknown. Lovers? Two strangers at the wrong place at the wrong time?

What else did Cross know? The man with the shotgun was waiting for Cross and Slurpy. Of that, there was no doubt. And why was that? Cross couldn't be sure. But he knew that it ended with the murder weapon in his and Slurpy's possession. The question then became, was Cross the intended set-up? Maybe the killer or killers wanted Cross to take the fall. Specifically Cross. True? Cross couldn't be certain of that even though it felt that way. If Cross was the real target, maybe the bodies in the trunk were a pretext, related to nothing else, not even to each other. They were used to get to Cross.

'You must think pretty highly of yourself,' Cross said to himself.

Either way, how did they know Cross, or anyone for that matter, would be there to repo the car the same evening the victims met their fate? Then there was a phone call to let the police know where they could find him, Slurpy, the two dead bodies and the shotgun.

It all seemed to come down to Edelman. And he would be profoundly, eternally quiet.

Cross clicked the mute button and sound burst into the room.

A very blonde, doll-like woman read a few headlines to tease for the news that would follow nearly endless commercials. Once the dancing mops had saved the day it was clear that the bodies in the trunk led the news.

'Police are asking for help in the murder of Marshall Talbot and an unidentified woman.' A police sketch of a woman appeared on screen. She appeared to be Hispanic, perhaps Middle Eastern. 'Police are seeking information about the woman shown here in a police sketch. Both Mr Talbot and the other victim were found in the trunk of a repossessed automobile, both apparently dead from shotgun wounds.'

The face of Lieutenant Rafferty appeared on screen, a microphone in front of his mouth.

'What have police learned about the repo case so far?' asked a disembodied voice.

'We know very little at this point. We are in the preliminary stages of the investigation. With the help of the coroner and medical examiner, we are developing a time line and are questioning everyone who might be able to shed some light on the case. We are confident that we will be able to apprehend those responsible for these deaths.'

'I understand that you are questioning a private investigator, the person driving the car at the time of the discovery of the bodies.'

'We are questioning everyone.'

'Is the investigator ... let me see ... Howard Cross a suspect?'

'In this stage of the investigation almost everyone is a potential suspect.'

'He *is* being held for questioning,' the voice asked. 'Isn't that right?'

'We are not going to go into any information regarding people of interest at this point. Thank you.'

'I'd like to follow up on the death of Chester Thurman who was killed by police that night.'

'We'll be getting back to you when we have more to say.'

'The public has a right to know,' the voice said.

'Of course. And they will know. At the moment we need to make sure we don't jeopardize the investigation and that we protect the rights of every citizen. Thank you. We'll keep you informed.'

Rafferty was good on camera, Cross thought. Unfortunately though, Howard Cross was now in the public domain. 'Howard?' Of course, he didn't like 'Howie' either, but a guy has to have a name. He was about to shut the television off when the next story picked up on Edelman's death.

'Indianapolis police have their hands full,' said the blonde woman behind the desk. 'We've just learned that Irving Edelman, owner of the car lot where the repo murders were uncovered, was found dead in his home in an apparent suicide. Arnie is at the Edelman house on the city's Northside. What do we know about this, Arnie?'

'What the police will tell us is that Irving Edelman was found dead in his garage with a noose around his neck. Police will not confirm the suicide theory saying that they are waiting for the coroner to make a statement and that it might take a few days before that ruling will be made. We do not know who found Mr Edelman or what other information they might have gathered so far. All we know is that city hall recently boasted of a declining murder rate. The number of homicides in the last few days has to worry them.' Arnie looked into the camera for a few serious moments before the camera went back to the perfectly coiffed anchor.

'I'm sure the mayor has something to say about this,' she said. 'Thanks, Arnie. Now for news from the Indianapolis Motor Speedway. Members of the—'

Cross clicked it off. He finished his noon breakfast and sipped the last of the coffee. Time to do something. But what? Edelman was dead. That left the police, who weren't known for sharing with a civilian let alone a suspect. And members of the family weren't any more likely to consent to an interview with the likes of Cross.

After letting Casey out and then back in,

Cross showered, shaved and slipped on jeans and an old madras shirt which he left untucked.

'What do rich people have that most people don't?' he asked Einstein, who seemed bored at the attention. 'They have help. People who do their cooking and cleaning and gardening and who knows what?'

He punched in the numbers.

'You've reached the law offices of James Fenimore Kowalski. Please leave a brief message at the tone.'

'Kowalski. This is Cross. I want to know where Raymond Taupin lives and he isn't listed anywhere. Give me a call at...'

'Taupin lives in some fucking McMansion up north,' the lawyer said, speaking over the outgoing message.

'That narrows it,' Cross said.

'Hold your horses. Wait.'

There was a long silence followed by an address.

'But you'll never get in,' Kowalski said.

'I know. I thought I'd wait outside and talk to the help.'

'Interesting.'

'I don't have anything else.'

'If you get anything, let me know. I'll do what I can to take that old blood-sucking bat down.'

'You should see a shrink about your hatred of the upper classes,' Cross said, teasing.

'I love the rich,' Kowalski said. 'Rather, I'd like to be rich. And some rich people are lovely and cool and admirable and pleasantly humble, but Taupin is a sneaky, condescending, conniving creep. I mean that from the bottom of my heart. He has no class. He has no redeeming value.'

'OK, I understand. He's not a give-his-money-through-a-foundation kind of guy.'

'He funds nonprofits. These are the nonprofits that make sure politicians who pamper the rich get re-elected.'

'I see.'

'In other words, I'll help you.'

'Let me get a start on this first. So you are one of those famous left-wingers I've heard so much about?' Cross asked.

'Oh no. I'm not a radical. I'm more of a left-breaster than a left winger. Moving a little left seems like a correct direction after the last decade. You?'

'I just want to stay out of prison,' Cross said.

'I guess that makes you the wishbone.'

It was a drive into uber-Republican country and into a ritzy if somewhat gaudy development. Taupin lived in what Kowalski called a Mc-Mansion – a large, imposing, fairly recently built home on a proportionately too small lot. Homes of a similar size were perched on hillets on all the curving streets of the neighborhood.

The closeness of the neighbors made it difficult to stake out the place, to see who came and went. It wasn't likely he could get away with scanning the day's mail to see what kind of services the Taupins paid for. But he was fortunate to see that there was a tiny sign in the corner of the front yard that said 'GreenLawn-Kare.' It was a start.

He Googled the firm on his new iPhone and found its offices were in nearby Carmel, pronounced like the candy, not like the California town.

GreenLawnKare was in a well-kempt, well-landscaped, one-story building with a two-story corrugated steel building in back. From the lobby, Cross could see a glassed-in conference room and some offices leading back. The workers and equipment had to be in the back. The brochures said that the company provided complete landscape design. They also offered maintenance programs for lawns and gardens.

'How can I help you?' said an attractive woman in a flowered blouse over which she wore a green jacket with the company's name embroidered on the front.

'I'm not sure how to go about this,' Cross said, 'My car was hit. It was parked on the street and someone, I don't know who, put a huge dent in the door.'

'And you are here because...' She said this in a playful way, accented with a smile.

'Because I didn't see who did it and I think your crew was across the street at the Taupin's doing some work. I am hoping that maybe they got a glimpse of who might have banged it up.'

Her mind began to work. Cross supposed there were some options to weigh. Did they even want to get involved in something like this?

'Just a question or two. Probably nobody saw it, but I really don't like the hit and run thing. I'd have at least left a note.'

'Wait here.'

When she came back she brought a man in a green coat she introduced as Alex. 'Dwight is down in Broad Ripple this morning with his team. I don't really think that it'd be proper to have you talk to him while he's on the job. I'd be happy to forward your phone number to him and he can call you if he wants to.'

'That's very reasonable,' Cross said, 'but I have to get to Albuquerque. And I need to get this resolved. I promise you, Alex, that I will be brief. I'll ask if he knows anything about the dent. If he says 'no,' then I'll move on. If he says 'yes,' I'll just ask him what he knows. And that's it. No muss. No fuss.'

This was Cross at his friendliest and simplest – a very easy-going guy just asking a friend for a favor. It earned him an address in Broad Ripple, a former little town on its own and now swallowed up by the sprawling city of Indianapolis.

The area was toward the north end of the canal that begins in downtown Indianapolis and ends at a former Monon Railroad stop. Now, both the graveled path along the still water of the canal and the stretch where train tracks once were are paths for runners, bicyclists, and dog walkers. Homes along the canal were often unusual and ranged from high-styled and expensive to remodeled river shacks. One of Cross's favorites, a big, beautiful deco home once occupied by the actress Frances Farmer, was near the home where Dwight and his two co-workers trimmed hedges and cared for the lush green lawns many Americans are addicted to.

'Dwight!' Cross called out, getting out of his car and moving toward the workers. All three looked up. But only one, presumably Dwight, stepped forward.

'Alex called and said you were on your way. But I don't think I can be of any help. I didn't see anybody banging into a car.'

'I was afraid of that. I kind of think that it may have been one of Mr Taupin's people. Knowing Raymond, I mean, I don't want to speak ill of anyone, but knowing Raymond Taupin, it's not likely he'd leave a note.'

Dwight laughed. 'You got that right.'

'Isn't a good boss, I take it?' Cross said.

'Oh, don't see him much. But he tried to put the squeeze on me once.'

'What do you mean?'

'Well, wanted me to just work for him private. Come out on my day off and work for him. He'd pay me less than he'd pay GreenLawn-Kare but more than the company'd pay me. I told him that would get me fired. And it wasn't right. Man, I saw the look on his face. It was like instant, spittin' hate. Then a smile came all over him and he said I could just work for him permanent. He had a place up on Lake Wawasee, and between those two places, it'd keep me busy.'

'I take it you told him no,' Cross said.

Dwight nodded, but his eyes squinted a bit, from caution, not the sun. Cross told himself to go for it. Now was the time. He reached in his pocket, pulled out a copy of the photograph from the autopsy.

'You ever see this girl around the house?'

Dwight looked at him, suspicions confirmed. 'No car got bumped.'

'No. I'm trying to find the person who killed her.'

Dwight shook his head. 'I don't know anything. I'm serious. If I did, I'd help you out. I promise you that. Why didn't you just start out being honest?'

'That's a strategy that doesn't usually work for me,' Cross said.

'Give it a chance,' Dwight said.

Lake Wawasee. The name wasn't entirely foreign, but he knew nothing about it. It was Google-time again. Broad Ripple was only minutes from home.

Neither Casey nor Einstein managed to get up to welcome Cross home. It was warm everywhere even inside his tile-walled house. He plucked a beer from the refrigerator and settled in with his computer. He typed Lake Wawasee into the Google box and was surprised that he got the spelling right.

Biggest lake in Indiana, if you didn't count that portion of Lake Michigan that dipped into the state's northern border. But aside from the great lakes, this was one big lake for him never to have heard of it. It was known for its clear water and the number of plush cottages that surrounded it. Who knew? He thought he probably should have. Summer homes for the rich? It was near Syracuse, Indiana, not on any major interstates. Maybe a three-hour drive from Indianapolis. Weekend escape for the busy executive. A place to send the wife and kids when school is out and daddy doesn't want to be bothered. A connection between Raymond Taupin and his son-in-law's death may not exist. Curious though, Cross thought.

Kowalski called and before the lawyer could relate why, Cross launched into his Lake Wawasee discovery.

'You are one goddamned fantastic private investigator,' Kowalski said with dramatic effect. 'And ... a great American. I've been gathering some financial information on Taupin. I always wanted to do this, but I never had a reason before. He's one wealthy human being or whatever species he is. He has a holding company that owns holding companies that own a jillion small businesses and pieces of a jillion other businesses.'

'What's a jillion, Kowalski?'

'A hundred gazillion. Everybody knows that. Anyway, Taupin is involved in publishing, gravel, insurance, construction companies, laundromats, strip malls, garbage, you name it. And he's bought all sorts of local and regional franchises: from fast food to oil change drive-thrus.'

'Damn,' Cross said.

'There are names I can't decipher. Corporations with names that mean nothing to me. He collects businesses like some people collect stamps. As I understand it, he buys some to drain them of their resources, when the parts are more valuable than the whole. He buys others so that one business will feed another. I've never seen a game like this.'

'All legal.'

'Yeah. No numbers racquet or anything like it. All legal. He may be unethical, but it appears he keeps it all legal.'

'Anything come up on the son-in-law, Marshall?' Cross asked.

'He's not on the board of any of the businesses as far as I can tell, but it appears his wife and daughter are.'

'You think the deaths are connected to Taupin, then?' Cross asked.

'One huge hunch, not a grain of evidence. We know who the girl was?'

'Not yet. I think I can get Collins to tell me what he knows when he knows it. On the other hand I'm one jerk of the leash from prison.'

'You're a realist Cross. I like that in a guy. Otherwise, you OK?'

'I am. Can you stop here and check on the cat over the weekend, maybe Saturday? I'm going up home and I'm taking Casey with me. And Maya and I may go have some fun at the lake.'

'Let me know what you find out,' Kowalski said.

'Thanks,' Cross said as Kowalski disconnected.

NINE

Despite a recent refresher course in Mexico, Shanahan's way of the spook was still rusty. He finally got away from his tail so Channarong could do what he was asked to do – follow the follower. Back in his room at the hotel, the impact of what had just happened hit him hard. Maureen had set upon a task that would have been far too dangerous even if she were experienced in such things. He could feel the fear in the pit of his stomach. It came from both the thoughts of what could happen and the very clear fact that he was powerless to do anything about it.

Bangkok was a city of eight million people and if you include the neighboring provinces, it covers three thousand square miles. At minimum it goes out twenty miles in all directions. Needles and haystacks? It seemed more like a grain of salt in the Sahara desert. So when the phone rang, Shanahan was more than hopeful. He allowed a rare optimism to enter his mind.

'Channarong,' the voice said. 'I'm downstairs. May I come up?'

This is why optimism didn't agree with him.

His stomach sank again.

'Please,' Shanahan said. He was at least pleased to have someone there who might be able to help.

Shanahan immediately called down and ordered up four beers. They followed surprisingly fast on the heels of Channarong's arrival. Channarong declined, but when pressed in the mildest possible way, he accepted the chilled bottle. He reported what he'd found out.

'The kid used his cell phone. Made two calls. Spoke briefly. He came back here and was replaced by a middle-aged man.'

'Thai?'

'Thai.'

'Did you follow the boy?'

'I did. He went to an apartment building. He had a key. I have an address. I'll give it to you.'

'Do you know this place?' Shanahan asked him, handing him the paper he'd received from the man on the bench.

'I don't know anyone named Moran and I don't know the bar,' Channarong said, sitting down, rereading the note. He took a sip from the beer. 'Most clubs have some sort of relationship with the police and they are often connected to even more questionable businesses and questionable people, balancing somewhere in between.'

'All are prostitution rings?'

'You need to know that while there are a lot of dark and predatory dealings in the sex business here, the Thai people do not have the same horror that most Americans do about sex. Some girls are brought down from up North, some sold by their families who know what it is about, some are fooled into the business, and many do it because it is a way of earning money, more money than they can make any-where else. So, if you go in with the notion that the people you are talking to are the scum of the earth...'

'I won't,' Shanahan said, interrupting the dissertation. 'To the best of your knowledge I'm not volunteering to be killed or kidnapped if I go there?'

'No guarantees.'

'Maureen is missing,' Shanahan said. He was quick and brief, afraid he might get emotional.

Channarong's pleasant but unexpressive face showed surprise for a moment, then concern.

'She followed the man who gave me this note,' Shanahan continued. 'I've heard nothing since.'

Channarong looked at his watch. He took a deep breath.

'Then you have one more reason to keep the appointment.'

Shanahan nodded his agreement.

'Should I call the police?'

'You'd get the tourist police, not what you need right now. And even they would laugh at you. She hasn't been gone that long and the streets are safe,' Channarong said. 'Was the man Thai?'

Shanahan shook his head 'no.'

'How was he dressed?'

'Well.'

Shanahan went to the balcony, went outside, walking into a hot, stinking wall of air.

Channarong followed.

'Mr Shanahan. Most of our crimes are what are called "non-confrontational," mostly purse snatchers and pick pockets. We have less violent crime than almost any large city you can mention. She's been gone two hours. That's not long. It could take her longer than that to get back by taxi considering the traffic.'

'I hope so.'

'So do I. What do you want me to do with the tail outside?'

'I just need to know where one of them lives,' Shanahan said. 'We've got that. Thanks for your help.'

'I can hang awhile if you...'

It always amazed Shanahan that Channarong had such a flair for casual English.

'No, that's fine. I'll call you tomorrow.'

'You need me tonight for the meeting?'

Shanahan thought for a moment.

'No, I'll take care of it.'

'I can go as a customer. Have a drink. Admire the girls. I don't know you.'

Shanahan nodded his agreement. Whether Channarong's motives were for profit, it didn't matter. It was a good idea. Shanahan was a stranger. There were things he could not know.

'By the way, not all girls are girls in Thailand. That's especially true on *Soi* Cowboy. And some are pretty convincing.'

Shanahan nodded. It didn't matter. Shanahan wasn't interested in meeting girls, real or not, and he didn't spend time judging other people. His mother used to tell him not to criticize other people unless he had walked a mile in their shoes. That was a bit of advice he held on to.

But he'd have no trouble judging anyone who brought harm to Maureen.

Time moved slowly, uneasily, afternoon into evening. The small hotel room had become a cage. He couldn't leave for fear she would call. The only recourse he had was to meet the man at the Kitty Club on *Soi* Cowboy at eleven, at the urging of the man she followed.

A key turning in the lock brought him from a light sleep. The sudden light suddenly blinded him and when she came into focus, she looked fuzzy for a few moments.

'Sitting in the dark?' she asked.

He was glad she was all right, angry that she had done what she did and, and at the same time fearful that he had slept through his appointment on *Soi* Cowboy. He knew he should go embrace her. It was what he wanted to do, but he was frozen by the conflicts in his mind.

'He went to the police station,' she said, looking exhausted and puzzled.

He stood, walked to her. He held both her hands.

'You shouldn't have done it,' he said as gently as he could.

'Why? Because I am a woman and I should let the man of the house do it?'

Usually, there was a lightness in their conversation, often belying deep feeling, but a lightness nevertheless. No lightness here.

'No. I may be old and very rusty,' Shanahan said, 'but I was trained to do this. Would you want me to come to your real estate office and take over a big sale?'

'I wanted to help.'

'I know. And you do. No one in my life has ever been more help to me. But I am not strong enough to deal with the idea of losing you.'

There was a long, hard silence.

'I'm not all that delicate, Shanahan.'

He said nothing.

She looked him in the eye. 'I've followed a man before without him knowing it.'

He saw the evil twinkle in her eye, and the ever-so-slight curve to her lips.

'He went into the police station, you say?'

'Yes,' she said, sitting on the edge of the bed. She took off her shoes. 'I waited outside. I waited for two hours. He didn't come out, so I figured he either worked there or they arrested him. It took me a while to get back.'

'And he didn't see you?'

'He didn't.'

'You hungry?'

'Have we met?'

He looked at his watch. 'I think we have time to freshen up and get a nice dinner somewhere close.'

'What do you mean "we might have time?"'

'I have to meet a guy at a strip club later.'

'And who might that be?'

'I think it's the guy you've been following.'

'I'll go with you,' she said.

'What? And blow your cover. No such thing.'

She gave him the look.

Shanahan came out of the bathroom, saw his beloved conked out on the bed. He looked down. An angel. Maureen's auburn hair splayed across the blanket. Dinner and a couple of drinks did her in. He was happy for her – and a little jealous. He too was tired. He had not had so much physical activity in one day, had not had such emotional upheaval since Maureen was taken from him before. He wanted sleep too.

He put a blanket from the closet over her. It may be hot and humid outside. Inside, the rattling air conditioner evened things out. He wrote her a note. He nodded to the guard who stood on the stairs and punched in the elevator button. In the lobby, he stopped at a little stand where he bought a thin, plastic poncho. Last night the rain came with the unexpected suddenness of a home invasion and he wasn't sure how late he would be out.

After bargaining with the driver, they tuk-tuk'd the relatively short distance to *Soi* Cowboy. He had left early enough to ensure he'd get there in plenty of time to keep the appointment and to wander around, get the lay of the land, before the meeting. He wanted to know about back doors and what else was going on in the neighborhood. Were there police around? Were there gangs? There weren't. Mostly tourists. Mostly male tourists.

He went into the bar early as well to see what was going on, get a good sense of the space, upstairs, downstairs, if there were little corridors leading off to who knows where. These kinds of places hadn't changed much since he wandered about Southeast Asia and Indonesia so many years ago. Girls dancing. Girls at the bar. Girls wanting drinks bought for them. Prettier girls than he remembered in his now slip-sliding past. And if they weren't girls, acknowledging the doubt Channarong planted in his brain, they were doing a great job of being girls.

It mattered little to Shanahan. He wasn't in the market for the goods being sold, except for a glass of whiskey with a beer chaser. He went to the bar, squeezed in, tried not to look at the scantily clad women who might take the glance as encouragement. Busy place. Older men, some Asian, some not. The only women were the bar girls, not as scantily clad as those on stage. He thought of Harry's bar. Maybe he should suggest Harry change the ambience. A couple of these lovelies – and all it would take is a couple – would definitely liven the place up.

All right, he said to himself. He noted the door in the back covered in red leather. He noticed a hallway that probably led to rest rooms. He'd check that out. There was a stair-way that wound back behind the bar and to a second floor. If there was a downstairs, which he doubted because of the heavy rains, he didn't see the way there from the bar itself.

After finding out the hallway to the lavatories went only to the lavatories, he came back into the main room, watched the girls on stage shed more garments, leaning against a back wall. So young. So young. At eleven twenty-five, he saw Channarong come in the front door. His friend went to the bar as if he knew the place, blended in perfectly.

At eleven thirty precisely, Shanahan went through the red leather door.

TEN

Cross loaded some clothing, a camera, binoculars and tools into the Trooper. With the dog, Casey, as his co-pilot, the two of them set out for Eaton, a few miles north of Muncie and in the general direction of Lake Wawasee. Kowalski had agreed to look in on Einstein, but at his age the elderly cat – as long as he had some water and food – was perfectly happy to be left alone.

The plan was to get to his parents' farm early to pick everyone up for a day at the lake. Once Kowalski learned that Taupin had property at the lake, he used the county land office to locate the parcel. Cross downloaded a Google map of the area and specifically the lake itself, with Taupin's home marked. As they boated the large lake, Cross would take a look at the Taupin home, hopefully identified by the satellite photo Google provided. What he thought he'd find he wasn't sure. But this is how he did his work. Just gather as much information as you can and see where it leads.

The sky was clear and blue. So was the lake. Maya, at six, was happy. Even Cross's father and mother seemed to enjoy the break in their routines. Mom had fixed fried chicken, baked beans, and potato salad. His father had packed another cooler with beer and soda. The rented speedboat cut through the water easily, gliding past homes that opened out and down to the lake. Most of the properties had piers that extended from their back lawns out into the water. Barbeques were fired up and badminton and volleyball games were underway on the shore. There were sailboats and pontoons and fishing boats moving about on a glistening surface that extended for miles.

Cross, who received general directions from the boat rental operator, was heading toward the area where the Taupins had their summer cottage.

'When can I go swimming?' Maya asked.

'When we get to the swimming area.'

'There's water here,' she insisted.

'It's illegal to swim here. And it's too deep.'

Maya shook her head. The expression on her face asked the question, 'Why am I surrounded by fools?'

Cross's father laughed. 'All that time in Hawaii, she's practically a mermaid.'

'Mermaiden,' Cross corrected.

'We'll stop by the park, have a little picnic and then after a little wait, we'll go for a dip in the lake,' his mother told Maya. 'OK?'

Casey, who had been extremely nervous about floating around on the water, eventually found a spot, and clunked his bones down.

Cross worried about his mother. They had applied spf fifty sun block. She nonetheless looked as if she had either just heard a dirty joke or was getting more sun than she should. A few more minutes. No street numbers on the lake, but Cross was pretty sure the three-story home, nearly all windows on this side, was the Taupins. It was the biggest on this part of the lake and it had an extra-long pier in order to accommodate a yacht of ocean-going proportions and a seaplane. Nothing was going on outside but the gentle bobbing of the sea craft. Cross smiled. The multi-millionaire known for his cheap ways had a few luxury items.

The sky was blue. The sunlight bounced off the caps of the gentle waves. The clouds were storybook white and fluffy. It was an American Kodak moment – happy and golden. Cross took his camera from the bag and, while it looked like he was taking a typical family photograph – Dad, the kid, the grandparents and family dog – he was also recording the numbers on the plane and the name of the boat: *Ruby Tuesday*.

Cross didn't know whether any of this mattered, whether in this wholesome scene there was some level of evil or not, but the trip was worthwhile. What did surprise him was the seaplane gently rising and falling on the tiniest of tides. There weren't many of them on the lake, but it made sense. It was more than two or three hours to Indianapolis by car, nearly all of it on slow-going secondary roads. If Cross wasn't mistaken, there was a small airport in Fishers, near the low-profile tycoon's city home. Home to home in what? Half an hour?

'Who wants fried chicken?' Cross asked happily as he cut left, or port as some more experienced seafarers might say.

The sign on the red leather door said:
EMPLOYEES ONLY.
On the other side was a long, dark hallway with double-door wide openings along the way. Each was draped with muslin. Soft light and muffled voices spilled through the pleasantly shrouded doorways. Shanahan walked slowly, waiting to be intercepted or to find a doorway open and inviting.

At the end of the hall was an elevator. One button. Shanahan pushed it. He hesitated for a moment before stepping in. He'd come this far. Inside there were two buttons. One was lit – the floor he was on. He pushed the other. The door closed and Shanahan found himself in a softly lit space that moved smoothly. When the doors opened, he stepped into what appeared to be immaculate space. White walls, pale gray carpeting, a white sofa with matching chairs. There was a sense of style. But the style was sterile. It was a clear contrast to the bar below, where the walls, and tables, and floor had a sensuous, perhaps living patina.

A woman in white clothing appeared and

112

pointed toward Shanahan's shoes. He took them off while she pulled some blue-green paper slippers from a box. He slipped them on and she nodded for him to follow. The air was cool, but there was no sound of air conditioning. The air was clean as well. Filtered.

They turned, went through an arched doorway and into a larger room, though of the same coloration and purity. The man, slender as a reed and ageless, sat on a large upholstered silver gray chair. He wore a white robe, trimmed in gold. A second look and Shanahan could pick up a few more details. The skin was a little too tight at the neck. The flesh was a little too tight on the bone. Before him on a small table was what Shanahan thought to be a glass of iced tea.

The man looked up. His eyes were bright. This wasn't the man who sat beside him on the bench in the park.

'Why are you here?' the man asked with a mix of impatience and confusion.

'I was told to come here.'

'I meant why are you here? In Thailand. I would have thought you were long gone by now. You should be you know.'

'I'm looking for Fritz Shanahan.'

The man had a wide smile. His face crinkled in amusement.

'How very poetic,' the man said, nodding toward a chair that was a match to his own.

'Why is that poetic?' Shanahan asked, sitting.

'Though it's a little adolescent, there's something poetic about a man looking for himself. There is something profoundly sad, though. You, a man of such experience approaching the endgame of his life without the knowledge he was born with.'

'Looking for myself?' Shanahan decided it might be wiser to let this man do all the talking.

'It is what you said. You think a beard makes you a different man than you were before you grew it?'

Shanahan shook his head 'no.'

'It's very brave and perhaps a little adolescent as well,' the man smiled again, 'to come back here.' The man reached for his glass. His fingers were long and narrow, bony and old.

Shanahan thought the man and his apartment were pretentious, affected. Then again, he reminded himself, he thought his own beard was an affectation. He would shave it when he returned home.

'I am not Fritz Shanahan looking for myself,' Shanahan said, though he had given thought to the idea of keeping the lie alive. But, given what he'd learned so far, being Fritz might be more dangerous than being Dietrich. 'I'm his brother, Dietrich.'

Shanahan wasn't sure he'd ever really seen anyone demonstrate the expression 'taken aback' so well. It was as if the little man had received some sort of tiny slap from an invisible villain. Recovering, he smiled as broadly as he had done before.

'You are a rogue, Fritz,' the man said. 'You almost convinced me for a split second. Interesting dodge. But you won't pull it off. You'll have to do something better than that. A little cosmetic surgery, perhaps. In the interim, no doubt a very short one, you have places to go and promises to keep.'

Thai though the man was, his English was without accent. The words 'rogue' and 'dodge,' were interesting choices.

'You know,' the man continued, 'that I've always given you more room than anyone else, but there are limits to my patience even for someone as charming as you.'

'Charming?' Shanahan asked. It wasn't a word usually used to describe his personality. 'Perhaps Fritz got a bit more of the Blarney Stone than I did,' Shanahan said. 'I assure you I'm not charming and I'm not Fritz.'

The man got up from his chair, plucking a pair of glasses from his robe pocket, and walked toward Shanahan and examined his face. He reached down and lifted up Shanahan's left hand. He stepped back.

'You seem to have grown your pinkie back,' he said as he went back to his chair.

'It's from the lizard side of the family.'

'Fritz would smile when he said something like that,' the man said.

'You are beginning to get the picture.'

'You don't fall down on the floor and kick and

bite and generally scare off the clientele do you?'

'Not recently. Why do you ask?'

The man smiled. 'You brother has these fits from time to time. Some people are frightened of him. They think he is possessed.'

'What do you think?'

'I think we're all possessed.' The man smiled again, shook his head. 'What brought you to me?'

'A man told me to come here and ask for Moran?'

'Who is Moran?'

'I have no idea,' Shanahan said. 'Aren't you Moran?'

The man laughed. 'No, and you aren't Fritz. Am I asleep or in a silly play?'

'All I know is I'm Dietrich Shanahan and I was told to come here to find my brother.'

'What are we going to do with two of you? One was more than enough.'

'You have any idea where he is?'

He stood. 'I thought I did. But it is you instead. Happy hunting, Mr Shanahan.'

The elevator brought Shanahan back to the hallway as half a dozen young, slender half-naked girls, having finished a shift, came back giggling, slipping behind the translucent drapery. He passed unnoticed until the red door. A few in the bar looked his way as he came from a 'no admittance' door. He glanced at the bar. Chan-

116

narong was still there. The number of customers had increased. The girls on the stage looked as if they were doing the 'Dance of the Seven Veils,' bringing back a long-ago memory just as odd as the last few minutes.

Outside, the neon lights from the cluster of clubs in the *soi* bounced around the wet streets and walls. People moved about, many of them in deep, but slightly drunken lust. He slipped on his plastic poncho and headed in the drizzle for the hotel. He would ask Channarong to do what he could to find out the name of the man in the white room and in what businesses, besides girls, he was engaged.

On the way back to the hotel, Shanahan tried to figure out what he learned from the meeting. It appeared that Fritz would be even harder to locate than he thought. He wasn't just hiding from the police as Shanahan had suspected, but also from folks he worked with. He found out that his brother looked a lot like him. They bore a striking resemblance when they were young, he remembered, but time and trouble can play havoc with the genes. On the other hand, Shanahan was aware that the man in the white room might be playing him. He reminded himself he was a stranger in a strange land and what appeared to be to a mind like his, might not be.

Maureen was awake, wrapped in a blanket, sitting in a chair with a rum and tonic.

'You left me behind,' she said.

'I did.'

She nodded, smiled. She wasn't going to make anything of it. It was one of the many reasons he loved her. She never pouted. Get even, maybe. But she didn't pout.

'What did you find out?'

He told her.

'Hmmnn, two Shanahans? This I have to see. Perhaps these people out to find your brother won't have to worry. There's a very good chance you'll kill each other.'

Shanahan smiled.

'What?' she said, eyes wide, mouth open. 'You smiled. Do you realize this is the fifth time in all our time together I've seen you smile.'

'You're counting them?'

'Five is not a hard number to keep track of. The point is: you smiled.'

'I promise, I'll be more careful in the future.'

Cross took Casey out for a walk in the dewy morning. He had the old Catahoula hound on a leash because he had the genes of a pig-herder and tended to have an attitude toward the farm animals, particularly Maya's goat.

Breakfast awaited him. A big breakfast. His normal pot of coffee and maybe a piece of toast would be replaced with a three-egg omelet, roasted potatoes and sausage. It was a farmer's breakfast, but on this occasion it would not go to waste or waist. He had determined that Sunday's chore would be to fix the roof. He had purchased the shingles that last time he was up.

Once he got into it, he didn't mind this kind of work. Manual labor, especially the simple kind, meant he could think more clearly about other things. He worked until the August noon sun made it torture. He gave in to an old Adirondack chair facing a field of corn, a bottle of cold beer, and his thoughts.

Who was the man who held the shotgun? Not Taupin. And the girl in the trunk? Had the police an identity yet? The son-in-law lived in Woodruff Place on Middle Drive. Woodruff place was composed of three wide streets, each with a grass median and fountains at the mid-street turnarounds. Once an expensive neighborhood, it fell on hard times. Many of the old Victorians were subdivided into cheap apartments. Now on its way back, it still seemed to attract the more adventurous of the city's citizens – not something he thought Mr Taupin would appreciate. Was young Marshall Talbot a rebel? That was a reach, but he should spend some time on the lives of the victims. Marshall Talbot shouldn't be too difficult.

He took a sip of beer and looked out over the field. This might have been his life. Probably wouldn't have worked. The days of the family farm were receding. This one was merely a token. A couple of cows in the barn. Two dozen chickens or so, a young goat, and a large garden. Fields of corn and soybeans, along with an orchard on one side, surrounded the farm. None belonged to his parents. They had sold them off,

119

one parcel at a time, just to stay alive. But they knew no other way to live.

People do what they have to do to survive, Cross thought. Whose survival depended on the deaths of the two people he was suspected of killing? And Edelman?

If he had stayed here, Cross thought, shaking off the images of the dead, would he have married a local girl, settled down, raised a family?

ELEVEN

Shanahan left his sleeping beauty just after daybreak. Outside the heat hit him, surrounded him, and seemed on the verge of suffocating him. And to think, he thought, this was the coolest part of the day. He would be in it just as long as it took him to get a cup of coffee and read the newspaper. He looked around to see if the tail was still on him. He didn't spot anyone. Could be the earlier tail belonged to the man in the white room and that the man thought that his dealings with Shanahan were over.

They weren't. He would call Channarong at a more civilized hour and find out more about this man who claimed to have mistaken Shanahan's identity. For the moment, this was his best if not quite only lead. Channarong had given him the address of one of the young men following him as well. As the coffee nudged his sleepy mind and the air conditioning cooled him down, he also remembered Maureen telling him she followed the man who sat on the bench to a police station, where he remained for at least a couple of hours.

* * *

Channarong again sat with them at breakfast.

'I'd like for you to find out about the man upstairs,' Shanahan began after the three of them exchanged greetings.

'God, you mean?' Maureen asked, grinning cat-like.

'Upstairs in the bar.'

'I know some things already,' Channarong said. 'I ran into an old friend who was chatting up one of the girls.' Channarong told Shanahan the man's name, but it had endless syllables, and they agreed that from now on they'd call him Mr White. 'He treats the girls better than most. They say he is good natured and generous.'

'He also speaks English very well,' Shanahan said.

'He does. That's not unusual for people in his line of work in Bangkok. He is a little frightened of germs. I was told that when he bought the bar, he completely remodeled the upstairs. Half of it is devoted to rooms for the girls and guys to spend time together.'

Maureen smiled.

'The other half,' Channarong continued, 'is his apartment. The air conditioning operates in conjunction with an air filter. He rarely goes out.'

'Any connection with rubies?' Maureen asked.

'None was mentioned.'

'Maureen followed the man who provided me

with Mr White's invitation to a police station.'

Channarong shrugged. 'The police are very much involved in Mr White's kind of business.'

'If that is his only business.'

'Well, he has other bars, other girls,' Channarong said. 'My friend says he has a private room in each one.'

'Does he have a police record?' Shanahan asked.

'I'll see,' Channarong said, taking a moment to form an answer. 'I'll do what I can.'

'I'm doubling what we pay you,' Shanahan said.

'No need.'

'You are doing far more than what we agreed. Are you willing to continue to help in that way? I could use your help.'

Maureen looked surprised.

'A smile last night and now you are asking for help?' She turned toward Channarong. 'Maybe they kidnapped Shanahan last night and this is Fritz after all.'

Channarong smiled and agreed to help.

It might have been the heat or the thought of traipsing about the backstreets of Bangkok that caused her to bow out of a trip to find the young man who followed Shanahan yesterday. Channarong suggested she go to the Oriental Hotel. The hotel had an amazing number of restaurants to choose from. The concierge, Channarong told her, would provide her with many shopping options as well.

'You got her at restaurants,' Shanahan said.

Maureen made a face, but she knew it was true.

'The object,' Channarong said, 'is never to be more than a few minutes away from an air-conditioned mall, hotel or restaurant.'

Shanahan, like other *farangs*, couldn't seem to stop perspiring even if he stood still. Breathing too seemed a struggle. Escaping from the frying pan of an Indiana August he had jumped into a Bangkok fire. He would have to endure it. They would be going to neighborhoods not noted for multi-storied malls and elegant hotels.

The traffic was gruesome. Channarong had a van for the day and he seemed to have the same aggressive driving behavior as the rest of the vehicles on the wide expressway. They dodged motorbikes, buses, vans, tuk-tuks, trucks – all of whom seemed to be engaged in a race. Overhead, the BTS Skytrain whisked folks around without the practiced confusion below.

Before long they were on narrower busy streets, but with the same dodging and weaving, with pedestrians added to the mix. Shanahan had no idea where he was or even in what direction they were heading. When the streets narrowed again, the traffic thinned out until there was none. The buildings that lined the streets became more and more ramshackle as they continued until they became little more than temporary structures, obviously cobbled together with remnants of other structures. Walls, in many cases, seemed to merely lean on one another to stay vertical.

Channarong pulled over.

'Be sure you lock everything,' he said as he got out of the van. Shanahan followed. They walked into a building that had been abandoned before it was completely built. It wasn't that old. Finances ran out. There were piles of clothing on the concrete floor, but little other evidence of human habitation. Soon they were in an empty space between buildings. The ground was muddy. Hoses and barrels were scattered around. To the left were three elephants. They noticed but seemed unconcerned by Channarong and Shanahan's presence.

In a second building, very similar to the first, they saw a number of dark-skinned young men. They looked up. Puzzled, they muttered to themselves in Thai.

Channarong said something. Shanahan didn't understand the question or the answers but saw the shaking of heads. More conversation. At one point all eyes traveled to Shanahan, then back to Channarong, who began handing over money to those who had talked. Others began to talk. Channarong, out of baht, put his hand out for more of the colorful currency. Shanahan obliged. Channarong pulled out the larger bills and handed them back.

Each of the seven or eight boys was on his feet, babbling louder and louder, vying for

Channarong's attention and reward.

'Most of the boys are *mahouts*,' Channarong said as the two stopped to look at the elephants on their way back to the van.

'*Mahouts*?'

'They tend to the elephants. They are friends, the elephants and the boys.'

'What do they do with them?' Shanahan asked.

'Take them out into the city at night to beg or maybe entertain visitors. Nothing else the elephants can do anymore. They are not needed for labor. There's no place in the wild for them to go. With the tips both the boys and the elephants can eat.' He tugged briefly at Shanahan's arm. 'Let's go.'

'I didn't get a close look at the boy who followed me,' Shanahan said.

'No,' Channarong said. 'He spends a lot of time here. Many of the *mahouts* who hang out together here take jobs for the police, including following people during the day. Mostly drugs, but they have worked with murder investigations.'

'Murder?'

Channarong nodded.

'What about smuggling?'

Channarong gave a 'who knows' shrug. 'You never know, there's always someone somewhere who expects a cut of anything going on. Could be rubies.'

'Where are we going?'

'Police?' Channarong asked.

Shanahan nodded. 'You have names.'

'You'll have to do this alone,' Channarong said. 'I'll drop you off.'

'A place you cannot go?' Shanahan asked.

Channarong nodded. 'Forbidden,' he smiled, 'but only if I want to enjoy my life.' He turned back on to a wide expressway. 'The officer I'm suggesting you talk to speaks English. At least well enough.'

When he was dropped off a block away from the station, Channarong said not to mention his name. And that whatever Shanahan did he was not to allow himself to be redirected to the tourist police. This wasn't a tourist matter, he said.

Once inside and after successfully maneuvering beyond the suggestion that he not talk to the tourist police, he was taken to the officer whose name Channarong had written down for him. Shanahan was unable to pronounce the name and when addressing the Police Lieutenant Colonel, Shanahan addressed him as Colonel, which was met with approval.

'I have a couple of things to ask about,' Shanahan said.

The officer nodded toward a chair in his small, relatively plain office. He was somewhere between thirty and fifty years old and slender, as were most Thais. In fact most Thais were about half as big around as their counterparts in the Midwest.

Shanahan sat. 'One is that I have been followed and I believe it is possible the police are the ones who believe I should be monitored.'

'We are not following you,' the officer said. 'If we were, you would not know it.'

Shanahan nodded. He would have liked to have challenged the statement, but thought it unwise at the moment.

'My brother is a man named Fritz Shanahan. You know him?'

The Lieutenant Colonel maintained his poker face, said nothing.

'I'm trying to find him.'

'Why is that?'

'Family reunion,' Shanahan said. 'We're getting old, Fritz and I. And I'd like to make amends.'

'Why did you come here?'

'To talk to you.'

'How is it you came to ask for me?'

'I'm not really sure,' Shanahan said. 'I've talked to many people. I talked with the fellow who lives above the Kitty Club on *Soi* Cowboy. You know him?'

The officer stood, came around from behind his desk.

'Have you had a chance to dine on one of the Riverboats? I can recommend one. The food is good and the views at night are spectacular. You will have a different view of some of the temples you have visited. And for your lovely traveling companion a rich and romantic cultural experience.'

He spoke English very well and was intentionally letting Shanahan know that the two of them were being watched.

'Once I find Fritz, I'll be able to relax and enjoy the scenery and then go home, no bother to anybody.'

'Mr Shanahan, people come here for many reasons. Most come for the exotic nature of Thailand, the spicy food and the beautiful women. If you are a sports person, you'll see the finest kickboxing in the world. Many come to live out a fantasy. Some come here to lose themselves for a while or forever. Thailand can be a friendly, welcoming place. However, it can be treacherous for those who try to turn over every rock and for those who spend too much time in the darker places of Thailand's soul. My hope for you is that when you leave Thailand you will have many happy, light-filled memories.'

'Me too.'

He gave a slight bow and Shanahan knew the meeting had come to an end. The problem was that he knew little more than when he started out. By this point he hoped he would know the connection between the young man who tailed him, the man who sat beside him at Lumpini Park, Mr White, and now the Lieutenant Colonel of the police.

Maureen, climbing out of the rooftop pool, gave Shanahan, who was just stepping in, a brief rundown of her enjoyable afternoon, but only provided the high points because she wanted to know what Shanahan found out. He told her – in very general terms He swam a few laps, and sat in the hazy, carbon-laced sunshine with her for a while, before the two of them cooled off with beer, showered, napped, and prepared for an evening out.

'Someone advised me to take you off on a dinner boat at night,' Shanahan said.

'Are you going to listen to his advice?'

'That one piece of it, yes.'

'What else did he say? It was a he, right?' Maureen asked.

'Yes, a he, and he wanted to talk about rocks and dark places.'

'We are at a disadvantage here,' she said. When he didn't respond, she continued. 'You know, your brother, even if he can be found, might not want to be found.'

Shanahan nodded. 'I know. If I find him and he wants me to mind my own business, I will.'

'Sure,' she said.

The night was as the Lieutenant Colonel promised. Though there was no way to find any stars in the night sky, the many boats on the river were lit, as were many temples posing, it seems, as fairylands. The dinner boats were often two-story, golden inside, sounds of happiness drifting from them. Inside their floating dining rooms were elaborately costumed dancers, Thai

130

music, exotic and colorful drinks, as well as the scents of curry, coriander and ginger.

When the food was served, they were pleasantly surprised by how many unfamiliar flavors could be so wonderfully combined. They had been warned about the spices. Maureen told the waiter that while they were somewhat adventurous, they were, after all, used to bland food.

'It is good to be cautious and not foolish,' the waiter said and smiled.

'That's always good advice,' Shanahan said.

They ordered a bottle of wine because of the description on the menu:

Light pail color. Flourish and fruity nose. Dry, nervous, but not too acid.

'I've never had a nervous wine,' Shanahan said.

'How about a foolish wine,' Maureen said.

'We may have just ordered it.'

When they later walked by a girly bar, she asked, 'If you hadn't met me, do you think you'd consider retiring here in Thailand?'

'What I'd be doing is sitting in a bar all night with whiskey and beer, maybe watching a baseball game. I doubt if I would have had the energy to pack up and move here, though the beer is cheaper and one can wait for death just about anywhere.'

'And the beautiful women?' she asked.

'There could be no other woman in my life,' he said.

131

For a moment he expected a funny, flippant response, but he knew he had said it in far too serious a tone. She said nothing.

TWELVE

Cross had driven home late Sunday night, after his parents and Maya were in bed. He enjoyed the drive. It was so quiet on the highways and he could keep the window open, letting in the cool night air. Casey seemed to appreciate it as well, occasionally poking his head out of the window on the passenger side.

In the scheme of things the idea of a Monday morning usually meant nothing. However, devoting weekends to the family in Eaton meant there was some order in his life. And with two days of investigation not exploited and a murder charge a prosecutor's whim away, he felt the need to get busy on the deaths that weighed heavily on his mind and threatened his freedom – maybe his life.

Cross invested in a 'people search' on the Internet and by paying a small fee got a little more information on Taupin's son-in-law. It included the current address, not quite current, considering the situation, and all his previous addresses. If the address in Woodruff Place was still occupied by Mrs Taupin-Talbot, perhaps he might be able to talk to her. He might also be able to get some opinions from neighbors at his previous address. On second thought, he wouldn't bother the widow, for now. It would likely only irritate her and therefore irritate the police and he would like to avoid them for as long as he could.

But that wasn't meant to be. He was pulled from the shower by the phone ringing. Cross found the smooth, confident voice of Lieutenant Collins on the other end.

'Cross,' Collins said, 'need you to be at the City-County building at three this afternoon.'

'Should I bring a toothbrush?'

'You never know. You'll be meeting with the deputy DA. If you don't behave, there is always the threat of incarceration.' He said 'incarceration,' drawing its syllables out for emphasis.

Cross got the room number and the name of the ADA. The name was Lauren Saddler.

'Oh, Lieutenant,' Cross said, catching the officer before he hung up. 'Do we have an identity on the female victim?'

'No. A puzzle. We're pretty sure she has Latin ancestry, if that means anything. Nothing from missing persons. That's all I have. Good luck, Cross.'

A dial tone.

'You've never seen a naked man before?' he asked Einstein who had quietly appeared, sitting, and staring up at him. Cross went back to the bathroom to towel off and develop a plan for the day that included this added calendar item.

An elderly gentleman, who lived across the street from the victim's home in Woodruff Place, was the only neighbor available shortly before noon on a workday morning. He had not seen anything out of the ordinary at the Talbot's house. He had no recollection of seeing a woman who could be Hispanic at any time. But, he said, he didn't make it a practice to spy on the people in the neighborhood.

'A changing neighborhood,' Cross said.

'Back and forth, back and forth,' the man said, using his hands to illustrate movement. 'The place was a rat hole for a while, then came all the artists. Now, you got folks moving in and trying to make it look like it did when they wrote about it in the book.'

'The book?'

The Magnificent Ambersons,' he said. 'There was a book and a movie. Took place right here in Woodruff Place. It was a grand place then.'

'Still is,' Cross said. 'What do you know of the Talbots?'

'Weren't here long before he died.'

'They seem happy?'

'Yes. At first anyway.'

'What do you mean "at first"?'

'They didn't seem to be doing things together. I used to see 'em out in the yard, gardening together, fixing things up, two of 'em driving away together. Then it was just like two separate people comin' and goin'.'

'They argue?'

'Didn't see any of that.'

'Any other visitors?'

'Sometimes an older man would come by, usually after the boy went to work.'

'What was he like?'

'Just a man. Average height. Wore a suit, hair all slicked back. Had black rimmed spectacles. Looked like a banker or an accountant.'

'Conservative.'

'That would be good to say about him. Drove a big old black Buick.'

'He came by himself?'

'He came around dinner one time. One time as far as I know. He came with a woman about his same age. They went in. Stayed awhile. Young Mrs Talbot walked them to their car just before dark. Like I say, I don't pay much attention to what people do around here. Not my business.'

Talbot's previous address was in Irvington, another old community where homes were being restored, often by young marrieds. The community was less grand, but there was a pleasant small-town feeling to the area. The home that Talbot occupied before his marriage to the Taupin daughter was one of the smaller two-stories, red-brick, covered with ivy.

It struck Cross that Talbot was a bit of a romantic. His impression was confirmed by a woman who was putting brick down in a walkway that went from the street to the front door

136

of the house just to the north of Talbot's old place.

'You're ambitious,' Cross said to her as she patted down the sand she sprinkled between the bricks.

She looked up. She was attractive. A blond with a bit of hair that had escaped her headband.

'I have my moments,' she said.

'I'm doing a little investigation into the life of Marshall Talbot.'

She shook her head, then stood up, wiped the palms of her hands on her white shorts.

'Oh, that is so, so sad,' she said.

'You knew him?'

'Know? I'm not sure I did. But I liked him. He was kind of shy, kept to himself. You saw him walk his dog in the morning and then again in the evening. It was so clear he loved that dog. And the dog loved him. He wasn't active in the association, but if we asked for money for something, he always gave. He always waved, but tended not to stop and chat.'

'Quiet guy?' Cross said, trying to keep the conversation going.

'Yes, we had a book drive. Just after Katrina, a bunch of us decided to get some books together for the libraries in New Orleans. He came through with several boxes of books. They were good books, classics, high quality modern novels, histories. He was just such a decent guy.'

'But you didn't know him,' Cross reminded her.

'It was the feeling you had when you were around him. Maybe a little innocent, maybe a little sad.'

'Did you ever see him with a woman with dark hair, maybe Latin or Middle Eastern?'

She thought for a moment, again brushed the hair from her eyes.

'No,' she said. 'Shortly before he put his house up, his wife-to-be dropped by from time to time. Never really saw anyone else there.'

'What was the wife like?' Cross asked.

'I don't know. I noticed her one day. And the "For Sale" sign went up the next.'

Cross got the name of the real estate company. If he wanted more, he'd have to come back after working hours. He checked his watch. He wanted to squeeze in a lunch before heading downtown to see Lauren Saddler. Or he could have lunch downtown.

Though there were parking garages closer to the City County building, a vertical glass box, he parked at Circle Centre – a downtown mall. He'd grab a quick bite in the food court, stop at Borders on the walk back to the DA's office. Next, he'd see if he could find the listing agent for Talbot's home in Irvington. It was likely the rep who listed this one also handled the purchase of the one in Woodruff Place.

The Deputy DA's office was seventies cool. It

matched the building, but was newer. The Deputy DA was probably born in the seventies and was extremely 'cool' in the parlance of the era. Hard edges and sleek lines seemed to dominate the atmosphere.

'We don't know what to do with you,' she said, motioning him to sit down in what appeared to be a stylish but uncomfortable chair.

'You are not alone,' Cross said.

'I know you,' she said. An unkindly smile appeared on her face.

'Generically is what you mean, as in you know my type, right?'

'Right.'

She looked pinched. He thought she'd be quite remarkable if she would relax a little. After all, he was the one in trouble. Not her.

'And that is not a good thing, I'm guessing.'

'Right again.' She shook her head. 'Unmarried, up late repossessing cars and hanging out with...' She couldn't find the right word. 'How old are you?'

'I only tell my friends,' Cross said. All along he knew what he shouldn't say, but the words came out on their own.

She picked up the file and looked at it. She shook her head again.

'You know, Lieutenant Collins vouches for you. So do a few others on the force. Others say you are an irresponsible smart-ass. And whether you did it or not, the world would be better off without you messing around in it. What do you think?'

'I think we could do something other than play dominant and submissive,' Cross said. He regretted saying it. He regretted it *as* he said it. 'I'm kind of in the middle of that whole scene.'

'Well,' she said, looking at him directly in the eyes, 'today you are a submissive.' She went around her desk to her chair. 'Say, "yes ma'am."'

'Yes ma'am.' He gave in to a smile. She repressed hers.

She read the narrative of the case out loud in a monotone.

'Do you have any corrections or additions to make?' she asked.

'Just one. Slurpy wasn't making a threatening move toward the police.'

'Did he have a weapon?'

'Yes,' Cross said.

'Did he put it down when he was told?'

'No.'

'Was he coming toward police officers?'

'Yes, but...'

'No buts.'

'Yes buts. He held it high, away from his body. He probably couldn't hear the instructions with all the policemen yelling at him at the same time.'

'Is that all you wish to say about the events of that day?'

'Yes ma'am.'

'About Mr Edelman,' she went on, 'how is it

you were at the scene of his death?'

'I was not only at the scene, I called it in.' He wanted to be sure that point was clear. He had called it in.

'Once more, Mr Cross. How is it you were at the scene of his death?'

'I drove there to talk to him.'

'What about?'

'You have that in your files don't you?'

'Humor me,' she said.

'I believe I was set up. Someone wanted me to drive the car with the bodies in it so I would take the fall for the crime. The only person who would know for sure where I was going and what I was planning to do was Edelman.'

'Why would he set you up?'

'That's what I wanted to talk to him about. Why are you talking directly to me? At this point, it should be the police, shouldn't it?'

'Probably, but you have a complicated relationship with the police.'

'You think they would give me a break, help me beat a murder rap?'

'Or they might help you take the fall,' she said. 'I wanted to see for myself.'

'Have you?'

She shrugged. 'Didn't change much. I could make a case against you. Probably get a conviction.'

He wanted to ask what she was waiting for? But he didn't want to nudge her in that direction. He'd done enough damage already.

'Is it just the "probably" that's holding you back?'

She nodded.

'But you are getting pressured, aren't you?' Cross asked.

Lauren Saddler looked at him for a few long moments, said nothing. Finally, she broke the silence. 'You're on a short leash. And I'd advise you not to strain too hard against it.'

Cross stopped by his place on the way to the real estate office with Lauren Saddler's hint of a smile drifting back and forth through the gray matter of his brain. He let Casey out, filled Einstein's bowl with dry food and put food down for the Catahoula. He didn't feel guilty for not playing with them. He'd spent days with them before and they barely moved. A hot day like today and they moved less. Casey was all business with his business. He was back at the door in less than a minute.

Mark Graber was the real estate agent who worked with Sarah Taupin-Talbot. It took Cross about twenty minutes to track him down and, posing as a potential home seller, convince the agent to stop by his place. Cross used Graber's travel time to down a very cold Asahi Dry. On hot days, he liked lighter beers.

Cross saw the guy, suit coat tossed back over his shoulder, casing the grounds as he slowly came up the lawn and through the gate into the inner yard. They shook hands at the door and

Graber refused the offer of beer until Cross asked him a second time. He seemed grateful.

'This is a strange one, isn't it?' Graber said, even before he took the 30-second tour.

'Let me show you the East Wing,' Cross said.

They walked through the double, arched doorway and then down the steps into a large, cool room. There was a fireplace on one wall and a wall of paned glass doors on the opposite wall. The doors opened out on to a couple of pines and a small metal table and some chairs.

'Cool in here,' Graber said.

'The walls are big clay tile blocks. Thick. The roof is covered with clay tiles...'

'I noticed that. Beautiful. Expensive to repair,' Graber said. 'You said Sarah Talbot recommended me.'

Cross saw the furrowed brow.

'Marshall actually.'

'Oh.'

That seemed to relieve him.

'Being dead, I ... you know.'

'Sure,' Graber said, not wanting to talk about deaths. 'Messy business.'

'Yeah.'

'So...' Graber said, looking around, ready to get back to what he'd come to do.

'You ever meet the Missus?'

Graber nodded. 'Working with her now. She doesn't want to stay in Woodruff Place, given the situation.'

'I don't blame her.'

'It's still a little rough around there.'

'What's she like?'

Graber gave Cross a strange look.

'I mean I knew Marsh, but you know he was a quiet guy. I was always curious about the kind of woman ... you know.'

Graber walked back up the stairs and into the middle room, then into the kitchen, which wasn't exactly gourmet ready. He looked around. This kind of property was probably a little below his usual standards.

'I'm sorry, not high-end enough?'

'It's a strange one,' Graber said, on the verge of laughter.

'Used to be a chauffeur's quarters. Turned the garage into a living room. Kind of patched up other areas.'

'You have the neighborhood going for you,' Graber said. 'Why are you giving this up?'

'This was my artist phase,' Cross lied. 'I'm ready for real comfort with very little maintenance. I'm tired of mowing lawns.'

'Sarah is a Taupin,' Graber said.

'What?'

'You asked about the missus.'

'Oh, yes,' Cross said. 'What does that mean?'

'Being a Taupin, she knows what she wants and what she doesn't want and she has...' He drifted off trying to find the right words.

'...high expectations?'

'Yeah, that's a good word. She has every right to be demanding.'

144

'She must be really broken up about all this,' Cross said.

'They don't show their emotions, the Taupins. Everything is close to the chest. You don't get in. Don't know what their lives are like really.'

'You know Raymond?'

'Yeah, I do. I do a lot for the family.' He caught himself. 'In the way of real estate.'

'I heard they had a place up at Lake Wawasee.'

Graber was clearly shocked. Did he know? Or was Cross not supposed to know?

'Didn't know about that,' Graber said.

'What do you think it's worth?' Cross asked.

'How would I know ... oh ... you mean your place. I'd have to run some reports. And that's not going to be easy. I mean, one bedroom. No offense, but who has a one bedroom home, especially in this neighborhood? But you know, there's somebody out there who might like this.'

Cross knew of no other way to spend the evening productively than to track down everything he could on Taupin. And the only means he had was the Internet. By eight he was bleary-eyed and numb. He called Bazbeaux in Broad Ripple and had them send over a pizza. Good as it was, it only deadened him further. It didn't matter. An arrest could come at any moment. He had to get what he could get before the hammer came down.

What he found out was that the son-in-law,

145

the victim, was not a board member of any of Raymond Taupin's corporations. However, Taupin's wife, Cheryl, was on every board as was Taupin's daughter Sarah. There was another oddity. Someone named E. V. Lancaster was also listed on all of Taupin's boards. These were the only constants.

Marshall Talbot was nearly invisible. However he was listed on a professional social network that linked people who had common past associations and allowed for the interested to contact them. It listed Talbot as the executive director of a human rights foundation. It was a prestigious enough job, one that would earn him respect, but not one to pay more than a modest salary. It could support a fixer-upper in Irvington and possibly a larger, but not ostentatious home in Woodruff Place. He had graduated from Notre Dame and attended Stanford Law School. He was on the board of several nonprofit organizations, all of which were doing something generally acknowledged to be good for humankind.

As he clicked off his computer and switched off the lights, he wasn't sure he had found anything useful. He couldn't be sure. He reminded himself that the trail of the murderer still led to the Taupins.

THIRTEEN

The previous evening had been pleasant. More than pleasant; for the first time Shanahan felt as if he were on vacation. Even the 'nervous' and slightly sweet wine turned out to be good. In the air conditioning they slept well. Getting up earlier than Maureen, as usual, Shanahan realized he was victim to a routine. His walk for coffee and a newspaper, a return to the room to freshen up and have breakfast in the hotel with Maureen, all were predictable. No doubt Channarong would join them in the hotel dining room. If there was anyone out there who wanted to do them harm, predictability was dangerous.

When Channarong called, Shanahan suggested they meet somewhere else for breakfast. The guide suggested a dim-sum place in Chinatown. They would meet there.

'I have something to show you,' Channarong said before disconnecting.

'Chinese for breakfast?' Maureen asked when she found out where they were going.

'You don't think the Chinese have breakfast? I understand they make a delicious porridge.'

147

'Porridge.' She looked at him with a Mona Lisa smile. 'All right, bring on the porridge.'

'To tell you the truth, it's more like an early lunch,' Shanahan said, looking at his watch. 'They're serving at eleven.'

They found a taxi. At the intersection, a flock of motorbikes gathered in front of them, each with their lawnmower motors straining to get the go.

The restaurant was large and loud. The main room was two-stories high, with mammoth square columns every ten or twelve feet. It was grand, but sheer size had replaced decoration. The waiters, all young Chinese it appeared, wore white coats and pushed stainless steel carts built to carry a dozen trays full of small dishes. Access was from the side.

Shanahan felt as if he had stepped back in time. He had been in such places during his time in Malaysia and his trips to Hong Kong. But all of that was long ago and he wondered how many of these kinds of place – white coats in this heat – were left. Of course the cold stone of the walls and floors helped cool off the place and overhead fans that dropped twelve feet from the ceiling were keeping it as cool as possible without air conditioning.

Channarong was waiting for them at a table well in the middle of the great room. He stood, shook hands with Shanahan, and nodded graciously to Maureen.

'What a place,' Maureen said.

'I'm afraid I'll have to interpret for you. Most of the waiters here speak only Chinese and Thai.'

A cart was rolled up and the waiter pulled out the first of many trays he would display for inspection.

Midway through the 'breakfast,' which included porridge, Shanahan asked Channarong what he wanted to show him.

Channarong presented a photograph. It was grainy, but clear enough for Shanahan to see a man that looked much like himself. It was a strange feeling. He hadn't remembered his brother resembling him so much during the childhood years that he knew him. He showed it to Maureen.

'It's a little eerie,' she said.

'Where did you get this?' Shanahan asked.

'I got that from a friend at the police department. It's probably ten years old.' The arrival of another cart interrupted the conversation and after consulting with Maureen, he ordered shrimp and chive dumplings and turnip cake.

'I need to tell you something else,' Channarong said. 'I told the *mahouts* that there would be a reward for information about Fritz Shanahan. I gave each of them a copy of the picture.'

'How much is the reward?'

'Twenty-five hundred baht,' Channarong said, 'about seventy-five dollars.'

'Cheap,' Maureen said. 'But why would they know anything about him or how to find out

149

information? There are, what, eight million people who live in Bangkok?'

'Money is a motivation. They know people who know people who know people. Eventually we are all connected. There are a few bars just for the expats. And we can narrow that down to English-speaking bars. Whether he speaks Thai or other languages, it's likely that he visits at least one place where English is spoken. If you are an American, you will tire of Thai food. You will want to read an English or American book. Even the people who choose to live here, need a break from Thai culture once in a while. And we know where the British go, where the Americans go and so on. It's our business. Literally.'

The food was good; but Channarong was right, Shanahan was already longing for some sausage, northern beans, potatoes. He also realized he had come to appreciate Channarong. He kept the investigation going. He understood that offering seventy-five dollars of Shanahan's money was an economically effective way of getting information. He didn't need permission to do it.

'We still don't know whether these people trailing us are connected to each other,' Shanahan said.

'No, we don't. And they could be connected but want different things.'

'Then why are they working together?' Maureen asked.

'You see, that is the way it works here. The police, the criminals, the business people, the army – they all jump sides when it is convenient. One day one is your friend, the next your enemy. It is difficult for the western mind, perhaps.'

'I'm not so sure we're all that different. What did you tell your band of private investigators?'

'Connections were the Kitty Club, your Mr White, rubies, smuggling, Americans in occasional trouble with the law.'

'Key words in a Google search,' Maureen said.

'It's our version,' Channarong said.

'Why wouldn't the kids just make up information and we go off on a wild goose chase?'

'They won't. But they might sell whatever information they got from us to another interested party.' Obviously noting Shanahan's disapproval, he continued, 'Fulfilling both contracts.'

'Whew,' Maureen said, but was distracted by the arrival of a cart and Maureen spotted the soft shell crab. Channarong translated and when he was done he told them he had something else.

'I feel like a fifth wheel,' Shanahan said.

'I know how things work here, that's all,' Channarong said. 'Tonight we can hit some of the expatriate bars and see if there's anything we can learn.'

'And what kind of bars are these?' Maureen asked.

Shanahan looked at Channarong. 'They are discreet bars where Westerners go to drink scotch and engage in men talk.'

'I see. Men talk. Are there women there?'

Now it was Channarong's turn to look at Shanahan.

'No stripping, right?' Shanahan asked.

'No stripping,' Channarong said. 'Very discreet. Quiet, but, I'm sorry, a Western woman would discourage conversation.'

Maureen shook her head and nodded when Channarong translated the food on the tray as mango pudding.

'Imagine a baby shower,' Shanahan said. 'Men aren't invited...'

'A baby shower? Is that the best you can do?'

'Well really, there are places women don't want men around.'

She grinned broadly. 'I understand, but it is fun to see you squirm.'

There wasn't a lot for Shanahan to do, other than wait. He had planted seeds in the gem district. He had apparently stirred up interest with Mr White and with the police. Channarong, using the promise of reward, had sent the *Mahouts* on an information gathering mission. The afternoon would roll out its empty hours, he thought, and he had no idea of how to fill them. He might as well give in and enjoy it.

The roof-top pool was rarely used during the day. But there were bars and lights that suggested that maybe it came to life in the evening when the heat was bearable and the darkness hid smog in the air. He swam four full laps while Maureen prepared to get into the pool. He climbed out, struggling a bit for his breath. He dried himself off and stretched on the lounge chair that looked down the length of the pool.

A shower, nap and dinner. Shanahan felt better than he had in quite awhile. The sun, an occasional swim and afterwards naps to replenish his energy. Maureen let him know she didn't mind missing the men's club and would spend the evening with rum and tonic and a good book. Perhaps a late evening swim.

'They have a bar up on the roof. I'll mingle, you know,' she said grinning, 'with the crowd.'

'What crowd?'

'I'll find a crowd.'

'You'll create a crowd.'

'Whatever's necessary.'

It wasn't only Western women who were rare visitors, but also Thai men. Channarong wandered about the Night Market, very close to the two clubs Shanahan would visit. The first had a handsome bar that ran the length of the front room. Occupying the other two-thirds of the room were white linen-topped tables. There were half a dozen women around tending to Caucasian guests. The women were dressed well and Shanahan thought they were available for more than mere companionship, but if so, it

153

wasn't obvious. Discretion ruled. One would, in a sense, likely court the object of his affection and remuneration would be understood to be a gift. At bars like the one owned by Mr White, things were less subtle – the girls wore numbers.

Shanahan sat at the bar and was at once given a cool, damp towel to remove the thin layer of perspiration that had gathered on his face. The bartender was an attractive woman, who was slightly older than the other women. She also broadcasted her authority. No question she ran the place.

He ordered a beer and noticed that the back bar was filled with bottles of Scotch. There were names on them and they were marked at the level of liquid inside. It really was a club. People bought their own bottles and were served from them.

When he noticed she was between tasks, he asked her to look at the photograph. She did, looking back and forth between Shanahan and the photograph.

'You have any idea where I might find him?'

'Is this a joke?' she asked without an ounce of hostility, a slight, amused smile on her face.

Shanahan took a chance. He held his hands forward, touching one pinkie finger and then the other.

'That's not me,' Shanahan said.

She nodded. 'That's Fritz's,' she said. She shook her head to dispel the confusion. 'I just thought you ... Fritz grew a beard.'

'You know where he is?'

She shook her head 'no.'

'When was the last time you saw him?'

'Two weeks ago, maybe three.'

'You have any idea where he might be?'

'That's the way it is around here. You see somebody every day for six months then, poof.'

'He have a bottle up there?' Shanahan nodded toward the back bar.

She pointed to it. Fritz's bottle of Scotch was three-quarters full.

'I wondered why you ordered a beer. You never ordered a beer after dark.'

'Thank you.' He finished his beer, left a generous tip and left, going across the alley between booths selling all sorts of trinkets, wallets, scarves, Buddhas, on his way to the second bar.

It was clear he had just entered a bar that catered to a less moneyed clientele. The table tops were not covered. The bar was slightly battered. The women were dressed more casually, more Western. But again, none of the girls pressed the clients to buy them drinks – all more polite than their counterparts in the States. The girls were there to join a table if invited. There was a woman, also slightly older than the others, tending bar. How many of these kinds of places existed in Bangkok? Would he need to go to them all?

He ordered a beer, and was given a knowing look.

'I'm not much for beards,' she said.

'I'm not sure I am either.'

'If you're trying to hide it won't work. Beer tonight? You have work to do?'

She went to the end of the bar to pick up where she left off – chatting with one of the girls in Thai. Lots of laughs and nudges. He noticed the same line of bottles at the back of the bar. Shanahan waited but finally interrupted them to ask the question.

Shanahan had to show her and her friend that he had ten fingers before they believed him.

'I thought you lost some weight,' the younger woman said. 'You're his brother.'

'I am. I'm trying to find him.'

'I didn't know anything about his private life,' the bartender said.

'Does he have a bottle here?'

'Yes.'

'Which one is it?'

'You want him to buy you a drink?'

The bottle was half full or half empty. Shanahan wasn't sure which.

'Sure. If he asks, tell him he bought a drink for his brother Deets.' He handed her a card. She put it next to Fritz's bottle on the shelf.

Shanahan, a bourbon or Irish whiskey drinker, wasn't a fan of Scotch. But this seemed appropriate.

FOURTEEN

The lead story in the *Indianapolis Star* recapped and updated what the police were willing to say about the murders. Cross sat in the middle room with his coffee, Casey asleep at his feet and Einstein on top of the table where a slice of sunlight landed. For the most part the story confirmed what he already knew, but it was the first time the public knew the police were connecting Edelman's suicide with the bodies in the trunk. They also said they were questioning someone who had ties with all three deaths. No name was given, but he knew that would be him. Also missing was any mention of the fact that the murder weapon was not your average shotgun. Homicide made it a practice to hide from the public some evidence that only the murderer would know.

The other item of interest he found in the paper was that Marshall Talbot would be buried at two that afternoon at Crown Hill Cemetery. According to the story, only family and invited friends would be permitted to attend the service. However, by omission perhaps, the burial was not private. Perhaps not, he said. It was possible that he wouldn't be allowed near the family and he wasn't sure he wanted to given his status as a suspect, likely the prime suspect.

He got up and went to the bedroom closet. Was there anything in there he could wear to such a solemn occasion?

Cross stopped by Harry's for a beer and to see if Shanahan had contacted him. He hadn't. It was a wasted trip and Cross was pissed that he'd gone out of his way to make it. Harry was in such a dismal mood that Cross downed his beer quickly, grabbed a hamburger at a fast food restaurant before driving to the Crown Hill Cemetery. He remembered that John Dillinger, subject of recent discussions with Kowalski, was buried there among such luminaries as Jefferson Davis, a former president, and several past Indiana authors, governors and senators.

The place was beautiful. One could usually count on the grounds keepers for cemeteries and golf courses. But it was clear that Cross would get no where near the people gathering at the burial site. There were off-duty police checking lists on both sides of a cordoned-off area. People were still arriving.

Cross scouted the area and, having brought with him a pair of binoculars, found high ground not all that far away. He drove further back and when he got out of the Trooper, he carried with him a bouquet of bargain flowers

158

he'd picked up from a supermarket. He walked about pretending to look for the gravestone of a friend or relative, but in reality he was trying to find the best vantage point from which to scope out the mourners.

What a good idea, he thought, as he focused in on the group. Gathered together on the left were the Taupins. He recognized Raymond from occasional news reports. He wore a gray pin-striped suit that hung on his thin frame like the cheap suit that it was. His thinning hair was slicked back as if he didn't realize people could see through the greasy strands to his balding skull. Beside him was his one and only wife Cheryl who was somewhere around sixty and a student of the Tammy Faye School of Beauty. She had attempted to paint her way back to twenty nine. This seemed appropriate for the Taupins who were prominent social and fiscal conservatives. Sitting in a chair in front of them, wearing expensive sunglasses, was Sarah Taupin-Talbot, grieving widow.

There were others, perhaps brothers or cousins or business partners of the Taupins. Judging by their close proximity to the grave-site, he guessed this second group represented the Talbots, the deceased family and close friends. Two stood out. One was a big guy in an ill-fitting black suit. His hair was closely crop-ped. His face was as immobile as granite. The second was a blond fellow who also stood near the family. He, like the family, tossed earth on the coffin. But his coloring suggested he might not be a family member. Cross would bet that the young man was Marshall Talbot's best buddy.

That's the one he would track. Parents often either fail to know the truth about their children or, at least, want to hide anything that might harm the memory of them. Best friends were better as a source for both character and deeds. By the time the gathering broke up, Cross situated himself just outside the gate, where he waited for the blond young man to exit. He was by himself. Cross memorized his license plate number in the event he lost his prey in traffic.

He didn't lose him. He followed the BMW east on 38th Street, and right on Pennsylvania over the Fall Creek bridge, past the grand Central Library and eventually to the Lockerbie area of the city. Cross intercepted him as he was about to enter what was called the Old Glove Factory, a building in the heart of a historic district, where warehouses had morphed into attractive and coveted condos.

'I'm sorry to trouble you, but I saw you at the burial and I wanted to chat with you.'

The whites of his eyes were red. He took out a handkerchief and swiped it across his nose.

'What on earth about?'

'I'm a private investigator. I'm trying to find out who murdered Marshall.'

'Let's see something. I.D. something.' He

waited.

Cross showed him his license.

'I'm guessing you're his best friend,' Cross said.

The guy was still trying to determine if he should talk to a stranger, licensed or not.

'All I want to do is find out what kind of guy he was,' Cross continued.

'He was a great friend, a good person,' the guy said but couldn't give up his concern about Cross. 'Who are you working for?'

Cross was prepared to answer.

'It wouldn't be right for me to disclose this right now.'

The blond guy shook his head in disgust. 'You working for the Taupins?'

'No. But don't keep asking who.'

'Well I'm not in the mood for disclosure right now either.' He had the main lobby key in his hand but he smartly didn't open the door fearing Cross might follow him in. He wanted to wait until Cross had left.

'I'm working for me,' Cross said.

'I don't understand.'

'Do you want to keep talking out here?'

'I need more before I let some stranger in my apartment.'

'Well this may not help, but I repo'd the car that had his body in the trunk. As a result, there are those who think I killed him.'

'You knew Marshall?'

'A complete stranger as was the girl found in

161

the trunk with him.'

'Come on up,' he said, as if he were angry with himself for the decision he'd made.

The living room was large with a wall of windows looking over the quaint neighborhood in what used to be called Germantown. The condo was filled with furniture and accessories Cross would describe as modern. They looked good against the brick and concrete walls.

'Sorry, the maid is due tomorrow. Gets a little rough. You want a drink?'

A maid, Cross thought longingly.

'If you are.'

'I have to. What do you want?' He headed toward the kitchen, which opened over a bar into the living room.

'Whatever you're having.'

'What do you want to know?'

Cross sat in what looked to be the most comfortable of the chairs. He saw a hallway that led to more – at least one bedroom.

'What kind of guy was he?'

'Big question,' the guy said.

'One of his neighbors said he was shy.'

'He could be seen that way. He never wanted to impose on anyone else. He was unselfish to a fault.'

The guy came in carrying two glasses of clear liquid with ice and a lime.

'Gin and tonic,' he said, handing Cross one of the glasses and seating himself on the sofa.

'I should have introduced myself. My name's Cross.'

'Thad Moore, or did you know?'

'I didn't. Just seemed like you'd be the guy who knew about Marshall.'

'We go way back. Park Tudor.'

'Rich kids.' The drink was nearly all gin, very little tonic.

Thad Moore smiled. 'There's rich and then there's rich.'

'Which were you?'

'Rich I guess.'

'And Marshall.'

'Just rich, like me.'

'Now a delicate question. Were there any skeletons in his closet? A secret drug addict, a foot fetish, gay, anything?'

'He drank, every once in awhile too much. We used to smoke dope when we were in high school. If he had been gay, he would have simply been gay. He wasn't, but he saw no shame in it. No skeletons.'

'You were his best friend?'

'I would have died for him,' he said, voice breaking. With sheer will he pushed back tears. He took half his drink in one gulp.

'The Taupins,' Cross said.

'Assholes.'

'He married into the family. Did he think differently?'

'He wouldn't have said what I just said. But he didn't like them. He hated it when he had to visit them.'

'Is Sarah different?'

'She's a bitch. She's no different.'

'So how did that work?'

He finished his drink and went to get another. 'You ready?'

'Not yet,' Cross said.

'He believed he saw something in her. And I think this obsession of his to rescue the poor, the tired and the humbled masses, or however that's phrased, kicked in and he wanted to save her from the Taupins, from her own family.'

'You seem angry. Did you two fight over her?'

'I am angry. And we always fought. You know what he said when I showed him my new Beamer?'

'What?'

'He said, "do you know the difference between a BMW and a porcupine?" Then he answered, "with a porcupine the pricks are on the outside."'

He laughed. He caught himself.

'That was all right with you?' Cross asked.

'Sure. That's how we talked. He hid his sentimentality around me, but he thought the best of people. I don't. And it appears I'm fucking right.'

Cross slid the photograph from his pocket. He set it down on the table beside him and put his hand over half of it, covering the body of Marshall Talbot.

164

'Come here a minute, if you will, tell me if you know this girl.'

He came over. He looked at her.

'No. Never saw her before. She was with him?'

'They were found together.'

He shook his head.

'Was he having an affair on the side?'

'No.

'He's human, Thad. He couldn't be tempted?'

'He couldn't. He simply couldn't. He was so honest, so loyal, so true to his word. He couldn't have had an affair.'

'How is it they moved to Woodruff Place? It seemed like an odd location for Sarah.'

'It was. It was the compromise. She wouldn't move to Irvington, the snob. He lived in a great neighborhood. So they compromised with Woodruff Place – you know the Magnificent Ambersons, history, big homes, and all that – and that way neither one of them was happy.'

'He didn't give her everything she wanted?'

'Whatever I told you about him wanting to help and do the right thing didn't mean he was pushover. He was tough as nails for a cause and he put his foot down with Sarah over where he'd live. He wouldn't live in what he considered to be the very snooty Carmel. And he said he'd never live in a McMansion.'

Before Cross left, Thad had consumed three no doubt very strong drinks. He promised he'd do anything he could to help Cross or the police find the murderer.

'You have to go out for anything?' Cross asked as he headed toward the door.

'No, why?'

'Just thought if you needed anything I could pick it up.'

'I have enough gin in the house.'

Cross stopped by the grocery on Illinois and 52nd and picked up a steak and a bottle of wine. Casey went out into the twilight and spent a little longer than usual. He must have caught the scent of something wild. The neighborhood had various critters roaming about: possums, squirrels, raccoons. As old as he was, the old hound couldn't resist the scent of the wild.

There was a call from Kowalski on the answering machine.

'I have a wonderful evening planned. And I'd like to see the evening through. So don't kill anybody until tomorrow. But give me a quick call. Let me know where things stand.'

Cross called him.

'Anything new?'

'Not really. Nobody knows the female victim. But according to Marshall's best friend, the two wouldn't have been an item. Marshall Talbot was a saint.'

'What's he doing with the Taupins?'

'He wanted to save the daughter from herself,' Cross said.

'You know the old bastard bought some land

once. On it were a couple of buildings that were historic landmarks. That little problem would have prevented him from selling it for development. He had them torn down and then told the authorities that it was a mistake, the wrecking crew got the wrong address. Oops, it was all a big mistake. He paid a fine that was more than covered by the highly profitable sale price he got for the land once the obstacle of "historic status" had been removed.'

'Nasty man.'

'Lots of stories, but he wasn't exactly the mafia type.'

'You're saying he wouldn't sink so low as to hire someone to make a hit?'

'Morally, I don't think he'd quibble about having someone shot, but it's hard for me to imagine that he's that tough. It's a big jump from code violations or squeezing a business dry to bumping a guy off. He operated within the law, often barely and was willing to pay the price if caught.'

'Never enter a battle you can't win...'

'Right. Murder is a helluva risk.'

'So is keeping you on the line.'

Cross might have thanked him for checking in, but Kowalski was someone else who didn't like sentimentality.

FIFTEEN

Morning rituals completed and nothing on the agenda, Shanahan went to the rooftop pool, which he and Maureen had to themselves. There was almost a hint of blue in the sky, and the air was not so rancidly thick as it would become as the day wore on. Maureen swam gracefully, effortlessly, it seemed. Shanahan watched until he was interrupted by a young man in a white shirt and black pants.

'Are you Mr Shanahan?' the boy asked.

Told that he was, the boy handed Shanahan a note, scribbled in Thai. Shanahan recognized the phone number as Channarong's and assumed he was supposed to call him.

He mimed phone call to Maureen and descended the stairs to his room.

'We have an address for Fritz,' Channarong said. 'One of the *mahouts* came through.'

'That's impressive,' Shanahan said. 'I suspect he's not there, but I think we should look around, don't you think?'

Channarong picked them up in front of the hotel. The taxi took the three of them across town to an unremarkable area of multi-story modern buildings. They stopped in front of the address the *mahout* had for Fritz Shanahan. It wasn't the dirty, rundown place of a man on the run that Shanahan would have imagined. It was a clean, new building settled in a slum. The manager, a thin woman with hawk-like eyes, denied there was a Shanahan in 403. She brought out a ledger, on which 'Feiht' had been penciled in beside the room number.

'No Shanahan,' she said, not quite pronouncing it right. She said it while casting furtive glances at the old detective. The way her eyes moved it looked as if she were trying to look behind his beard. 'Look like you,' she said. It was an accusation.

Channarong said something in Thai. She said something back.

'I told her you were his brother. She thinks you are him. Apparently, Mr Feiht is two weeks late on the rent.'

'How much is it?' Shanahan asked.

He asked her and she responded, face forward, but eyes on Shanahan.

'Five thousand baht.'

Shanahan dug in his pocket. 'Tell her she can have it if she let's us in and leaves us alone.'

'Pig in a poke,' Maureen said. 'The place might be spotless.'

'That will tell me something too.'

Like the exterior of the building, the interior of the apartment was a small, but clean one-

169

bedroom with a small balcony that overlooked a swimming pool. The air conditioning was off. Shanahan switched it on. The room was tidy and held very little that was personal.

'You want me to sit here and look pretty or do you want me to help?' Maureen asked.

'Looking pretty would be enough, but if you want, you could go in the bedroom. Search the drawers and closets, all the clothing.'

'What am I looking for?'

'Anything that's not clothing. Pieces of paper, maps, correspondence, anything.'

'And me?' Channarong was smiling.

'You can just sit there and look pretty, if you like.'

'I'll go talk to the manager, see what she knows,' Channarong said.

Shanahan started to push the button on the answering machine, but had second thoughts. 'Wait a minute,' he said to Channarong, 'let's listen to the messages. Someone might have left a message in Thai.' He pushed the button.

'You know, Fritz, it would be so much better, if you know what I mean, for you to come by and see me rather than for me to spend so much time trying to find you. Under the right circumstances, all can be forgiven.'

'That was Mr White,' Shanahan said.

'His English is good.'

The second message was in Thai. Channarong waited until the caller disconnected.

'I don't know who was speaking, but it said

170

that you were looking for him.'

'Hmmn,' Shanahan said. 'But it came too late.'

'Unless your brother checks his answering machine.'

'Probably not. Calls can be traced.'

There were no other calls.

The call from Mr White was before Shanahan met with him. The second call came in after Shanahan had met with him. The calls revealed only two things, which Shanahan had already suspected: Mr White wanted to find Fritz, and Fritz spoke Thai.

Channarong left to talk with the manager. Shanahan poked around the living room. It was tidy and held no clues to anything. There were a couple of English-language newspapers on the kitchen table. The last date put Fritz's departure no earlier than the fifteenth of the previous month. That was probably when he took off.

The bathroom had the usual: a couple of cheap, throwaway razors, shaving cream, toothpaste, deodorant, a bottle of aspirin. All items easily left behind to suggest that he might or might not have planned to return. He'd check the bedroom. Maureen was going through the pockets of a jacket left in the closet.

'Odds and ends in the drawers,' she said. 'Couple of socks with holes in them and some tattered underwear.'

Shanahan glanced around. No luggage of any

kind. That indicated to him that Fritz probably hadn't been abducted. It didn't clear up for sure whether he planned to return. If Shanahan were a betting man, he'd bet Fritz had no intention of coming back. Leaving a few things and not closing out with the apartment manager was a smart tactic against his pursuers. Using a fake name meant he felt threatened.

When Channarong came back he said that the only thing that the manager recollected was that Mr Feiht had inquired about the weather in the North. 'It was an incidental thought after I badgered her about everything he ever told her.'

'North?'

'Chiang Mai, maybe,' Channarong said. 'It's fairly close to routes coming from Burma.'

'And?' Maureen asked.

'The best rubies are smuggled in from Burma.'

'He went south,' Shanahan said. Channarong gave him an odd look. 'He had to have gone south,' the old detective said. 'He's running away. He needs to cool off. If he went to ruby country he's more likely to run into someone he knows.'

'Why would he...?' Maureen began.

'He told her in the subtlest way so that it would appear the information she revealed would be by accident on her and Fritz's part.'

'She hasn't been questioned,' Channarong said.

'Yet.'

'What's south?' Shanahan asked Channarong.

'He'd go to Phuket to have the most escape options,' Channarong said. 'On each side of a long narrow strip of land is water. On one side you have the Gulf of Thailand and the South China Sea and on the other is the Andaman Sea, which is part of the Indian Ocean. That area has countless islands.'

'How do we get there?'

'Fourteen hours by train,' Channarong said.

'Or?' Maureen said.

'One hour by plane. And a short bus trip, depending on where you're going. Into Phuket City or Patong or some other place.'

'How hot is it down there?' Shanahan asked.

'The air is better. There are sea breezes,' Channarong said, smiling. 'I say it's a net gain.'

'Net gain,' Shanahan repeated. 'You should hang with a better crowd. You'll go with us?'

'I'm afraid I can't. And if I did I wouldn't be worth much,' he said. 'I don't know that area very well. I can connect you with someone down there. He is a little ... uh ... unpredictable, but he is a good person.'

Shanahan had little choice.

It was still early in the day when the plane lifted off. Shanahan wondered if he'd been followed. He didn't want to bring Fritz's enemies along. On the other hand, when they figured out he didn't know where his brother was, they seemed to lose interest in him. And Shanahan couldn't be sure that Fritz was in the South. He might have gone to Cambodia or Vietnam. He might have gone north after all. He could be in Milwaukee for all he knew.

But he also believed that to have survived for so long in a foreign environment, Fritz had to be pretty savvy. As Channarong said, the South afforded two coasts from which to launch a boat in the middle of the night. It allowed him a certain cover. As a *farang* in a place with so many tourists he wouldn't stand out. Also, as Channarong told them, Phuket was about as far away from the business of smuggling rubies as one could get and still be in Thailand. That kind of business happened much further north.

Maureen sat by the window and looked out. She was happy to be out of Bangkok, Shanahan thought, and happier still to be heading toward palm trees, sunny beaches and sea breezes. Shanahan reached a decision of his own. He decided that if he couldn't pick up the trail in Phuket, he'd stop looking and would feel at least slightly better that he had tried to find him. The world was too big and his funds were too small for this to go on too long.

Channarong had made hotel arrangements, putting them in a non-glitzy hotel slightly off the beaten track, up and away but not far from the boisterous Patong Beach. Once Shanahan was there, Channarong promised to call him to set up a meeting with the new guide.

'What are you going to say to him?' Maureen

asked.

'Who?' Shanahan knew the 'who' she was referring to, but he hoped he could avoid an answer.

'Your brother.' She gave him the look she always gave him when he used a cheap ploy for delay or outright evasion.

'I don't know.'

'Are you nervous?'

'I don't know.'

'What do you want from him?' she asked.

'You're not going to give up, are you?'

'Yeah, I'm giving up now,' she said. 'I just don't want you to get hurt.'

He wanted to ask what she meant, but that would keep the conversation going and the burrowing deeper. He didn't want that. He simply didn't know. And that had been gnawing at him since the dreams began. What could either of them expect after all this time?

Channarong had described their accommodations accurately. They were fine, though – clean if a little ragged. There was a small kitchen, air conditioning, a big, comfortable bed, and a wide balcony that provided a view, distant though it was, to the ocean.

As Maureen and Shanahan unloaded their bags, the phone rang. It was Channarong.

'You have a shadow,' Channarong said.

'That means I exist,' Shanahan said.

'That means someone is following you. They

had you at the airport in Bangkok.'

'How do you know?'

'When you checked in, a man followed you to the counter, asked where you were going. He reappeared with a ticket and got on the same plane. I talked to the attendant he talked to.'

'You followed me into the airport? Why?'

'Our friend, Mr Kowalski, told me to make sure I kept you safe while you were in Bangkok.'

'Beyond the call,' Shanahan said. He was impressed but also deeply disturbed that if he was right about Fritz being in Phuket, he had led his pursuers to him. 'Thanks. Let's hold off on our new Phuket guide. I'll let you know if I change my mind. How will I recognize the tail?'

'Not by looks. A male Thai, maybe about thirty-five...'

'Everybody could be thirty-five here.'

'Dark hair, brown eyes,' Channarong said. Shanahan could imagine him smiling. 'He has an odd tic,' Channarong added. 'He exercises his hands. If you have a cat you'd recognize the movement. It's what a cat does sometimes when it can't find something to scratch.'

'He splays his fingers and then closes part way?'

'He did that while waiting for you to finish getting your boarding pass. And again while you were waiting to board the plane. He was behind you.'

While Shanahan was wondering what to do about this development, Channarong continued. 'You might have a few hours before your phone is tapped.'

'Thanks for everything,' Shanahan said.

Shanahan took Maureen outside and they walked down to where the land began to drop off. Below and to the right was Patong, the epicenter of boisterous tourism. Down to the left were other beaches with less development. He could smell the salt in the air and realized he could breath again.

'We're being followed.' Shanahan explained the situation. 'What we have to do is pretend we've given up on our search, that we're staying a few days to have a short vacation before we leave. When we're in town, I want you to call Cross from a public phone or buy a cell phone and tell him to give us a call tomorrow evening and ask us about our progress in finding Fritz.'

'Why me?'

'I want to see who is paying attention to your leaving the table.'

'Then we lay low for a couple of days?' Maureen asked.

'Maybe not exactly low.'

'Have fun,' she said.

'Go down to Patong, have a few drinks, a nice dinner.'

'Was this part of your job in the Army? Laying low and having dinner and drinks?'

'Sometimes.'

'Did you have someone run into town and make phone calls for you?'

'It was a long time ago,' he said.

She gave him that knowing look. It said without uttering a word, 'you have no secrets from me.'

SIXTEEN

Cross now had a sense of some of the personalities who might be involved in the deaths. He had yet to gauge Raymond Taupin's wife and he had not found the man who came at him with the shotgun that evening. He was glad to have a sense of something other than the haunting image of Edelman at the end of rope, an image with which he had spent a good portion of the night grappling.

Now, having let Casey have his morning stroll in the yard beyond the front door and feeding Einstein, Cross realized he had to face the day, reminded himself that he had to make it productive. His freedom being at the pleasure of others was in danger of suspension at any moment. With morning coffee, he went over the records of Raymond Taupin, deciding to search for the man whose name was on the board of nearly all of Taupin's companies.

E. V. Lancaster proved elusive on the Internet. None of Cross's searches yielded a clue to Lancaster's biography or whereabouts. He called a few of Taupin's businesses to ask for Lancaster. They had no idea who he was. And when Cross would say that he was on the board of the company, the invariable answer is that they don't work with the board. Mr Taupin does.

Cross called Collins and peppered the homicide lieutenant with a series of questions. Had they identified the female victim? 'Nope.' Had they found any link between Edelman and the crime? 'You,' the lieutenant said. Had they traced the shotgun to anyone? 'Nope.' Anything new at all? 'Additional frustration and pressure.' From whom? 'Guess.' They suspect anyone from the Taupin family? 'No comment.' Do you know an E. V. Lancaster? 'Nope.' Could they see if there is a criminal background attached to the name? 'Maybe.'

'You probably weren't that good with essay questions,' Cross said to Collins.

'And you were probably the clown at the back of the classroom making faces.'

'I'll call you this afternoon about Lancaster.'

'I'm working for you now?'

'You always were. I am a taxpayer.'

'Yeah, I bet you contributed mightily to tax revenues.'

Cross, feeling like a telemarketer, called his parents. Maya was fine. She was outside with Cross senior. They were still doing their morning chores. Chores. The farm was the only place he heard the word. 'And we're all doing very well,' his mother said. 'You usually don't call this soon after a visit. Is there something wrong?'

'No, you guys were on my mind. I felt like calling.'

'Your father is almost completely back to normal. It was like the heart attack never happened.'

'Good.'

'And Maya goes to school in a couple of weeks.'

Cross sat back in his chair. He looked around. Casey and Einstein were asleep. What Cross needed to do was look through Edelman's stuff, but daylight wasn't made for a break-in. His decision to go back up to the lake was merely to do something rather than nothing to alter a path to prison. He'd get up there by noon. He'd spend a few hours and be back to meet Casey and Einstein's dinner expectations.

He gathered his usual stakeout gear, modified for a couple of sun scorching hours on a boat. Binoculars, hat, sunscreen, sunglasses, water, a Snickers bar, a book, a gun.

Outside, he noticed a black Chrysler sedan, the ominous style favored by high testosterone males, parked half a block away. He allowed himself only a glance. It may be nothing, but he knew the cars that usually parked on the street. He'd lived there for ten years. It seemed out of place among the Volvos and Saabs.

Cross pulled away from the curb, then made a U-turn so not only would he pass by the car, but, if he was followed, it would force the driver to make a U-turn himself. There was someone in the driver's seat. A male. But the man's head was turned away. He looked in the rearview mirror. He was well-practiced in reading numbers and letters backwards, quickly, and memorizing them. Cross felt his heartbeat accelerate. It wasn't fear. It was a little bit of gamesmanship and it was a lot of satisfaction, knowing that – unless this was the police – this would connect him to people worried about him nosing around. But he would not let them follow him up to Lake Wawasee.

He pulled into the grocery store to buy a couple of extra bottles of water and called Kowalski. He explained his situation.

They agreed to meet at a gas station on Michigan Road. Cross needed to fill the tank anyway. It was a long drive and he didn't want a gas stop to come in the middle of something important. While Cross was at the pump, the Chrysler pulled into a 7-11 parking lot across the street.

When Kowalski arrived, riding his Harley, he pulled up next to the Chrysler and engaged the driver in conversation, blocking his view of Cross, who used the moment to feel the underside of his car and find a tracking device. In a few moments, Kowalski pulled into the gas station and went inside to talk to the attendant. He ignored Cross who attached the device to Kowalski's bike.

Cross pulled over to the tire pump, checked the pressure on one of his tires, while Kowalski used the rest room. Kowalksi pulled out first, followed by Cross in what would seem, they hoped, coincidence.

Cross drove east and eventually pulled into the parking lot of Keystone at the Crossing, a shopping center. Kowalski kept close. If all went well, after a vehicular dance in the lot, the tail would lose Cross and follow the electronic beeps now coming from Kowalski's Harley.

Cross was in the first hour of his dog day afternoon – without the dog, this time. Casey was not fond, Cross discovered from the last outing, of the heat or the water. He liked solid ground and plenty of shade. After all, Cross thought, the dog's ancestors herded pigs, not ducks. The plane was gone. The boat was docked. The house was quiet but there was activity inside. People appeared and disappeared in the huge, paned windows. It was about one when a young girl who looked to be Hispanic or perhaps Middle Eastern, came out to the table on the Taupin's lawn. She opened the umbrella and went back inside. In minutes, she returned with a pitcher of something that looked as if it could be filled with lemonade or margaritas and glasses that suggested the latter. She went back inside.

Two women, one a younger version of the other, with sandy blond hair, pant suits, straw hats and sunglasses, found their way to the table and sat. The first woman returned with plates,

183

each with a sandwich and a green salad. The server asked them something and was waved off by the older woman. It was a rude dismissal – as if the server were some sort of annoying puppy.

Mother and daughter spoke, occasionally leaning in, toward each other. If they were not trading government secrets under the yellow umbrella they were engaged in some serious gossip. Cross tried to read lips, but couldn't make anything out. He unwrapped the end of a Snicker's bar. He had packed it next to the cold water, so it held together pretty well despite the heat.

He picked up the paperback he'd packed and read a few paragraphs before he realized he wasn't in the mood. He called Kowalski to ask about his stalker. Kowalski, along the way back to his place, located a blue Trooper in front of a Chinese restaurant and put the tracking device on it.

'Your guy was pissed.'

'Ouch,' Cross said. 'You waited?'

'No fun without seeing the results. The guy quizzed the senior citizen who claimed the Trooper. The Chrysler peeled some angry rubber getting out of there. And what are you doing, my friend?' Kowalski asked.

'Sitting in a boat on a lake watching two rich women on shore drink their lunch.'

'Jealous?'

'I could do with some tequila. If it's in a

margarita, so be it.'

'Get anything?'

'They have a maid,' Cross said.

'The two women? Mother and daughter?'

'I think so,' Cross said. 'And the maid looks a little bit like the Jane Doe.'

'You staying awhile?'

'I'm roasting out here. I'm going to call it quits.'

'You run the plate?'

'I called Collins. He's supposed to call me back.'

Collins did call back. Cross's cell wiggled in his pocket like an electronic fish. The car that followed Cross belonged to Richard Talbot, thirty-four. 'License says six foot three, two hundred and forty pounds.' He gave Cross the address in Fountain Square.

'Got anything for me?' Collins asked.

'You know that Taupin has a home on Lake Wawasee?'

'So, what difference does that make?'

'He owns a plane that can land on water.'

'Again, does this matter?' Collins asked.

'It might. Have you ruled out the family?'

'I'm trying to. So these observations, what am I to make of them?'

'I'm playing ball, Ace.'

Collins laughed. 'You know my real name?'

'Yes.'

'Don't ever use it.'

'OK. How's Lauren?' Cross asked. He wasn't sure why. The woman had stayed in his mind in ways that weren't connected to his dilemma.

'How's Lauren? You're getting real familiar all of a sudden. Calling me Ace, asking about Lauren. We're not a team.'

'Ms Saddler, then. How's Ms Saddler, Mr Collins?'

'Lieutenant Collins,' Collins said. 'I imagine she's OK, but we don't talk about feelings.'

'Richard Talbot. Victim's brother, cousin, what?' Cross said, changing the subject.

'Brother. Older brother,' Collins said. 'Cross, don't go busting down his door, OK? We'll ask him what he's doing. Appreciate the cooperation.'

'You'll pass that on to Ms Saddler.'

'Cross,' the cop said with warning in his voice.

'Ace,' Cross matched tone for tone, 'I was on your team once upon a time. I know how it works. I don't want any part of it. I know what the big blue line is capable of. And that leads me to this: I don't want to spend the rest of my life in jail because you can't find the real perp.'

Collins laughed.

'I know,' Collins said without malice. 'I'm playing nice, Cross. For now.'

'Me too.'

The black Chrysler was parked where it was before, half way down the street from his house. The car itself seemed demonic, waiting like a stalking animal, waiting for the right moment to pounce. Cross could confront him now or wait. Nature was calling and he had a bag full of stuff to get inside. He waved, but went up the steps across the yard toward the gate and inside. Casey exited as Cross entered, also to answer the call.

Cross heard the front door shut. When he came into the middle room, he saw the wide silhouette of a man backlit by the strong light coming in through the window. Casey barked, but it was hushed because he was on the other side of the front door. It was a smart move, keeping the dog out of potential hostilities.

'You go by Rick, Rickey, Richard or Dick?' Cross asked. Getting names right was fresh on his mind.

'Doesn't matter, I'm only going to visit you once, and it's not friendly.'

'This just isn't my day,' Cross said.

'No, it isn't.'

'I think I'm going to become a bartender. Everybody likes bartenders. You want to sit down or do you want to stand there looking all Smokey the Bear?'

Despite his heft, he was quick. He covered the seven feet between him and Cross with such speed the detective's reaction was totally instinctive. Cross stepped to his left where there was just enough space to accommodate him, and put his foot out to trip the big guy. The thud

187

was so loud Cross thought the man's fall had broken the floor.

The man was up on his haunches before Cross could get to him, jumping up and lunging at the same time. Cross dropped back as quickly as he could. The attacker grabbed Cross's waist as he went down. Cross brought his knee up, catching the guy in the face. The man fell forward, his head hitting the wood floor with a thud. Cross grabbed an arm, pulled it back, and stepped on his neck.

'I'm very sorry about your brother,' Cross said, his voice and body strained from holding the guy down. 'From all accounts he was genuinely a good person. I did not kill him and I am devoting, for selfish reasons, whatever time it takes to find out who did kill him and the girl. Do you understand?'

No answer.

Cross pressed down his foot harder. 'Grunt once for yes and two for no.'

'All right.'

Cross moved away and as the big guy got up, Cross plucked his handgun – a small Sig-Sauer P232 – from the bag. He sat in the comfortable chair, the handgun in his lap and motioned for Talbot to sit in the other.

'You're in my house. You get tough or you don't cooperate, you die and I just put a knife in your hand and tell people it was self-defense. Got it.'

Talbot straightened himself and sat down.

Cross remembered him from the burial ceremony. He was the man that stood in back of his family, alone. Now, he was red-faced. Anger, fear and embarrassment all mixed up.

'I didn't kill your brother,' Cross said.

'Why should I believe you?'

'I don't know. Why would you think I did?'

'You had the bodies in your trunk, man.'

'Not in my trunk. In the trunk of the car I was confiscating for the guy who financed the sale. How the bodies ended up in the trunk I don't know. Could be you for all I know.' It was clear Talbot was keeping his body in that chair out of sheer will.

'Where did you go? When you lost me.'

'You don't have any right to that information,' Cross said.

'I want my brother's killer,' he said.

'So do I. Tell me about your brother.'

'Nothing to tell. He was good. A good person. Foreign to me as an Eskimo.'

'You're not a good person?'

'Not like him. He believed that anyone and anything could be turned around. All we have to do is work at it. He worked at it. Somebody killed him. Here's me. The older brother, as miserable a son of a bitch as there ever was. I don't take shit from anybody.'

'What do you know about his life, who he knew, who tried to make his life miserable...'

'Don't know anybody who didn't like him, except maybe his wife's family. I don't think they disliked him so much as they saw him as a failure and they didn't want their daughter to marry somebody like him.'

'He ran a foundation,' Cross said.

'They thought it was left wing and, of course, it was nonprofit. He was never going to be a successful business man. And he didn't agree with the Taupins politically. There was so much they couldn't talk about. Marsh could only speak of the weather at family dinners.'

'I met Thad Moore.'

'A little dweeb, but an OK guy. He and Marsh were friends since first grade.'

Richard Talbot had calmed down, but his chest was still heaving and anger still filled his eyes. He stood up abruptly and Cross tightened his grip on the gun.

'You tell me what I can do to help you get the...' He laughed. 'No words for it. I'll help you. Now about me coming after you? I slipped or you wouldn't be as pretty as you are now.'

'I'll take that as a compliment,' Cross said. 'You stop following me, OK?'

'OK. And you remember,' he said with a threat back in his voice, 'I want a shot at this guy.' He nodded as if confirming his own words. He walked out in a way that suggested he had restored at least some of his dignity.

'They sleep a lot,' Cross said. He was on his third tequila, sipping it straight. He was answering Maureen's inquiry about Casey and

Einstein.

'Did I wake you up?' Maureen asked.

'Nope. How are you and Shanahan?'

'We're in Phuket. We're not sure why, but the trail ended in Bangkok. Shanahan deduced his brother might be down here. It's nice down here. I called to ask you to call us at the hotel tomorrow morning ... that is your tomorrow morning. And you need to ask us if we found Fritz.'

'OK,' Cross said. 'Why am I doing that?'

'Because by then our hotel phone is likely to be bugged. I'm calling from a pay phone in another hotel.'

'I see. You having fun?'

'Yes,' Maureen said. Cross thought it seemed an unqualified 'yes.'

'Well, like I said, the kids are fine. Very easy. Casey doesn't like boats, I found out.'

'Four feet on solid ground at all times. If you lift him up he gets this silly expression on his face.'

'I do too,' Cross said.

'Everything all right?' Maureen asked.

'The usual,' Cross said, taking another sip.

SEVENTEEN

The morning in Phuket disrupted Shanahan's morning routine. The coffee, retrieved from the small lobby, was made from a jar of instant powder and not quite steaming water. The English language newspaper, if there was one, would be a long walk down to the beach front. The only good news is that the call from Cross came through and Maureen adroitly provided the intended misinformation.

'How are the animals?'

'Happy and sleepy,' Cross said. 'How are you coming on locating Shanahan's brother?'

'We had to give it up,' Maureen said. 'It was just impossible. We lost whatever scent we had in Bangkok. It's unfortunate.'

'So when are you coming back?'

'I've talked Shanahan into hanging around for a little while. We spent so much money and took such a long trip, it seemed a waste if we didn't take a few days and just enjoy the trip.'

'How's Bangkok?'

'We're down in Phuket now. Beautiful and the air is so clean.'

'Maybe your pal can get a little color. Tell him

192

he can go surfing.'

'I'll tell him. I'm sure he'll have something for you to do,' Maureen said to Cross who began to laugh. 'Everything all right there?' she asked.

'Don't hurry back. Enjoy yourself. You guys should check out Thai boxing.'

'I'm not fond of seeing people beating other people up,' she said looking at Shanahan. 'But some people in this room don't seem to mind.'

'I'm sure you can find something fun to do,' Cross said.

'I'm thinking breakfast right now. Probably in Patong.'

Shanahan, standing beside Maureen, was pleased at the improvisation. She had told the possible phone tap listener where they'd be and when they'd be there.

'Good work about the breakfast,' he said after she said goodbye to Cross. She gave Shanahan a puzzled look. 'We might be able to pick up our tail while we have our coffee.'

She smiled. 'All I wanted to do is have breakfast.'

And breakfast she had, out in the open in a café just across a road from the beach. It was already hot and would probably have been unbearable, if it had not been early morning and had they not spent so many days in the suffocating, thick heat of Bangkok. The restaurant was unpretentious, busy and full of tourists. Other than servers, there weren't many Thais. Many of the customers, obviously normally pale, appeared pink in their colorful clothes and seemed to be divided into two distinct groups – those cheerfully starting their days and those waiting for the effects of the previous night to disappear.

A man appeared at the table next to theirs. He stood out not only because he appeared to be Thai, but because his clothing looked European. He wore a handsome straw hat, a silk shirt restrained in its color and design, white linen pants and leather sandals. The man nodded hello when Shanahan first noticed him.

'What brings you to Phuket?' The man directed his question to Maureen in perfect English.

'At first business, now just pleasure,' Maureen said.

Shanahan leaned across the table and whispered in her ear: 'In a few moments, turn away from him, pretend he doesn't exist. Now say something to me about how silly I am.'

Maureen laughed. 'Maybe tonight. We have a few days, you know.'

'I hope your business trip was successful,' the man said.

She shrugged, picked up her menu and moved her body, so that he was looking at a shoulder and the back of her head. Shanahan, in sunglasses, pretended to focus on the menu as well. After a few quiet moments had passed, Shanahan picked up the tell-tale movement. The stranger's right hand opened from a fist to fingers splayed outward, then back, then outward. It was the tic that Channarong described.

'I know what I want,' Shanahan said, putting the menu down and taking a deep breath.

'Me too,' Maureen said, eyes reengaging with the man at the next table.

'I hope I was not too nosy,' he said, 'I travel a lot and I'm just interested in other people's stories.'

'Don't worry, we just let hunger get the best of us. I was afraid the waiter would come and we wouldn't be ready.'

'Americans,' he said with kindly amusement.

'We weren't really here on business in the economic sense,' Shanahan said. 'I was trying to find my brother. We were separated in our youth and well ... it's late in our lives. We thought we'd take a vacation where we understood he was living. But it appears he has taken off again.'

'You don't know where he has gone?'

'No way to know.'

'So you came here?'

'We heard so many lovely things about Phuket.'

'We spent a good deal of money to get here,' Shanahan said, trying to be more sociable than he was. He was not good at being chatty. 'We decided to see a little more of your fine country before we leave.'

'Not my country,' he said, smiling. 'I am a visitor too.' He looked at his watch and excused himself. 'I'll have to grab something on the run. So nice to meet you. Enjoy your stay.'

He was gone.

'He was down to business,' Maureen said. 'You think he buys the story and is headed back to Bangkok?'

'I think we wait a day or two anyway before we do some serious hunting. We'll do tourist things. I'm sure there's a boat ride to somewhere and temples and hotels.'

The problem was, though, that even if Fritz were in the area as Shanahan theorized, it still didn't mean they could find him. But with the stranger in Phuket it was too early to be showing photographs around.

As Shanahan faced the day, Cross went out into the night. He had set his alarm for three a.m. Casey came in the bathroom to see what had disturbed the routine and, apparently satisfied, went back the way he came. The drive to the Eastside was quiet. Moisture saturated the air. Having stopped a few blocks from Edelman's used car lot and in dark clothes, Cross walked the rest of the way. By walking, he thought, he reduced the chances of being seen.

The streets, still hot from the August sun, sent steam up from the asphalt and the wet air made the lights from the streetlamps fuzzy. He dodged these soft pools of light.

He jimmied the back door of the office. He hoped it wouldn't be in vain. The police might have taken his financial records to help determine if this was a suicide. In fact, they should have. But it was likely they couldn't find the hidden records. Cross clicked on his two-foot-long flashlight – which could double as a weapon – running the beam across debris. The degree of the mess suggested it wasn't a forensic cop who did the tossing.

Though he wasn't exactly sure what his predecessors were looking for, he figured it was probably the same thing he was after. Because the mess was so comprehensive, it suggested the intruders might not have found what they were looking for. And that probably meant that what Cross wanted wasn't in the wreckage. Or, all of what they needed was on the old computer. The box was gone. The screen remained. But what Cross wanted wasn't something Edelman would keep out in the open. The only difference between himself and the people who made the mess is that Cross knew where Edelman kept the vodka. And putting the beam of light on the sailfish, it appeared it had not been touched.

There it was. Behind three bottles of Absolut was an expandable file and a big checkbook, the kind that businesses use. He pulled out the checkbook, sat it on the desk. The account was a bank in Montana. The folder was thick. Notes had been scribbled on yellow legal pads, napkins, the margins of columns in magazines, the back of envelopes. All informal, and, if Cross was right, incriminating.

Satisfied, he grabbed the folder, the check book and a bottle of unopened Vodka. What he was doing was highly illegal. But compared to the hovering murder charge, it was nothing. He made his way back to the Trooper and back across town, getting off the Interstate Loop at 56th and crossing back to his place via Kessler Boulevard.

It was as if all human life had been sucked from the planet. The late night celebrants were climbing into bed and the early morning workers had yet to stir.

When the light began to seep in through the windows, Cross switched from vodka to coffee. Since you're up, Einstein seemed to say with his nagging meow, feed me. Cross went through the morning routine earlier than usual and sat back down to the papers before him. The pieces were coming together. Edelman did not own the car lot or his house. The business appeared to be making a profit and the house paid off. Both were legally owned by two different Raymond Taupin corporations. Based on the information Kowalski gathered, the name E. V. Lancaster was listed as a shareholder and board member. Judging by the scrambled notes, Taupin's opportunity came during Edelman's divorce. No doubt Taupin stepped in to help Edelman financially during an expensive divorce. And Edelman had no idea just how expensive Taupin's help would be until it was too late.

The problem was, according to Edelman's scribbles, that Taupin was squeezing harder and harder, every bit of blood out of the turnip. And Edelman, feeling the pinch, was doing a little investigating on his own – keeping a separate set of books. Edelman had notes that paralleled Kowalski's, listing all of Taupin's companies and names. Edelman, on the brink of financial ruin, might have challenged Taupin. And the bodies might have been designed to send Edelman a message. But why would Taupin kill his son-in-law and some woman to make a point?

Cross sat back, pulled off his latex gloves. It didn't make sense. The other thing that didn't make a lot of sense was a note with several different phone numbers with country codes that turned out to be Colombia, South America. The girl? If Edelman did commit suicide why didn't he see to it that incriminating evidence got to the police in the event of his death – or before? If he didn't do himself in why was he killed before the killers found what they were looking for?

Cross would call Kowalksi and fill him in, but not until the sun came up a little higher. He took all of Edelman's papers to a copy house and, with latex gloves back on, made a copy of everything.

When he got back, he called Kowalski.

'Give them the copies,' the lawyer said. 'I'll find a lock-box for the originals.'

'You don't trust the DA?'

'I don't trust Taupin,' Kowalski said. 'His slimy hands are all over everything. He is well-connected to the city council and has been known to push the mayor around. I think you should get the young-uns out of your house. When you drop off the box, bring Casey and Einstein. They can stay here. You heard from the world travelers?'

'Something odd going on. They're in Phuket and they believe they've picked up a tail who might have their phone lines tapped.'

'Sounds like a good time. Wish I was there. Anyway, I've got an extra piece of halibut. So come up around dinner time.'

Kowalski, over grilled halibut, sautéed eggplant and chilled white wine, explained his concerns about the animals. If the DA had a sudden urge to have him arrested, they might arrive with guns drawn and dogs be damned. And if the murderer comes for you, you're all in jeopardy.

'In other words, I'm inches from the cliff?'

'You know Taupin is making their lives miserable – the cops, the DA, the mayor.'

They dined outside, Kowalski's bulldog, bored with his furry friends, slept in a little spot of evening sun. Though White River, as it wound through the strange little neighborhood known as Ravenswood, wasn't exactly the kind of river that songs were written about, it looked presentable as the sun prepared to set.

'I'm puzzled by the Taupins using muscle,' Kowalski said. 'The murders couldn't have been planned. He is the slimy type, but it's all done financially and the pressure he can bring to a situation with the powerful folks he knows and manipulates. It's all favor for favor or denial of a favor. Mafia-light.'

'Why do you have it in for Taupin?'

'The people downtown paint me as either a socialist or a Nazi. That's because they don't know the definition of either. I don't like the idea of somebody working real hard to set up a business honestly and then there's guys like Taupin who use insider knowledge, play fast and loose with regulations, and set up complicated business deals that blindside and bleed out their investors. That's why all these corporations have different names. When one goes rotten, the public doesn't associate the others with it.'

'Kind of creating a brand name.'

'Precisely. You have to take a special interest in him to put the pieces together and you'll never know when you have all the pieces.'

Cross told him about Edelman.

'My point, exactly. Taupin is a predator in an angel's tutu.'

'Angels wear tutus?' Cross asked.

'Meanwhile,' Kowalski said, ignoring the interruption, 'the guy trying to start a business on his own gets screwed over.'

201

'Survival of the fittest, Kowalski,' Cross said.

'Yeah, well I'm going to survive,' he said. He stood, went in the house. When he returned, he had a bottle of Scotch. 'And I'm going to see to it you do as well. How are Maya and your folks?'

'Maya's six inches taller, still tough as nails, and ready for first grade. She's going to be quite a woman.'

'The problem is will first grade be ready for her?'

'The folks are fine.'

'You still trying to keep the farmhouse standing?'

'Still trying. What are you up to?' Cross asked.

'Trying to keep an eighteen-year-old male out of jail for having consensual sex with a seventeen-year-old female. Prudery dies hard here in the Midwest.' He laughed, shook his head. 'They're five months apart in age, but they insist on going for statutory rape.' Kowalski poured them each two fingers of Scotch. Kowalski sat back. 'Anything else I should know?' he asked.

'It's a long shot, but on notes Edelman made, most of them about Taupin and money, he scribbled phone numbers. They had a Colombia country code.'

Kowalski's eyes widened. 'He can't be into drugs. I mean he's a major league asshole, but he'd be out of his league...'

'The girl in the trunk could be South American.'

'You call the numbers?'

'Don't speak Spanish.'

'I do,' Kowalksi said.

'Anything you can't do?'

'I can't get Angelina Jolie to return my calls.'

They sat for a moment.

'This doesn't make any sense. Taupin and women and drugs. Not at all his style.'

EIGHTEEN

Shanahan wouldn't have enjoyed himself had Maureen not been there. The waiting would simply be dead time. And the varieties of exoticism that existed at this southernmost tip of Thailand would not be so entertaining if he weren't seeing it through Maureen's eyes. Her curiosity and excitement were his.

Yesterday's dedication to look like tourists worked. They became tourists. Whether it was the splendor of the Wat Chalong temple, the flirtatious ladyboys on Bangia Road or the sweaty Muay Thai warriors in the boxing ring, they shared experiences that brought them even closer.

It was a new morning. Shanahan believed that to be safe they would play their game for one more day and begin the search tomorrow.

'Have you dreamt of him?' Maureen asked as they breakfasted at the same place as yesterday when they met the man with the twitchy fingers.

'Not since I've been in Thailand. Not once that I remember,' he said. He waited for the follow-up question. It didn't come. She was

204

respecting his desire not to discuss his feelings. But he was feeling more relaxed about things. It wasn't that he came from some fast-paced world from which he would have to chill, it was because time was slowing, moving at a less urgent pace. But finding his brother hadn't become less urgent. Yet because of the pace, the air and the warmth, Shanahan found patience. He also believed – and it was uncharacteristic for him to believe without evidence – that Fritz was nearby.

'We are still looking, aren't we?'

'We are.'

Maureen ate the apple-like jujube at breakfast. It was one of the many tropical fruits not seen on the shelves of Indianapolis supermarkets. She had already tasted the juicy lychee and the sweet longan. Advised early by Channarong, she did not partake of the smelly Durian. In fact, some taxi drivers, Channarong told her, refused to pick up fares when the ugly fruit was included in the baggage.

'Today?' she asked.

'You decide. I saw you looking through the pamphlets last night.'

'Let's plan on lunch in Phuket City,' she said. 'They have an old town.'

'Old towns are almost always worthwhile,' Shanahan said. 'Ye Olde Papaya Shoppe.'

'Sarcasm doesn't become you,' she said, giving him an ambivalent grin.

'Old towns are charming like old people.'

'I agree,' she said. 'I'll be agreeing more as time goes on and so will you.'

Tourism dominated Old Town. The rest of Phuket City was what one expects of a more ordinary capital. It was neither quaint nor glitzy. It was, instead, the heart of Phuket Province administration and seemed oriented to meet the needs of its citizens rather than visitors. There was a locally well-attended outdoor food market, definitely not trendy. Basic grains, fruits and vegetables. The two of them had been the only Caucasian faces in the crowd.

As they had lunch at an Old Town eatery, amidst what Maureen's brochure called 'Portugese Colonial' architecture, Shanahan looked over a map of the big island they were on to see at least a dozen other islands that could be reached by a small boat. Surrounding Phuket City were mountains of jungle. Surviving might be a problem but disappearing would be easy. While he could not get into Fritz's head exactly, he knew what most people do on the run, the places they hide and the other requirements of their survival – if nothing else, sleep and food.

Shanahan knew that his search was based on suppositions and speculations. Fritz could be up north around Chang Mai, still in Bangkok or some isolated Thai village. He could be in Vietnam or Cambodia. He could be in Las Vegas. Shanahan chose Phuket for two reasons. One, if he were some place else the odds were a billion to one he could figure out where. Two, he believed that because he left his last dwelling in extreme haste, he might have some unfinished business in Thailand, and Phuket was as far away from the ruby business as one could get and still be in Thailand.

If he couldn't be found here, Shanahan would be forced to give up his search. And he could console himself and perhaps confront his dream – he had at least tried to find his brother.

'He worked alone,' Shanahan said to Maureen who seemed surprised he spoke.

She nodded.

'He wouldn't be staying with friends. He's staying by himself. That means that from time to time he needs provisions. If he's down here, whether he's on some outlying island or somewhere in Phuket, he'll need something to eat.'

'And drink, probably. He is a Shanahan.' It was Shanahan's turn to nod. 'The market.'

'Which one?' Shanahan asked.

At a hotel, Shanahan made the phone call to Channarong to the number of the throwaway cell he'd provided his Bangkok guide. Shanahan made his requests.

'Tomorrow morning at ten a.m. I'll meet him there, his name's Billy, right? And he'll have it with him? Don't call me if you can't do it,' Shanahan told him.

They took a tuk-tuk back the 30 miles from Phuket City to their modest hotel near Patong

Beach. They brought with them a bottle of rum and some tonic water for Maureen and whiskey and beer for Shanahan.

They sat outside as night fell, content to do nothing, say nothing, think of nothing, just enjoy the other's presence on the other side of the world. After a long and comfortable silence, Maureen spoke.

'What are you thinking?'

'Maybe this isn't the time to answer that question.'

'Sure it is. Do we have secrets?'

'Sometimes we do. Temporarily.'

'C'mon.'

'You know I'm not a religious person,' he said.

'I know.'

'If you need to have a service for me, please do. But I don't need one, don't want one.'

'I know.'

'I was thinking that I don't want to be in a box. I don't want to be put in a coffin when I die. I don't want my ashes in a box or a vase. I want the ashes to be tossed somewhere.'

'Where?'

He was pleased that she wasn't upset by the subject of his thoughts.

'Anywhere. On the lawn, in a park.'

'In the lily bed?'

'Good.'

'And if I go first, the same thing.' She sipped her drink.

When night had fully settled, Maureen told him not to stay out too late. She went inside. He never knew anyone who sensed his moods so well. And he never knew anyone he loved as much. So strange for that to happen to him at this time in his life. He had been so ready to leave everything behind. She wouldn't, couldn't go first.

He might have slept and he might not have. He didn't know. But he became aware of movement near him. Someone was in the seat beside him. And somehow he knew it wasn't Maureen.

'How did you find me?' It was the voice emanating from a vague shape in the darkness.

'You've haunted me for a long time,' Shanahan said.

'Have I?'

'Yes. And it seems the other way around. You found me.'

'You were on the trail. Anyone follow you?' Fritz asked.

'Maybe. We think we've thrown him off the scent. How did you know I was here?'

'I heard someone claiming to be my brother was asking questions. Thailand is a country of dark secrets. But if you're not afraid of the dark, you hear things. Then I saw you and your beautiful companion at the market in Phuket town.'

'How did you know it was me? It's been a long time.'

'I knew. What can I say?'

'Are you in danger?' Shanahan asked.

'Yes. Now, so are you.'

'Let me see your hands,' Shanahan said.

There was enough starlight to make out hands coming toward him. The left pinkie was gone.

'They weren't all that angry and they really didn't relish inflicting pain. They just wanted me to have a constant reminder not to mess with them.'

'And are you messing with them?'

'You have to remember that much about me.'

'Why haven't you left Dodge altogether?'

'I'm greedy. There is something I need to take with me. And it's difficult to get to at the moment.'

'Rubies?'

'Just one,' Fritz answered.

NINETEEN

It wasn't that the sound was loud, it was because it was strange – a combination of clicking and scratching, metal on metal. When his eyes opened the minimal light in his bedroom was gray, filmy. Cross pushed himself to focus and grasped what was happening. He rolled off his bed quickly. On his feet, he slipped on his jeans. He wouldn't have time to get to his gun and load it even though he was moving at the speed of light. The lock on his front door was an easy pick. He was surprised that the intruder wasn't already inside.

Behind the fireplace was a narrow space, used to house the broom and mop. The opening to it was behind a door that looked like a wall. He slipped inside and waited, hoping he wouldn't sneeze or cough, and tried to control his claustrophobia.

Cross heard the door open and he heard the creaking wooden floor in the middle room as the person crossed it. Cross wasn't frightened of a confrontation. Part of him wanted to engage. But he preferred, at this point, to see and not be seen, to think before acting. His life was on the line and he didn't want to do anything foolish. His place was small. It took less than a minute for the intruder to decide no one was home. Cross waited to hear the telltale creaking as the intruder made his way out. But no creaking came.

'This is Eddie,' the voice said. Was the voice talking to him? Had he figured out where Cross was hiding? Cross waited.

'Not here,' Eddie said, obviously on a cell phone. There was a pause. 'I don't know. You want me to wait for him to come back?'

'Shit,' Cross said in his mind.

'If he stayed over somewhere he'd come back here to freshen up. I'll stick around until noon or so,' Eddie said.

Cross heard creaks in the floor. Judging by the direction, Eddie must have made it to the center of the room, probably at Cross's desk. Yes, Cross thought, hearing the metal wheels of his desk chair slide back. That meant he was facing the door, away from Cross's location.

There was no light in the little space he occupied. He had already moved what he could trip over to the other side. What else was in there? He felt around the dark space very slowly and found what seemed like an extension cord. It wasn't much; but it was something. And Cross couldn't wait for six hours. Not in there.

Cross heard his Mac computer go on. The guy was going to poke around, learn what he could. Smart, Cross thought. He'd have done the same thing. It was good for Cross. He wanted the guy's concentration on something other than his immediate surroundings.

He waited a couple of minutes and then slowly opened the space. He stuck his head out. He could see the back of the man's head. He could also see a .38 resting beside the computer – within easy reach. Cross focused on both those things and those things only as he moved toward the victim.

Fortunately Cross was shoeless and fortunately, as well, he knew where the creaks were in the floor. He could walk straight out of his little hole and walk close to the far wall. He held the extension cord like it was a garrote. There was a moment when his movements struck him, cartoon like, Sylvester stalking Tweetie Pie.

Eddie uttered a sound unlike any Cross had heard before as the chord caught the intruder on the throat. Eddie lurched forward, reaching for the pistol. But Cross pulled back suddenly, the wheels of the chair slipping out from under its occupant. Cross reversed the direction of his pulling, bringing the body that landed on the floor, up to a straight sitting position so his captive wouldn't slip out of the cord.

Eddie reached back, gouging his nails into Cross's hands. Cross, crouched over Eddie, but still on his feet, straightened and kicked Eddie in the kidney. He dragged the more compliant victim back and then brought his head back hard on the floor. Cross moved toward the .38

and got it.

Eddie pulled the cord from his throat. His face was blood red, his eyes bloodshot. His breathing was labored.

'You're a dead man,' Eddie said hoarsely.

'You?' Cross said, shaking his head at the recognition. 'You think you're going to leave here alive?'

Eddie was the guy with the shotgun.

'You must be E. V. Lancaster,' Cross said. 'Taupin's silent partner.'

Eddie just stared at him as if his gaze were capable of murder.

'I want you to stand up slowly,' Cross said, 'and empty your pockets on the table there.'

Eddie continued his stare as he got to his feet.

'Empty your pockets.'

Eddie had a practiced glare. No blinks.

'If I haven't evaporated by now, I think your technique needs some work. I don't want to convince you how serious I am by first putting a hole in the floor then in your foot and then your knee ... you know where I'm going with this, right? We can skip the stages. Empty your pockets.'

Eddie smiled.

'One more time. I'm inches from being arrested for the murder of two people, possibly three. Do you think I'm worried about killing an obvious intruder with his own gun? Do you think I have one ounce of sympathy for a guy who set me up for a lethal injection?'

214

Eddie's smile seemed to dim a bit.

Sunglasses. Electronic gadget for a BMW. A wad of bills, mostly ones. Finally, a wallet.

Cross took the wallet and opened it one-handed.

The driver's license was displayed and with the advance of morning, Cross was able to read it:

Everley Vance Lancaster, it read. Fifty-two years old.

'Everley,' Cross said. 'What kind of name is that?' Cross didn't care one way or another, but he wanted to get under the man's skin.

The man didn't show any stress or anger. 'Resident of Warsaw, Indiana.'

'Warsaw? Orthopedic capital of the world,' Cross said, but he was more interested in the proximity of Warsaw to Lake Wawasee. Close. 'What are you? Taupin's gardener?' The guy replaced his glare with distant indifference. 'Why did you kill them? What did they do to deserve it?'

'You and I have nothing to talk about,' Lancaster said.

'Everley, we have all sorts of things to talk about. But I'm easily bored.'

The problem was that Cross didn't know what to do with him. He picked up Lancaster's cell phone, punched in redial.

'Lancaster,' a voice on the other end said. It was a statement not a question.

'This is Cross. I have something that belongs

215

to you.'

There was silence.

'Number here says I'm talking to Raymond Taupin.' There was no response. 'Cat got your tongue? I've got your hired hand here, a Mr Everley Vance Lancaster. I believe he is on the board of several of your businesses.'

The other party disconnected.

'Now what do I do with you?' Cross asked the man staring at him with absolutely no expression on his face.

As the sun rose, the light came in the room behind Lancaster. Cross decided to move around so the light would be in the intruder's eyes, not his. That's when he saw the image on the computer. It was a photograph of Maya in Cross's arms, smiles on their Halloween faces, pumpkins on the farmhouse porch behind them. He clicked off the photo and another appeared. This time the four of them – Cross, his parents and Maya, stood beside the mailbox. The rural route number was clearly marked on the outside of it as was the word, 'Eaton,' the small town where the Crosses lived.

Cross felt a moment of insurmountable panic before a clear, cold focus set in. There was no question now about what to do with Lancaster. No uncertainty. This was a man who likely shot two young people in cold blood. This was a man sent to kill him. There was nothing to keep him from getting at what was left of his family. Even if he were behind bars, what would keep

Lancaster from telling Taupin about Cross's family and what would keep Taupin from hiring someone else to do his dirty work?

Lancaster's expression had not changed.

'I think you went over the line,' Cross said. 'I suspect that before you die you're not going to tell me why you killed those two kids.'

Lancaster closed his eyes in what appeared to be a blink in slow motion.

'You don't have the cojones,' Lancaster said. He said it as a person who was intimate with Spanish would say it, the 'h' sound powered out of the throat with disgust.

'A few minutes ago you were right,' Cross said.

'You are a soft American,' Lancaster said. 'Where I come from we devour and spit out people like you.'

'Is that right?' Cross lifted the pistol higher, pointing it at Lancaster's forehead. 'You come from some place real special, I bet.' Cross said, doing his best to insult the man.

'Colombia,' he said proudly, defiantly. 'You do not know what a man is.'

Cross lowered the weapon, briefly looking away. Lancaster lunged forward. Cross shot him, the hole nearly centered in the intruder's forehead. The body continued its flight forward. Cross stepped out of the way.

'Well now,' Cross said, his body beginning to shake. He saw the bloody flotsam and jetsam that struck the window on the other side of the

217

room. The cold passion he felt moments ago turned into nausea.

He stepped outside to get some fresh air. A squirrel darted across his vision. He looked up. The sky was blue. The world hadn't noticed. The nausea passed. He stood for a moment, looking at the clouds. What should he do now? Hide the body? He was, after all, a suspect in two murders already and was connected to what was for the moment regarded as a suicide. That could turn back on him as well.

'I'm going for the big prize,' Cross told Kowalski. He had retrieved his cell phone and went back outside. He felt better out there.

'Yeah, what's that?'

'I just killed a man.'

'That's a helluva way to start the day. I usually have a cup of coffee.'

'A Colombian employee of Raymond Taupin, E. V. Lancaster.'

'Lancaster is Colombian?'

'I killed a man,' Cross repeated.

'Anyone with you?'

'Just the corpse. And he's not much in the way of company. What should I do?'

'You have to call the police,' Kowalski said.

'I need to put the pieces together before I'm locked away forever.'

'OK, OK. Let me think.'

Cross's brain went dead. If thoughts were to be had or solutions found, it would be up to Kowalski.

'All right. We can buy you time. I don't know what you can do with it, but I suspect you want to get to Taupin.'

'Yes.'

'You have transportation?'

'Yes,' Cross said. 'If the police haven't inventoried Edelman's car lot, I have a car no one knows about except you.'

'Go. I'll wait an hour and call your girlfriend, Lauren, and tell them you killed an attacker, that you are afraid for your life and then I can draw out negotiations for your surrender.'

Through the trees Cross noticed a car pull up. Because it was down a slope, all he could see was the color. Black. Probably a big, official, Ford Victoria. He decided not to wait for verification.

'Gotta go,' Cross said. He went inside, grabbed a shirt and some shoes, his own pistol and as the knock sounded on his front door, he was out the back, and over the fence. He slipped on his shoes and shirt, tucked the pistol in his pocket and headed for the Trooper.

Two things were on his mind. One was his family. He needed to see and talk to his parents and to Maya. Next was Lake Wawasee. He had to talk with the Taupin's daughter. He had to make the connection between the two victims He liked driving when he had to think, to solve problems. Once out of the city, with a quiet secondary highway ahead of him, he began to breathe more easily.

TWENTY

If Maureen were looking out of the window she would see only two vague human forms, ghosts in the darkness. If she were awake she might have heard their low, slow voices trying to reach across their boyhoods and into the long stretch of their very separate lives. Below them, down to the right were the distant sounds and glittering lights of revelry from popular beach-front clubs and down to the left was the dim glow of a sleepier beach, luminescence dissipated in the night. When the wind shifted, sometimes they could hear the regular rhythm of the waves as they erased evidence of the day's activity.

'Where have you been?' Fritz asked.

'Around. A lot of places. You?'

'I looked for you once I got free.'

'Free?'

'From the institutions. I was seventeen when I got out. Looked for you. Nobody home. Nobody around home. Nobody knew where anybody was.'

'Mother died. The old man went into a home.'

'Where'd you go?'

'Hopped the rails to the west. Then went into the Army,' Shanahan said.

'When?

'Soon as I could.'

There was no rush in their conversation, no excitement.

'He was bad news, wasn't he?'

'He was.' Shanahan understood the reference. It was their father. 'He died unhappy.'

'The world refused to acknowledge his way of doing things, seeing things. Thought I was evil,' Fritz said.

'The seizures?'

'Yeah, how'd you know?'

'Word around here is that you still have them.'

'When I go on a binge and forget my meds.'

'How long were you in an institution?'

'Two of them. Second one had a real doctor who figured out I had epilepsy, that I wasn't possessed by the devil.' He laughed. 'Though maybe I am.'

'Jury still out on that?'

'It's out until the end,' Fritz said. 'Then I went to a foster home. On to the Merchant Marines, fell in love or lust with Southeast Asia.' Another long, but strangely comfortable silence. 'This place can get into your soul if you let it.' More silence. 'You have a beautiful woman there.'

'True.'

'You have a good life?' Fritz asked.

'Can't complain. Especially the last few

years.'

'Why did you try to find me?'

'I told you. You haunted me. Couldn't get you out of my head. Curiosity maybe. Guilt maybe. I shouldn't have let them take you away.'

'You didn't let me down if that's what you think. You couldn't have done anything. Neither of us really knew what was going on. You know Dietrich, it's all all right. I mean it. This is good, you and I talking together. It's a way of wrapping things up. Right?'

'I'm not trying to hurry it any, but yes.'

It seemed right that the conversation should take place at night, in near dark – there was a moon and some stars. And in the near quiet there were occasional sounds from life below. Yet the moment was dreamlike, an aside from real life. He had inhabited that odd reality shortly after he'd been shot. The world would have seemed off kilter to a sane, everyday mind. But this was different. The unknown depths of the ocean below them and the unknown yawn of the dark universe made ordinary conversation seem unnecessary, petty. Yet they continued.

'You feel like an outlaw?' Shanahan asked.

'Why?'

'So many people are after you, including the Thai government. Smuggling is a criminal activity.'

'A little righteous, brother.' He laughed. 'Right and wrong, Dietrich? Well, look at it this

222

way. A bunch of corrupt generals are running Burma. I could also say ruining Burma. Money from rubies goes to them, not to the people in any way. As beautiful as it is, it's not a place for people to live. Elections ignored. Human rights. What human rights? Outside of the North Koreans, the Burmese are the most isolated in the world. Their quality of life sinks lower and lower as members of the junta get richer and richer. It's like the diamond mines in Africa, Dietrich. Labor and hardship gets you nothing. Treachery and greed win the day.'

Fritz stopped talking. Shanahan didn't fill the void.

After a minute or two, Fritz picked a dangling thread.

'So I thought I'd try treachery and greed.'

He took a deep breath then went quiet again. The night surrounded them again for a while. Then from the quiet, 'They also have the best rubies in the world, Dietrich. And I've seen a lot of rubies. What I have is one of the best and one of the largest.' Fritz scooted the chair closer to his brother. 'It's called a pigeon-blood ruby. Found nowhere else but Burma. It's more than seven karats. Only one larger has ever been found.'

'But you are on the run.'

'I am, Dietrich, but if you steal from thieves and deprive the corrupt of their take, have you done anything wrong?'

'No one appointed me judge. How do you get

the rubies out of the country?'

'You see that's the problem. If it were just a regular big karat ruby, you mount it on a cheap band with a cheap setting. The people at customs wouldn't know a quality ruby if it bit them. What I have is bound to call attention to itself. But that's the least of my problems. The moment I leave Thailand they'll know I have it. And I can't trust it with someone else. Can you think of a solution?'

'No,' Shanahan said.

'You ever learn to smile?' Fritz asked.

'Maybe I'm smiling now. Can you see me?'

'No. Are you smiling?'

'No. But I practice sometimes when nobody's looking.'

A chorus of high-pitched sounds came from below, then quieted.

'You gonna have a good life?' Fritz asked.

'As good as I have any right to,' Shanahan said.

'You really need to go,' Fritz said. 'It was good that you came. I think it was the right time. But now, you and I did what we had to do. And we settled it on the opposite side of the world from where it all began. Pretty amazing. Memories and all that. But I have things to do.'

'Afterward?'

He laughed. 'I'm too old to be running around like this. I'm past retirement. This is it. The big play. Cash in. Go some place warm. Chile, Vietnam, Arizona. Spend more time looking at

224

sunsets than sunrises. Get a bottle of Scotch. Find a woman like yours.'

They talked more. About what they remembered – where they used to swim when the August heat became unbearable. The dinner table, where silence was mandatory, about their teachers and the Travis family on the next farm down. The three Travis brothers were a mean lot. And the sister couldn't be counted out. But Fritz was right. The conversation was becoming forced and hollow as the morning crept up on the two old men and Fritz said goodbye. No hugs. No handshakes. A nod, maybe.

'We're probably going to stay a couple days. Drop by if you want,' Shanahan said as Fritz passed over the hill.

Fritz, who had stopped and looked at his brother in a gathering of gray light, shook his head and abandoned words.

'Why are you up so early?' Maureen asked groggily from the disheveled bed.

'Wrong question,' Shanahan said.

She lifted the shade by the bed. The morning gray had a touch of pink in it.

'Why are you up so late? Did you go out and find some young dancer?' she asked.

He believed she was teasing, but sleep dripped over the sarcasm.

'An old dancer maybe. Fritz.'

'Fritz was here.' She sat up, awake. 'Why didn't you...?' She shrugged, nodded. 'He

225

found you?'

Shanahan sat on the edge of the bed.

'He wants us to go. Right away.'

'Go where?'

'Away.'

'Why?'

'I don't know. Maybe he doesn't want us to get hurt. He's got a plan to strike it rich.'

'And?' she asked.

'Maybe he's afraid we'll screw it up. After all, I led somebody down here. And he's got this scheme to end all schemes.'

'Is he crazy?'

'Could be. Thinks he can get a couple of million for a ruby.'

'A million doesn't go as far as it used to,' Maureen said.

'How many million do we have?'

'Haven't counted lately,' she said, not missing a beat.

Shanahan slept a couple of hours but awakened in time for some coffee and his scheduled trip down to the sleepy beach where he was to meet Billy – the guy with the gun. When Maureen nudged him into consciousness, he was startled to find the sun, in full cheer, streaming in the open window. And for a moment, the previous evening's conversation with his brother was viewed as just another of those haunting dreams.

He showered, dressed and the two of them

descended to the quieter beach, where he was to meet 'Billy the Kid.' Compared to Bangkok, Phuket had outdoor air conditioning. And there was plenty of open space, which they traversed to get to the beach. If the bar was intended for tourists, it targeted the down and out. The structure, nearly a lean-to, was completely open to the beach. At the back, a bar occupied half the width. The other half housed a table, on which sat a large screen TV covered by a sheet, no doubt to protect it from the blowing sand. Behind and to the left of the bar, between it and the stairway, were rows of nails, each with a number, and some with keys. There was a second story over half the bar area – rooms for travelers. In the bar itself, there were two dozen tables on two levels, facing the highway and the beach beyond it. Each table was covered in a plastic tablecloth that was stapled to the wood.

Shanahan and Maureen took a seat on the top level, since it was shaded from the sun. She ordered a Thai iced-tea and he a coffee.

'It's too hot for coffee, isn't it?' she asked.

'The hot liquid brings up the body temperature, which, in effect, reduces the effect of the temperature of the air.'

'Well...' She didn't know what to say.

Seated at the table below were four men. From what Shanahan could tell, they spoke German. One of them had a few teeth missing and all of them looked as if their livelihoods, even if they weren't too lively, came from playing at the margins. And they hadn't just arrived in the sunny climate or in the bar. There were eight bottles of beer on the table and the bartender was bringing over four more.

A few minutes past ten, a young Thai came in. He wore a white tee-shirt, too large for his thin frame, a pair of baggy shorts and some flip-flops. He looked around, noticed Shanahan and nodded. However, he was ambushed by friendly calls from the table of Germans.

'Billy boy,' one called out in English. When Billy went over to them he and the guy who called him chatted in Thai. Shanahan could tell, even from a distance that the young man had something tucked in the waist under the shirt. Shanahan's desire for a subtle exchange of money and weapon wasn't likely to happen.

Laughter came from the table as the more boisterous German translated Billy's answers from Thai to German for the two others at the table. The young man smiled too, but it seemed forced. He wanted to get along, but he also wanted to get away. The German grabbed the boy's hand and with his other tried to reveal what was making the bulge at the boy's waist. The boy jumped back, squirmed, tried to slip free.

'Billy?' Shanahan called out.

The men at the table stopped talking and laughing and looked at Shanahan. The look wasn't friendly. How dare he spoil their fun. But Billy managed to slip free as the guys at the table let their attention shift.

'Come meet Maureen,' Shanahan said with uncharacteristic and insincere cheer.

The boy nodded to the table and headed toward Shanahan.

The man who seemed to be the group's leader shouted something at Shanahan. Shanahan waved as if he had understood the shout to be a friendly greeting.

Facing Shanahan and Maureen and with his back to the unhappy group below, the boy lifted his tee-shirt to reveal a revolver.

'You shouldn't be tucking that thing in your waist,' Shanahan said. 'Is it loaded?'

Billy shook his head 'no.' He reached in his pocket and pulled out a half dozen bullets. He looked around, then handed Shanahan the revolver. Shanahan took it below the table toward his lap. He shook his head as he looked at it. It was much too large and it hadn't been cared for.

'How much?'

'Fifty thousand baht.'

'No, no, no,' Shanahan said. 'I'm not buying a house.'

'You rent, maybe.'

'Maybe,' Shanahan placed the revolver in his lap. 'How much to rent?'

'One week, four thousand baht. You lose it, you buy it.' The boy who was no doubt using the phrase he was told to use, was still worried about what may be behind him.

Shanahan looked at Maureen. 'This is a peacemaker. A 357. Wild west all over again.' He looked at the boy. 'A week. You trust me?'

He nodded 'yes.'

Shanahan reached in his pocket. He had 3,500 baht. Maureen contributed a 500 bill. He was about to hide the revolver in Maureen's bag when he noticed the four Germans were making their way toward the table. Billy heard them and stepped back just as Shanahan brought up the gun and began to load it. He looked up at them as he slid the bullets into the chamber with slow deliberation.

The lead German looked down. Shanahan focused on the leader. The man's ugly face formed an equally ugly smile. The man gave a little wave. It was either a bye-bye or a dismissal. He turned to go. The other two followed him out. They crossed the road and headed toward a couple of other guys who were on the beach, smoking. They talked, looking back toward the bar from time to time.

TWENTY-ONE

A light rain fell. Thousands of tiny droplets dotted the still lake. Cross peered through his binoculars from under a yellow plastic-coated poncho. The seaplane bobbed gently in front of the slope that led up to the house. All evidence of daylight was nearly gone and the lights of the Taupin house made him jealous of the warmth, dryness and comfort that emanated from the windows.

Occasionally Cross could see people pass, the gold light behind them. He saw mother, daughter and maid. There were two men. One appeared to be in some sort of quasi-military garb. The other was Taupin himself. A rather ordinary looking man in his mid-fifties or early sixties. He wore a suit. The tie hadn't been pulled from the collar. The man didn't seem to adapt to the more casual atmosphere of a lake cottage. If there were additional folks, they hadn't yet passed by any of the lakeside windows.

Cross felt around for a Snicker's bar, found it and gave himself a reward for his patience – hours on the most unusual stakeout of his life.

The problem was, he admitted to himself, he didn't know what he was looking for. And if that were true, he questioned, would he know if he found it? He observed, but had no plan. Even so, he was sure the key to his freedom was inside that house, with those people.

Boredom had set in the first fifteen minutes. Hours later it was stupefying. He found his cell phone in his jacket pocket and – still under the tarp-like poncho – he dialed Kowalski.

'What's up?' Cross said.

'Is this a social call? Are we going to talk about what Madge said to Helen and what Marsha wore to the book club?'

'No.'

'You are bored out of your mind,' Kowalski said. 'Or you're in trouble. Otherwise you wouldn't call me, the trait I most admire in my friends.'

'I'm floating on a lake staring at the Taupin's grand lake house, trying to figure out what I'm doing on a lake looking at some goddam house.'

'Lauren Saddler asked about you,' Kowalski said.

'About why I disappeared and where was I?'

'Yes. You know, I think she kind of likes bad boys.'

'Am I a bad boy?'

'Yes you are, you are a bad boy, yes you are,' Kowalski said in a fake, precious voice.

'You know if I ride the lightning for killing

those two, I might as well go for three.'

'No more electric chairs. These days we kill people pharmaceutically. We're not barbarians.'

'Does she think I did it?'

'I don't know. Probably not. You have no motive. But the pressure's building. Taupin is on the phone with her twice a day.'

'He's here now,' Cross said, 'chatting comfortably in his own expensive home with some guy who looks like he's leading a safari through deepest Africa.'

'He has a pith helmet?'

'He has epaulets. Who has epaulets these days?'

'He deserves to die too,' Kowalski said.

'C'mon now, you're just trying to cheer me up.'

'What are you going to do? They're not likely to kill someone in front of the window.'

'I thought I'd think of something. But I haven't. Maybe when the lights are out, I'll go inside.'

'Maybe they have Dobermans.'

'I don't think so.'

'Maybe bwana is the guard for the nightshift.'

'Maybe. Maybe he is security. Taupin has to know about E.V.'s death.'

'By the noon news if not before.'

'Will Lauren go after him?'

'Lauren, is it? Kowalski asked. 'A bad boy like you must find tough, dominant women like

Lauren attractive.'

'Just how interested are you in my behavior, Dr Kowalski?'

'This is the end of my needs assessment.'

'Promise?' Nonetheless Cross thought of Maya's mother. She was tough, dominant. A disaster. When he fell in love he fell foolishly.

As Cross's thoughts drifted, Kowalski continued to talk. 'They are all afraid of Taupin.'

'Why are they afraid of him? I've seen him. He looks like a milquetoast.'

'He is a cold, calculating soulless money machine. He is the ultimate materialist, completely unscrupulous, not an ounce of sentiment. He could as easily cut off your hand as he could lick a stamp. And he would do neither unless there was something in it for him. What makes people afraid? I think they know that to get his way he would destroy their reputation, or sue them into oblivion. We're going to have to put him in a package, wrap it up and tie the ribbon around it. You interested?' Kowalski asked. 'If you are, find the Colombian connection.'

'I've been sitting in the bottom of a row boat for hours on end. I think I've shown my commitment to the project. I have no choice.'

'It's true,' Kowalski said. 'One of you is going down.'

'Where's your money?'

'On you.'

'Why?'

'Because of me.'

They talked more. The plan called for Cross to enter the house, but not until the house went dark and stayed dark for a couple of hours. He searched the boat for an anchor, found it, dropped it quietly off the side, all 30-feet of it. He arranged the stuff in the boat until he created a soft spot. He pulled the tarp over him, listened to the tiny drops hit the poncho and welcomed the damp onslaught of sleep.

No doubt in Cross's mind. They would have killed him right in the boat had they not wanted some information first. And because he was in the house, a few feet from Taupin himself, Cross was pretty sure that once they got what they wanted, he and his nosy ways would be eliminated.

The man with the epaulets – they were on a jacket likely bought from a travelers clothing catalog, one that dried easily and had secret pockets – had the weapon. He spoke softly and with a Spanish accent. He had dark hair and fair skin. He leaned against a cabinet that housed, Cross supposed, the good china.

Because Cross was duct-taped to a maple dining room chair he was unable to move; but he could see the budget motel art on the walls, the sanitized bric-a-brac scattered about, and mostly Raymond Taupin, almost cartoon-like in the simplicity of his physical presence. A blue suit, a white shirt, a red tie, black-rimmed glasses. The fabric of his suit hung on his frame like a plastic shower curtain.

Only once did Cross notice Taupin look at him. It was a demeaning experience. It was as if Taupin had stumbled across a pool of vomit. There was a mild disgust, but in the end it did not affect him because he would have someone else clean it up. It had been embarrassing enough being towed quietly to shore while he slept in the dimmest of morning light. It was a gun pressed upon his sore and weary body that brought him to groggy consciousness. They had towed his boat to shore while he slept. And then Cross had been marched from shore to dining room. But in Taupin's eyes, Cross wasn't worthy of a moment's concern.

Taupin and the man with the epaulets talked quietly in the kitchen. What were they discussing? Probably, Cross thought, whether or not it would be smarter to turn Cross over to the police or kill him. Letting him go with a warning wasn't a likely option.

The man reached in his pocket and pulled out Cross's handgun. How did they get it? He hadn't brought it along. The two chatted and the man was showing Taupin how it worked.

Cross noticed a young girl, the servant, peering around the door. She could see Cross and Cross could see her, but the other two couldn't. Cross, wrists taped to the arms of the chair and mouth taped shut, could move his fingers and he pointed to her, then made two finger movements suggesting someone running. He rolled his eyes in the direction of outside and looked at her as intensely as he could.

The man handed Taupin Cross's pistol. Taupin examined it, weighed it in his palm. Finally he gripped it and shot the man in the heart. There was a brief stunned look on the man's face. He dropped to the kitchen floor.

Cross's heart sank. He remembered the girl, looked at the doorway, hoping he wouldn't see her. She wasn't there and the only good news he could hope for was that she would escape. She had to know she was in danger. Taupin was wrapping things up, fixing the problem. Even so, he was shocked when Mrs Taupin arrived in her white sleeping clothes, looking angry until she took in the body on the floor and Cross restrained.

'What's going on Ray?'

'See what a mess you've made,' he said, his back to her. He turned toward her, raised his arm and fired. Upon her white sleeping gown there was an explosion of red. For a moment this all struck him as some surreal play. And he was a very, very captive audience. It was sick, disgusting. He looked at Taupin, looked at him for signs of sadness or anger or even madness.

Taupin came over to Cross, but not to engage him. He appeared to be checking the restraints. That was all. When Cross looked directly at Taupin he saw the eyes of an insect.

'Carolina,' he called as he retreated into the

hallway. He picked up a phone, pressed a button. 'Carolina, could you come down please.' His voice was calm. Normal. No stress. 'Carolina!' he shouted something in Spanish. There was no threat in his voice, but it was a firm request one wouldn't normally deny an employer.

Cross hoped the girl was not foolish enough to hide in the house. He hoped that she was not only able to escape and save her own life, but also to seek help. Taupin stood in the hallway, looking back at Cross. His head was cocked as if he were listening for something. The sound of Carolina moving probably. Cross only had a few moments to think. He wiped away thoughts of the farm in Eaton, his parents and little Maya trying to find her way in the world without him. He wiped away the despair that was creeping into his thoughts and tried to think as clearly and coldly as Taupin.

It was stone quiet, except for the light rain that pattered against the kitchen window.

Taupin has a daughter, Cross thought. Where was she?

Taupin went to the kitchen window, which overlooked the lake. His eyes followed something and Cross thought that he could see a slight furrowing of the man's brow. Cross was convinced the man wasn't mad. He was coherent. What he was doing was part of a plan, one that would solve a problem or provide an opportunity for gain. Cross believed that Taupin's actions had a coherent purpose. He was not planning a shoot-out with the police. With Cross's gun, Taupin shot the security person – who probably knew too much. With Cross's gun, Taupin shot his wife. She had made the mess, it seemed, and Raymond Taupin had to clean it up. She may have also been a witness against him.

The reason Cross was still alive was also part of the calculation. Cross figured that Taupin was smart enough to make sure the medical examiner would conclude the two victims were dead some amount of time before Cross, himself, was killed. The story would be about Taupin coming home and discovering what Cross had done. In self defense Taupin managed to shoot Cross who, as no one would doubt now, shot the son-in-law and the unknown woman.

There would be no one left to contradict Taupin's story. It would be all tied up in a bow as Kowalski suggested, but in the wrong box. Taupin understood that the perfect crime is one likely committed by one person.

Cross watched as Taupin grabbed a kitchen towel and wiped down Cross's pistol. He came back over to Cross and, without saying a word and standing to the side, forced open Cross fingers. After a brief struggle, Cross's finger was placed on the trigger. With Taupin's pressure, Cross involuntarily pulled the trigger. The bullet zinged through a cupboard on the far wall of the kitchen.

Taupin took the weapon, wiped off all but the handle and the trigger. Fingerprints and gunpowder residue would indict the detective. Taupin was both thorough and, in his own way, creative. He inherited a problem and turned it into an opportunity, just like those books that tell you how to be a success in business. Taupin would not only rid himself of all this pesky murder business, but likely as not cash in a large insurance policy on his wife. Using the towel to hold the tip, he put the weapon on the counter.

He still had not acknowledged Cross as anything more than a piece of the plot. Other than the necessity of putting Cross's identity on the murder weapon, he had ignored him. But Cross hadn't ignored him, watching how Taupin had methodically worked his plan. How long Cross had to live he didn't know. Taupin, knowing it was still early morning and knowing that he had plenty of time, probably wouldn't gamble on the medical examiner's expertise in the interpretation of the time line. After all, he was in no hurry. Maybe Cross had as much as an hour. Maybe not.

Taupin disappeared. It would do Cross no good. His wrists were taped to the chair arms and his ankles were taped to the legs, all limbs wrapped several times. He might be able to scoot, but what would happen when he got to the door? He couldn't open it. And if he did, he couldn't get down the steps. He envisioned his head smashed against the concrete walkway after the tumble. The alternative version wasn't any better. A bullet in the head. Taupin would come back in moments. And that would likely be it.

'Well Pauline, I see you are on the tracks again,' Kowalski said coming in the lakeside entrance.

Cross gave him as intense a look as he could.

'Don't worry ... oh shit...,' Kowalski said, seeing the two corpses. Then, more distracted than usual, he continued. 'The asshole is up putting some clothes in his car.' He pulled the tape from Cross's mouth.

'Blood spatter,' Cross said, smarting from the tape removal. 'He needs to get rid of the clothing with blood spatter. It wouldn't fit his story. He needs new clothing for my blood to spatter on.'

Kowalski went to the kitchen counter, pulled a knife from the woodblock, began to cut his friend's arms free. He did so with an approach far less casual than his entrance.

'And why are you still alive?' Kowalski asked.

'Time of death. The story is that I killed them and he finds me hovering over the body and shoots me.'

'His problems are solved he thinks,' Kowalski said. He started to reach for the gun on the counter.

'Don't,' Cross said. 'We're screwing up all sorts of evidence. Why are you here?'

'You want me to leave?' Kowalski smiled. 'I tried calling you at about five this morning. Your phone is dead. I thought it'd be a great ride up here. And it was. Nice lake.'

Taupin had come in and had done so quietly. He apparently saw that the chair was empty and he ran for it, back out the street-side door. They heard him hit the door. Kowalski and Cross went in pursuit, but could only watch as Taupin, in his Toyota, headed down the road.

'A Toyota, for God's sake!' Kowalski said as he pulled out his cell phone. He checked the time, punched in some numbers. 'Not even a Goddamn Lexus. The cheap-ass bastard. Lauren Saddler,' he said into the phone. He waited. 'Kowalski.' More time. 'Get me Saddler right now. It's about a couple of homicides.' He turned to Cross while they were fetching the assistant DA. 'You have a lot of s'plainin' to do, Lucy.'

He advised Lauren Saddler to grab the sanest of the homicide detectives and come up to Lake Wawasee. Told her to get a chopper if she could. He also told her to take care of the locals. He had no idea who policed the lake community. Saddler would have to take care of that angle.

TWENTY-TWO

'Let me get this straight,' Maureen said, 'you found your brother. You had a nice chat. He said he had something to do that would keep him occupied, really kind of telling you to stay out of his business. And he said that you should go on home.'

'Yes,' Shanahan said as they walked down the quiet beach. It was empty. They had spent the day before – after Shanahan woke up – shopping and eating and generally being in a crush of people on the other beach. This morning they were the sole inhabitants.

'Yet you bought a gun?' she asked.

'I rented a revolver,' he corrected her, instantly regretting it.

'Oh, that changes everything. Now I understand.' She picked up the pace of her walk, temporarily leaving Shanahan behind.

'You think we should go back?' Shanahan said.

She stopped, turned back.

'He was here last night, but we don't know if he's still here. Even if he is, it is doubtful we can find him. And if we find him, we might lead

243

whoever he's running from directly to him. Strikes me he knows what he's doing. He's managed to stay alive roughly the same number of years as you.'

Shanahan nodded. 'All true.'

'But?'

'An uneasy sense. I can't explain it.'

'I don't really want you killed.'

'That's very sweet.'

'You have a few good years left,' she said, smiling.

'I hate to see him not enjoy the prize of his life,' Shanahan said.

'And you?'

'I have my prize,' he said, kissing her on the forehead.

'I think we can allow you to skip ahead a few grades. I'll talk to the principal.' She paused to look at a large ship sliding along the horizon line.

When he looked back he saw four people coming their way. He couldn't see their faces. An early morning haze erased the detail. He was pretty sure they were the Germans from the other day. He was pretty sure they were drunk.

Shanahan touched Maureen's arm. 'Let's go up,' he said.

She gave him a look of amused puzzlement.

'Up, away from the water.' He looked toward the forms and her eyes followed his. The stumbling forms shouted in German. 'Probably nothing,' Shanahan said. 'But they could be trouble.' Had Maureen not been with him, he would have traveled on.

She nodded and the two of them moved up the slight hill and into the tall, coarse dune grass.

'You have your gun with you, right?' she asked.

'No. But I wouldn't want to shoot them anyway. Too much paperwork.'

In a few moments the four Germans were passing below them. He could not understand a word they were saying.

Shanahan and Maureen were quiet until they were out of earshot.

'You don't think they are connected to what your brother is doing?' Maureen asked.

'I don't know,' Shanahan said.

'There are thousands of people here from all over the world. Tourists, expatriates...'

'Criminals,' Shanahan added.

'Being at the same bar. Isn't that just too coincidental?'

'The bar wasn't open yet,' he said.

'What do you mean?'

'Bar wasn't supposed to open until noon. That's what the sign said, that's what the bartender told me when I stopped back.'

'So?'

'We were there a little before ten,' Shanahan said.

'Maybe the kid had an agreement with the owner.'

'The Germans were there before we were. Again, that may be nothing. But it's not necessarily a coincidence. And why are four Germans hanging around with each other night and day? They might be obnoxious tourists, but they're not expatriates, drunk day and night and sticking together like that. If they were expats, they'd have at least some semblance of a life.'

Back in their room, while Maureen poured some orange juice and doused it with a shot of rum, Shanahan took the 'Peacemaker' apart. It was rusty and corroded. There was every likelihood that if he fired the damned thing, it would explode and kill him rather than the person he wanted dead.

He knew enough about weapons, especially old, simply engineered revolvers, to make sure all the pieces were there and once they were cleaned and oiled, put back where they belonged. The hotel's resident handyman was able to supply him with some fine sandpaper and oil.

By the time he was done it was afternoon and Maureen was pleasantly buzzed, a condition that normally produced a cute silliness he enjoyed. However, he was concerned for her. Things seemed to be getting more serious. He didn't understand it himself. He had nothing to base it on. However, his awareness was heightened, his focus tighter, narrower. This usually preceded a real threat.

They were in the chairs, looking out over the ocean.

'Maureen?' He tried to sound casual. However, he knew he wasn't good at nonchalant. She turned toward him. She was in a pleasant space, it seemed. Good, he thought. 'I was thinking. I have a few loose ends to tie up, but we've pretty much done all we can do. Don't you think?'

Her look went from curious to suspicious.

'And?'

'And,' Shanahan continued, 'I was thinking that maybe ... you might want to go back, check in on the animals ... I mean both of us being away...' He struggled. She knew it.

'What loose ends do you need to tie up?' she asked.

He continued his struggle for words.

'Out with it,' she said and he wasn't exactly sure what kind of smile she had on her face.

'I want you to go home. I think it could get dangerous.'

'Why do you think that?' she asked.

'I can't explain it. I have this sense that...'

'Intuition?'

'Well, not exactly intuition.'

'Not like women's intuition?'

'Exactly, not at all like women's intuition. More like a hunch.'

'I see,' she said. 'Men have hunches.'

'Your right eyebrow is raised.'

'I suspect it is.'

'Why is that, Maureen?'

'It does that when people are disingenuous.'

'Well, put it down and we'll talk about it.'

'You'll be your usual candid self from now on?'

'Yes.'

'OK, as long as we're being up front about this, I'm not sure I should leave.'

'Why?'

'You're not thirty-five anymore.'

'Not for awhile now. But you did say I had a few good years left.'

He knew what she was driving at. He couldn't be trusted on his own in a difficult situation. That was why she came along in the first place.

'And how is it, that after all these years you've suddenly become your brother's keeper?'

'I can't explain any of this. None of it. Maybe I've lost my last marbles.'

Neither would say, at least out loud, that maybe what he was doing was only a show of his independence, a statement to her and to himself, that he could still make a difference.

'Me too. And I'm being selfish. If I'm here with you and can keep an eye on you, then I'm not worried. If I'm home, I would be worrying all the time.'

'So, no matter what we do, one of us is going to worry?'

'We could both go home,' she said.

'I can't do that. Not again.'

'Again?'

'It's complicated.'

'Feelings are complicated things, aren't they?' she asked.

'Yeah, and it's your fault. Before you none...'

'Sssshhhh,' she said, putting her finger to his lips.

'I'll go.' There was no self-pity in her comment, nor was it guilt-laden. She had come to that conclusion.

Even so, Shanahan felt like the heavy.

'It's something I *have* to do.'

'I know.'

'I've put you in too much danger already.' She looked at him in a way that he didn't understand. 'Listen,' he said. 'I couldn't live without you. No point.'

'And me?' she asked. 'It's the same.'

'Let me do this,' he said.

'I can't stop you.'

'You could, but...'

'I understand,' she said. She kissed him.

Shanahan didn't want her going back through Bangkok. He didn't trust anyone at the moment and who knew what would happen at the airport? They, whoever they were, could use her to get to Shanahan and to Fritz. Maureen found a flight leaving that afternoon leaving Phuket, headed to Singapore, where she would change planes for the U.S.

The goodbye was awkward. For the first time neither knew what to say and for the first time they were frightened by the silence.

'It will work out,' Shanahan finally said.

'We'll be fine?'

'We will. Call me when you get home.'

She nodded.

Shanahan waited at the airport until he was sure the plane had taken off. He looked around, saw no one especially suspicious. He knew that didn't mean there wasn't someone there to be wary of. He took a taxi back to the hotel, carrying with him a sense of loss. In his desire to keep Maureen out of danger, had he smothered the unnamable spirit they shared? It was something *he* had to do.

He was about to enter his room, when the maid hurriedly interceded. She carried a pail with bottles of cleaners inside, a mop and a small vacuum cleaner. She spoke apologetically in broken English – something about not getting to the room yet. Shanahan turned to walk away, maybe down into Patong for something to eat. He needed a distraction to lead him away from depressing introspection. He had gone a few feet when he felt immense heat and his body lifting off the ground. Then came the sound ... the world was ending, had to be the world was coming to an end.

TWENTY-THREE

The room held several people whose physical presence seemed larger than life. Lieutenant Collins sat on the corner of the conference table, his expensive pants sharply creased and shirt starched. He appeared to be in charge. This, despite the fact that Lauren Saddler was an assistant DA and looking both highly professional and very formidable. Cross's friend and attorney James Fenimore Kowalski was no slouch in the intimidation department either. He was a big man, bearded. His black, swept back hair had a streak of silver, as did his beard. He could have been cast as Zeus in a Greek drama.

Also in the room, seated at the far end, was Raymond Taupin who seemed to possess none of the materiality of the others. He was almost a minus presence, yet it was Taupin who had been the powerful destructive force. His attorney, Anthony Zarga, sat next to him. He looked competent, smart, comfortable. There were two uniformed IMPD officers and the police chief from the jurisdiction that oversaw residents of Lake Wawasee. They had, at Saddler's request, allowed Cross and Taupin to be taken to Indianapolis as part of an investigation of the crime that seemed to have originated in Indianapolis. The crimes were obviously related.

'Ms Saddler and I are here this late not because we get overtime,' Collins said, 'We don't. We're here because it seems most likely that the truth about these deaths is knowable and that the truth is in this room.'

Cross was impressed with Collins. He didn't dress like a cop and he didn't talk like one.

'As should be clear,' Anthony Zarga said, 'I represent Raymond Taupin and I question the notion that a sleazy private eye, who has been involved in other highly questionable deaths would be put on the same level as a man who has earned his place as a respected businessman and as a generous contributor to the community.'

'At the moment,' Saddler said, 'we're going with the idea that everyone is equal under the law. It's a bizarre idea, I know. But for now, let's give justice the benefit of the doubt.'

'Sleazy private eye, sleazy business man...' Kowalski finished the sentence visually, with a shrug.

Collins continued: 'Mr Taupin says that days ago Mr Cross broke into his home and was confronted by his son-in-law, Marshall Talbot. And that somewhere, perhaps outside, Cross shot him, taking his body and an unidentified woman, perhaps an innocent witness, and put them in the trunk of his car. He switched the bodies from his car to that of a repo for transport later. Mr Taupin says he believes that Cross returned to the lake house to take revenge for the pressure Mr Taupin put on Mr Cross. When he didn't find Mr Taupin at home, he shot Mrs Taupin and the security person. And had not Mr Taupin fled the scene, he would have been killed himself. Is that about it, Mr Taupin?'

Taupin nodded. Said nothing.

'Mr Cross has a different story,' Collins said. 'He was picking up a repo as directed by the owner of the car lot and financier of the car to be repo'd. He did not know, he says, there were bodies in the trunk. He and his associate, Chester Thurman, disarmed a man who threatened them with a shotgun and the man later broke into Cross's home, threatened Mr Cross and was subsequently shot. Cross, feeling as if he was about to go down for the murders, visited Mr Taupin's lake home, where he was taken hostage. Cross said that he was restrained by being taped to a chair, a situation verified by his attorney, who freed him. But earlier, while being restrained, Mr Cross said he witnessed Taupin shoot his security man and then his wife. He did so, Mr Cross said, using Mr Cross's weapon. How'd I do, Mr Cross?'

'Good. The condensed version, but good.'

The darkness outside and fluorescence inside turned the window glass into a mirror. It was after ten in the evening, having taken an entire day of negotiations to move the crux of the investigation from Kosciusko County to Indian-

253

apolis. It was a good thing, Cross thought. In Taupin's backyard and with the circumstances appearing as they did, he would likely be in jail.

'We're here in good faith,' Anthony Zarga said, 'to move this investigation forward. But to give equal status to Mr Cross doesn't serve justice nor does it serve my client. Your Mr Cross has been associated with other suspicious deaths. You, Mr Cross were seriously involved with a prostitute who had ties to the sex slave industry. You, Mr Cross were fired from the police department and make your living by stealing automobiles in the middle of the night. And now we have the criminal's lawyer colluding with his client, providing false evidence to support his client's ludicrous claims.'

'There is no jury here, counselor,' Kowalski said. 'Save the rhetoric.'

During the silence Zarga jumped back in. 'The most ridiculous accusation of all is that Mr Taupin killed the two victims found in the trunk. Mr Taupin was in Mexico City at the time of the first two deaths. His whereabouts can be tracked through passports, phone calls, and witnesses if need be. He wasn't anywhere near Indianapolis the day before and the day after the incident. The same can't be said for the sleazy Mr Cross who was taking the victims for a ride.'

Taupin, allowing a smidgeon of disgust to cross his face, glanced dismissively at Cross.

'And Mr Taupin is the top vampire in the

254

business world,' Kowalski said, 'buying businesses on the cheap and killing them off by slowly draining them of their assets. He tears down historic landmarks and...' Kowalksi paused. He looked around the room, smiling broadly. '...and seems to have questionable ties to Colombia.'

Cross was pretty sure he saw Taupin's eyes widen, an expressive a gesture as he had seen, even while the man was killing his wife. Cross looked at Kowalski, wondering what his attorney was up to. If it was a bluff, it worked.

'This isn't a business deal that went wrong, Mr Kowalski. Four people were killed. Mr Taupin had no motive to kill any of them.'

'We're jumping ahead,' Collins said. 'We appreciate everyone's voluntary participation in this unusual meeting. But rarely do we have a situation like this. Because you each accuse the other and claim to be an eyewitness to some of the deaths, at least one of you is a liar and a murderer. Down to two. We should be able to sort this out before the press does a number on both of you.'

Taupin looked at Collins without expression.

What followed were two hours of accusations and denials, character sanctifications and character slurs as well as the silence of the two who were being accused. Cross was determined to appear as calm and unconcerned as the praying mantis, Taupin himself.

'His wife was murdered!' Anthony Zarga

shouted in the midst of the fray. 'At what has to be the worst time in his life, Raymond Taupin has agreed to come down here and help the police, but the police seem determined to allow this criminal to debase the victim.' He looked to Taupin, who seemed more bored than torn up, 'If he were on some mad murderous binge, why on earth would he kill his wife and let this cretin live?'

'I can answer that,' Kowalski said.

'Let's go,' Zarga said to Taupin, who stood and readied himself in the same casual manner that he would to leave a dinner table. 'You have anything to say to or any questions to ask of my client, feel free to call me.'

He said this to Saddler, who said, 'One more question. Is your client involved in any way with Colombia or Colombians?'

'I occasionally have a cup of coffee,' Taupin said with a straight face. The two of them walked out.

Saddler turned to Kowalski. 'Your turn.'

Kowalski sighed. 'My coffee comes from Rawanda and Zimbabwe.'

'Your Colombia comment, what was that about?'

'Working on it.'

'You better work pretty fast,' Collins said. 'Taupin will be going to the press, armed with what went on here today. And your client will be raw meat thrown into the press cage.'

'The nice thing is it can't ruin me financially,'

Cross said, standing.

Lauren Saddler shook her head as she faced Cross.

'You claim that Taupin was responsible for four deaths including his son-in-law and worse, his wife. Yet he let you witness it. My guess is that his clothing will not show gunpowder residue. My guess is that only your fingerprints will be on the weapon. And what were you doing there? You weren't invited. And the only thing you have on your side is a witness, who is your lawyer and friend.'

Cross had no idea why they weren't arresting him. He knew how all of this would look to a jury. Maybe Saddler read his mind.

She pulled him away from Kowalski and she spoke in a near whisper.

'I know you didn't do it. There is no motive, but it sure as hell looks like you did. You have twenty-four hours, the time it will take for us to get the reports from the crime scene. After that, with the huge preponderance of evidence against you, I'll have no choice but to have you arrested, charged with murder, and request that the judge order you to be held in custody without bail.'

Once inside Kowalski's Ravenswood home, Cross settled on to the sofa and the attorney brought in a bottle of Powers Irish Whiskey, the bottle in one hand and two cups in the other. Casey had been at the door to welcome them, but seemed momentarily confused with the constant change in people and places as well as the odd times of their coming and going. Einstein didn't move. He was snuggled up with Kowalski's bulldog.

'Saddler's trying to help,' Kowalski said as he poured a generous shot into Cross's glass. 'So is Collins.'

'I know.'

'You have any thoughts?'

'The two girls.'

'Two?'

'The one in the trunk and the one in Taupin's house. The maid who ran away when she saw what was going on.'

'She saw what was going on?' Kowalski asked, an incredulous look on his face.

'She saw me strapped in the chair...'

'For God's sake, Cross why are you just telling me this now? Why didn't you say anything tonight?'

'I'm still sorting all of this out. I didn't want Taupin to know about her. He might be able to find her faster than we can. And he'd kill her. I don't know, but I get the impression that she's an immigrant, probably illegal. If so, she's long gone. I just wanted to keep her out of it for as long as I could.'

'And the one in the trunk?' Kowalski asked.

'Look enough alike that they could be related. Hispanic probably.'

'Colombian,' Kowalski said. 'Same as...'

'Yes.'

'You're just now...'

'It's just now coming together.' Cross took a deep sip. 'Taupin told his wife that she screwed everything up. Then he shot her.'

'We have to find the girl,' Kowalski said. 'We find her, she says you were bound in the chair, it's over. You're free.'

He fumbled in his pockets for awhile, finally pulling out a few business cards. He sorted through them. He picked up his cell.

'Collins,' Kowalski said connecting. 'I know, I know. Without sleep we go crazy. But you're a big, strong guy. You can stay up a little longer. Listen, you have to talk to the cops up at the lake. We're looking for a young Latina.' He turned to Cross. 'What does she look like?'

'Maybe five-foot two, skinny, long black hair, brown eyes. Last seen she was wearing a black polyester uniform.'

Kowalski repeated the description for Collins. 'Why? Because she saw Cross taped to the chair, maybe more. Fearing for her life, she took off. Possibly an immigrant. She could be undocumented. So she might be hiding. Hell,' he said, 'she's got to be hiding.'

Where would she hide, Cross asked himself. Might she have family? If so, were they in danger? Did she go to the neighbors? If so, the local police would have found her by now. If she were illegal, she would hide from the police, probably from everybody.

259

She was the key to all of this. She would not only validate Cross's claim he was taped to the chair, she might very well know who the girl was in the trunk. And who might want Marshall Talbot dead? That was how all of this started, Cross trying to figure out who killed Talbot and the girl and why.

'Get some sleep,' Kowalski said. 'You all stay here tonight. We'll plot something out in the morning.'

Cross figured he only had tomorrow.

By morning he discovered he'd have to face it exhausted. It was a rough and tumble attempt at slumber. It ended with him wrapped in his bedclothes, struggling to get free. It was nearly a Gordian knot, a situation that paralleled his own. How could he do what he needed to do in one day?

Kowalski was up and had fed the menagerie before Cross finished his shower. He had scrambled eggs and made coffee for Cross, who took them out in the yard to get some fresh air by the river.

'I'm beginning to feel like the little woman,' Kowalski said, stepping outside and lighting up a cigar.

'Yep, the little woman,' Cross said. 'Seeing you in a little cotton dress is the stuff of nightmares.' He sipped his coffee, looked at a branch moving down the river. He watched it hang up on the slight bend. 'Speaking of cotton dresses, can we find out what the woman in the trunk was wearing?'

'We can.'

'Can we find out who in this little group of killers and dead people had a license to fly?'

'We can. What did you do, have a telling dream last night?' Kowalski asked.

'I went through every second of every event that led to this,' Cross said. 'The guy with the shotgun, the police and the bodies in the trunk, Edelman's hanging, Lancaster's attack, and Raymond Taupin's blood-letting. That is when I wasn't strangling the pillow.'

'So you know what this is all about?'

'No. But I remember that the girl who peeked in and saw me at the lake house wore a black uniform. A maid's uniform. I thought then how strange. I didn't know that the hired help still dressed that way. The young woman in the trunk of the car I was sent to repo wore black. It didn't seem dressy. I think it was something a waitress would wear.'

'Or maid,' Kowalski said.

'Yes. She's probably an illegal alien. And if so, she's scared to death and probably has no place to go, let alone find a way to get there.'

Kowalski nodded. 'And the license?'

'They have a plane,' Cross said. 'I want to know which one is the pilot in the family. I want to know who flew it. And when? Can you do all of this?'

'And you, what are you doing?'

'Going fishing.'

TWENTY-FOUR

Shanahan was treated as an outpatient at the hospital in Phuket City. No serious damage was done – a couple of cuts on the arm where flesh struck rock instead of sand. Some friction burns and some bruises. But no concussion, no fractures. He fared better than the cleaning woman whose death was now on him. If not for his nosing around, she would be alive. Sometimes, if people elect to become involved in a dangerous situation, the victims can be less than sympathetic. However, this woman made no such deal. Her death was senseless and her murderer need not expect mercy.

Shanahan was on his way in a couple of hours. But just *where* was up in the air. His room at the inn didn't exist. And even if it did, he didn't want to stay there.

He stopped to buy a few clothes and some toiletries and to make a few calls. One was to Cross to request that he pick up Maureen at the airport. Cross seemed distracted, Shanahan thought, but agreed to make sure Maureen would be met.

He also called Bangkok. As he waited in the hospital and saw how professional the doctors

262

and nurses were, something that had troubled him earlier bubbled to the surface. He couldn't reconcile Channarong's professionalism with Billy the Kid's lack of it. The young man's absolute lack of discretion, not to mention the shabby shape the pistol was in, was an uncharacteristic recommendation. Shanahan had another discussion with his Bangkok guide.

Billy the Kid, said Channarong, was an ironic nickname. It was like calling a big guy 'Tiny' or a fat guy, 'Slim.' Billy was probably sixty and possessed a restrained personality.

Had Channarong heard from him?

'Not since I called him. I hadn't heard from either of you,' Channarong said, 'so I assumed everything went according to plan.'

'Thanks,' Shanahan said. He took a tuk-tuk, a form of transportation Shanahan thought of as a lawnmower with an awning, from Phuket City back to Patong Beach. There he sat, sipping a beer, and thinking about the situation. The Germans had bothered him before merely by their rude presence and barely contained threat of violence in the bar. They bothered him more now.

Shanahan decided that since the little bar on the other, very quiet beach, was the center of activity, that's where Shanahan would set up camp. Maybe it was just keeping your enemies closer or maybe not. In the end, he had to stay somewhere and he'd bet this was pretty cheap lodging.

But first, he went to the hotel where he and Maureen had stayed. He talked with the manager who seemed more than a little uneasy. Could be the explosion. Could be he was in on it. Could be that he couldn't answer the question. Had Shanahan brought the violence upon his little inn or did he have some responsibility for keeping his customers safe? No. Quite likely another innocent victim in a greedy competition.

Shanahan asked if he had any messages. There were none. The police were eager to talk with him. Not that eager, Shanahan thought. They would have come by the hospital. Shanahan trampled through the debris in his room. The room smelled of sulphur, some of it the smell of burnt wood. The room was covered in a gray residue. There was a singed piece of string wound around the doorknob on the inside. He went to the corner closet and knelt down to open the room safe. It wasn't destroyed. And it was operable. Shanahan plucked the gun from the safe. He put it in the plastic bag that held his new clothes.

The man who was the bartender, waiter and landlord looked at Shanahan strangely. It could have been Shanahan's post-bomb apparel or that the elderly man's luggage was a plastic bag; but this didn't appear to be a place with prohibitively high standards.

The room, on the second floor, had a window

that overlooked the ocean, but no balcony. It had no bath. The communal bathroom was down the hall. Everything in the room – a bureau, table, double bed – had been around awhile and showed it. On the other hand, the place was clean. One could mistake a closed window with an open one, the attention to cleanliness so observed. Even the bathroom, shared by the occupants of the six rooms on the floor, was spotless.

As nice as they were at the hospital, Shanahan hadn't showered and he had put on the old clothes. He went down the hall, his pistol buried under a towel, and showered in room temperature water, brushed his teeth, and put on his new clothing.

'A shiny new nickel,' Shanahan said to his reflection. He put the revolver in the canvas bag he had bought for that purpose and slung the bag over his shoulder. A different person he was, Shanahan thought, with a beard and now with a bag, not to mention these strange clothes. He went downstairs to see if food was available in the bar. There was, in fact, rice and some sort of fish in curry sauce which tasted especially good with beer.

He wasn't wrong about the Germans. They were staying at the same place. They came stumbling down from their upstairs rooms, grousing and complaining as they spilled into the bar area a half hour after Shanahan sat down. When they saw Shanahan, the only other customer in the place, there was a wide-eyed moment, followed by silence. Their conversations were held in uncharacteristic low tones. Next came the stolen glances.

Their behavior simply confirmed what Shanahan already believed. Running into the Germans wasn't a coincidence. Maybe this kind of behavior wouldn't hold up as evidence in a real court, but it was the kind of evidence, supported by a healthy paranoia, that had kept Shanahan alive all these years.

The four bottles of beer arrived and the table of Germans went about their business. That left Shanahan's mind where it had begun to go before they got there – back to Maureen. He worried about the chilly parting. It wasn't the first time he'd felt this gulf between them, but it didn't happen often or last long. This one felt the deepest. It might be a while before it was resolved.

There were times when he would slip back into his old ways, a kind of chauvinism born of duty. She would have none of it. And she would occasionally try to manage his investigations. But Shanahan knew it was almost always about her wanting to be part of his life as well as her concern for his safety. Whatever difficulties they had with each other – and they were remarkably few – would be settled within hours if not minutes.

This time he had mixed business with pleasure and though she was quite capable of taking care of herself, her presence became a liability to both of them. Her presence also erased the advantage of his having 'nothing to lose.'

The German who appeared to be in charge was a large man. He wore a faded Hawaiian-style shirt. He whispered something to the guy next to him, a skinny guy in an oversized tee shirt. After a brief exchange, the skinny guy got up from the table and headed out to the street, but not before he glanced quickly at Shanahan. This group of four ran counter to the stereotype of the intelligent German. But that didn't mean they weren't dangerous.

Shanahan instinctively felt his canvas bag to make sure the 'Peacemaker' was still inside. It was.

The table was quiet. Others drifted in. Shanahan's mind drifted from Maureen to his brother and how this all started. He had simply come across an old photograph. He was in the photograph as were his parents. And that could have been it, but for the bare leg of a child in the bottom right hand corner. Just the leg – as if the figure had not quite made it out of the picture. And now Shanahan was here – his reason for being here as vague as the dreams that haunted him.

After a whispered conversation, another at the table of Germans left. Outside, the man turned the opposite direction of the first. This left two of them, the larger man who seemed to be in charge and the one missing two front teeth.

These were thugs, Shanahan concluded – not a bright one among them. They had plotted one person leaves at a time; but if that was supposed to be some sort of spontaneous act, the whispering and the dutiful, almost robotic departure made it almost comedic.

There was a plan afoot, but for Shanahan the question was whether the plan had to do with him, his brother or some other no doubt foolish undertaking. In a few moments, the answer began to take shape. The two who had left, returned, guiding what appeared to be a nervous and reluctant fifth person to the table. He was seated near the large, Hawaiian-shirted man and the toothless one.

While Shanahan took in the tabletop drama, the big German looked Shanahan's way and smiled. It was the first time anyone at the table acknowledged him. The big man whispered something in the newcomer's ear. From the look on the newcomer's face he didn't find the information encouraging.

It was a show, Shanahan concluded. They were trying to intimidate him by intimidating another in his presence. Shanahan could confront them. He'd lose. He could call the police, but there were four of them, all four of them more fluent in the ways of Thai police and politics. He decided to deprive them of an audience. If they were doing it for him, then they'd no longer need to do it if he were gone.

* * *

268

An afternoon nap, dinner on the party beach of Patong, a kickboxing match, a stop at a liquor store to pick up a bottle of whiskey and a walk back up over the hill to his room above the bar. It was pitch black when he opened his eyes, stirred awake by the delicate picking of the lock. His revolver felt heavier than usual. He took aim at the door. He was about to pull the trigger when he heard the whisper.

'It's Fritz,' the voice said.

A flashlight beam crawled over Shanahan until it found his face.

'Good God, you were going to kill me?' the man said, slipping in and shutting the door behind him.

'Yep,' Shanahan said. 'You were within seconds of certain death.'

'That's how it is for me,' Fritz said, 'I live my life as if every moment precedes my death by seconds.'

Shanahan sat up in bed, his back against the wall, poured Fritz a drink. Fritz sat at the foot.

'I thought I said "goodbye",' Fritz said.

'It could have been "goodbye", but then here you are.'

'If you were someone else, I'd swear you stayed because of the ruby, but I suspect you've done it out of some altruistic sense of brotherly love ... or responsibility. What you've done, dear Dietrich, is jeopardize not only my fortune but my life. I have this under control. Of sorts.'

'Of sorts,' Shanahan repeated.

'Yes. But you should have followed your pretty woman back to wherever you came from. Lived out your life. We had our little family reunion. That should have taken care of the hauntings.'

'The Germans, are they after you?'

'No one's after me. They are all after the ruby. But yes, they work for a concern in Bangkok.'

'Are they capable of building a bomb?'

'Sure. What do they need? A clothes pin, some metal, some powder, a few wires, a battery and a fuse. A piece of cardboard is attached to a string. When the door opens the cardboard is pulled out allowing all the parts to come together for ignition.'

'You know a lot about this,' Shanahan said.

'I've been around.'

'Why are they stalking me?'

Shanahan knew why. He wanted Fritz to keep talking, to keep drinking.

'They know you are here for one of two reasons,' Fritz said. 'Maybe you're trying to help me. Not good. Or you want the ruby too. Even worse. You are not only dispensable but dispensing you is desirable.'

There was a long moment of silence, Shanahan seeing his brother's face, much more like his own in the near darkness.

His brother said, a serious tone in his voice, 'Why *are* you here?'

'I don't know.'

'You don't know?' Fritz asked incredulously.

'I never used to do anything without a clear purpose,' Shanahan said. 'That's not so true anymore.' He filled Fritz's glass.

'Just a feeling?' Fritz asked. There was accusation in his voice.

Shanahan growled a yes.

'What the hell do you do all day? I can't imagine you're much of a shopper and I doubt if you brought a surfboard along.'

'I eat, drink, look around for you. Back in Bangkok I squeezed in a couple of laps in the pool.'

'Not afraid to get in the water these days. Not afraid of sharks?'

'Not in the swimming pool.'

'Swim pretty good?'

'For a man of my age, maybe.'

Fritz leaned forward. 'So you're all settled down, a little house somewhere on a tree-lined street? A dog maybe?'

'Something like that.'

'What's wrong with you. The woman make you soft?'

'She made me better.'

'I'm just jealous. Pay no attention. I gotta get outta here.'

'Are there others after you?' Shanahan asked. He didn't want Fritz storming out just yet.

'Probably. And that's worse because if I can't see them, I don't know how to avoid them.'

'What will it take for you to get your treasure and get out of here?'

'You think I'm drawing this thing out? Jesus, Dietrich. It's a day-by-day, minute-by-minute situation. I'll know it when the moment is right and then I'll be gone. And let me remind you, this isn't a team effort, Dietrich. You screw this up, my boy, and I die, you will come to know what a haunting really is.'

'You'll chase me around hell, is that it?'

Fritz laughed and coughed. Shanahan handed him the bottle of whiskey.

'You know the old man could still be alive,' Fritz said. 'People live to be a hundred.'

'Speaking of hell, right? Anyway, we're the old men now.'

Fritz took another sip of whiskey.

'You're not drinking so much,' Fritz said.

'Yeah I am. You're just not paying attention. You have your mind on the loot.'

'You know this is it for me. This stupid ruby,' Fritz said, 'having it makes the difference between a life lived as a slimy, bottom-feeding parasite or as a legendary discoverer who lives out his life with at least a measure of respect. I won't be world famous. But among those who count I'll be a prince. No, a king. They'll talk about me long after I'm gone.' He went quiet again and Shanahan tipped the last of the whiskey into his brother's glass.

Fritz had been right about his brother's drinking. Shanahan sipped and sipped only a little. He knew that if Fritz had survived the life he said he lived, dodging between corrupt authorities and greedy thieves, he had survival skills. Following him in his territory at night wouldn't be easy. It was important for Shanahan to keep his senses about him and to dull his brother's.

The night was warm and the air thicker than usual this close to the sea. At four in the morning, there were no lights to be seen. Fritz made it easily out of the dark, empty bar that opened to the road, then to the beach. He walked along it, near the water, away from civilization. The moon wasn't helping. Last night it showed nothing. Tonight, just a sliver of it was enough for Shanahan to see a blurry shadow half walk, half stumble in the night.

For a moment, Fritz disappeared away from the water. Shanahan had let some distance intervene and worried that he had left too much, that he had lost him. But the shadow reappeared, dragging something behind him. Fritz pulled it into the surf and climbed in. Fritz began to paddle out to sea.

Shanahan couldn't believe that his brother could go very far in such an insubstantial craft. He waited. He estimated he had waited ten minutes before he heard the distant sound of an engine starting.

Fritz was hiding on an island. As clever as the old, retired intelligence sergeant might have thought he was – getting his brother tipsy enough to follow undetected – he was at a loss now.

TWENTY-FIVE

Cross stopped back at his place, showered and dressed as though he was heading to church – something he hadn't done since leaving home when he was 17. Cross headed for Eaton, Indiana before swinging northeast to Lake Wawasee. If this was to be his last day as a free man, then he would visit his parents and Maya, the little girl he left in their care.

The old farmhouse and what was left of the farm itself, sat on a back road away from town. It was the house he grew up in. Handsome, but neglected and slowly slipping back into nature.

'Breakfast?' his mother asked.

'Had some,' he said, looking out of the window. Maya, who had been playing with the goat on the grass between the house and the barn, noticed the car and came running in.

'What did you bring me?'

Cross laughed. She was her mother's daughter.

'Just me.'

'Oh,' she said, disappointment easily read on her face. 'OK,' she said. She grinned and reached out for Howie to hug her.

'What brings you up this way this morning?' his father asked, coming in from the bedroom, pulling his robe together. 'Or is this the week-end already?'

His father seemed to be getting smaller with each visit.

'No. I might have to be away for awhile,' Cross said, then interrupting himself. 'I could do with a cup of coffee.' As his mother retreated to the kitchen. 'So I thought I'd stop by for a short visit first.'

No point in alarming them yet.

'You're all dressed up,' his father said. 'A wedding or a funeral?'

'Don't know yet,' Cross said bewildering his parents. But they were used to such bewilderment when it came to their son.

They talked, mostly of his father's medical condition – recovering from a serious heart incident and his mother's misunderstanding with one of the neighbors. They talked about Maya's school year, which would begin in a few weeks and of the prospects for some sort of normal home life for her. Maya, bored with such conversation, deserted them, for the outside.

'We gonna get to keep her?' Cross senior asked.

'Nothing else to do,' Cross said. 'You OK with the way things are?'

'We are,' his mother said. 'We're just worried. Where are you off to?'

'Work may take me away. I wanted to spend some time with you before I went. It's a little up in the air. There's a chance I'll be here on the weekend. But I don't want you worrying if I'm not.'

Cross's phone rang. He got up and walked out on the front porch.

'Where are you?' Kowalski asked.

'Eaton. I'll be off to the lake soon.'

'The natives are restless. Taupin and his attorney are stirring up trouble with the city council and reporters are nipping at the DA's heels. Saddler really went out on a limb for you.'

'She knows Taupin is guilty. She knows who he is. I've got today. They gave me today to figure this out.'

'Things change, Cross.'

'They don't know where to find me.'

'I'm sorry,' Kowalski said, 'where did you say you were?'

'Thanks,' Cross said. He clicked off the phone, took out the battery. He walked out to the yard where Maya and her goat seemed to be having some sort of *tête á tête*. As he approached, the goat looked at him warily.

'You know I love you.' Cross dropped down on his haunches in front of Maya. The goat eyed him. Mischief was brewing. 'Join the club,' Cross said to the goat. 'You know that, right? That I love you.'

Maya was real quiet, staring at him, a look of

panic replaced by a kind of blankness. Finally she said, 'Oh silly.'

'I know. The thing is I might have to be gone awhile.'

She nodded.

He was sure Maya's mother was never this intimate, but he knew too that she left her daughter often and for long periods of time. She was used to it.

'You'll watch over them?' He nodded back to the house. 'You can do that?'

'Of course,' she said. 'What do you think?' She hit him playfully on the shoulder and ran off, followed by the frisky goat.

Driving was therapy. It always had been for Cross. After he'd killed the two men in a field, the men who had abducted Maya's mother some many months ago, he went on the long drive to Iowa to visit a friend. As the miles and miles of interstate crossing redundant flat fields of farmland passed by him he began to shed the stunning effect their deaths had upon him. This, in some ways, was worse. He had watched this man, with ice-cold purpose, kill a man and then his own wife. No anguish. No anger. It was an execution prompted by the ultimate in practicality. So cold, so inhuman it seemed to Cross that while his brain could process it in some fashion, his mind, colored by at least minimal humane expectations, could not.

The old highways between Eaton and the lake

required more attention than the interstate expressways between Indianapolis and Des Moines. There was no way to view far ahead of where he was. There were trees by the narrow pavement, sudden turns, hills. And the gritty world of rural Indiana's rotting fences and collapsing barns was closer to him. He wasn't passing by; he was passing through, his attention focusing on the slow decline and isolation of these parts.

There weren't enough miles to clear his head, to cleanse his thoughts by the time he arrived. There was a lot of light and heat left in the day. And though he was uncomfortable in his suit, he was likely to stir less suspicion should someone see him enter the Taupin house, especially with police tape surrounding the home. He got out of the car, retrieved his coat from the back seat, straightened his tie, and walked to the front door.

He looked around. It amazed him how high-end the homes were, how well kept. The street that, for all practical purposes, circled the lake was quiet. He saw not one living being as he went about manipulating the tumblers in the lock at the front door.

Indoors was all light and cheer – a living room ready for guests. It was spotless and there was enough daylight seeping in from the outside that Cross didn't have to bother with lights. The place was sealed, soundless except for the low hum of the air conditioner. Why was that still on? Cross walked across the thick carpet toward the kitchen and family room – both with a wall of windows looking out over a glistening lake.

He walked to the window in the dining area, avoiding the kitchen where he had witnessed the cold executions. The lake was alive. Sail boats, small yachts out in the middle. Rubber rafts and swimmers closer to shore.

Cross, giving the killing area only a glimpse, went toward the area where the girl, the one who witnessed him taped to the chair as the shots were fired, had come from. But there was nothing there. Just a wall. Unless she was a capable of voluntary invisibility there had to be a physical explanation. He pushed at the wall and nothing happened. He knocked on the wall and heard the hollowness behind it. He applied pressure and moved his hand to the right and though it offered resistance, it slid open. The light from the kitchen revealed only the first couple of steps leading down and into pitch-black darkness. He felt for a light switch. He couldn't find it. He went down a few steps, still couldn't find a switch.

He stepped back and up. He wouldn't go down there. He went to the kitchen, checked drawers and cupboards, looking for a flashlight. None. He debated about going back out to his car, but decided he would be chancing discovery. He remembered that in the formal dining room, off the living room, was a candelabra. It had candles. He also found matches in the kitchen drawer.

It felt a little medieval to descend the steps with candles ablaze. With the light he was able to see that the sliding door could be operated with a remote control as, no doubt, the lights. Downstairs was one large room. There were three single beds and three portable closets. An industrial-sized washer and an equally large dryer occupied one wall near the ironing board. He investigated the closets. One was empty, except for a couple of uniforms. The other two had some street clothes as well as uniforms.

There was a bathroom downstairs as well as a small refrigerator and a hot plate. There were no windows. Before he was done shedding the miniscule light around the room, he saw another stairway. He climbed up to a landing, where the stairs turned and went up another flight. He followed the steps, came upon a wall, slid it and found himself in a closet full of linen, towels, toilet tissue and cleaning materials. There was a door that opened to the upstairs hallway.

'Damn,' Cross said, now back in light. He remembered a trip to Charleston and a tour through a home built well before the civil war. What was astonishing then – and now – was that there were a number of back stairways behind the walls. They were unfinished, certainly not meant to be seen. They led to the kitchen and to the sleeping quarters of the slaves who served the household. They served almost invisibly, never using the main stairs, slipping in and out of rooms through closets so no one would see them making beds, cleaning fireplaces, lighting lanterns and drawing the drapery.

It was becoming clear to him now.

The Taupins lived rare and strange lives and needed to keep secrets. His thoughts were interrupted by a sound downstairs – a door or window shutting, perhaps. He had only to find out if the person doing the shutting had just left or just arrived. The situation seemed to demand both speed and caution. He chose speed, taking the stairs two at a time on his way down. But he was not fast enough.

He stood in the area between the living room and the kitchen-family room area, understanding more, putting the pieces together. Even so, it was difficult to shake the feeling that he was lost, that the future was hopeless. Whoever escaped from the house bore Cross's last chance.

He went to the window and looked out again. He looked at the boats, the frolicking good time of folks on a wholesome Midwest summer's day at the lake. He saw the Taupin's seaplane bobbing at the dock. Every last piece of the puzzle fell into place.

He found her there, in the plane, hiding in the back, under a tarp. It made sense. The girl had nowhere to go. Who would she trust? The neighbors? She had stayed by the house, going in for food and hiding in the plane when the house had visitors. She was obviously terrified, probably of him, probably of the prospect of being deported.

The drive back was difficult. He used the Taupin's still active phone line to call Kowalski and tell him what he was doing. While the young woman was convinced – she no doubt felt she had no choice – to accompany Cross back to Indianapolis, suspicion and fear showed in her eyes and cut deep across her face.

They met at Kowalski's office downtown, across from the 28-story box that housed the bureaucracy that ran the city and county including the police and the courts.

Kowalski had rounded up a professional translator, hooked up a small tape recorder, had a basket of sandwiches and sodas, and had calming music playing in the background.

Cross sat with them, listening to the young Carolina Perez tell her story:

The two women were cousins. Alejandra Toledo Perez was the woman who disappeared, she said. The two of them were running from death threats. The Perez family ran afoul of a Colombian paramilitary organization and were directed to an organization that apparently specialized in finding safe havens for people on the run. Often this meant a period of illegal status in the new host country.

She was told there would be a period of time when her freedom would be abridged, but she had no idea that she would be treated the way the Taupins had treated her. Was she ever forced into sexual situations? Kowalski asked through the translator. No. How did she find Raymond Taupin? He was rarely at the lake and ignored her. On the other hand Mrs Taupin was an 'evil' woman. She would slap her and poke her when Carolina didn't understand the request or reacted too slowly.

And Alejandra, what happened to her? Kowalski asked. One day she disappeared. Nothing was said.

Kowalski showed her photographs of E. V. Lancaster. He was the one who worked with the organization to place both of them with the Taupins. Kowalski showed her a photograph of Marshall Talbot. She nodded. She saw him sometimes with the Taupin's daughter. Did she see the young man with Alejandra at any time? No, she replied, but she saw him the day Alejandra disappeared.

Carolina asked what was going to happen to her. Kowalski told her he was a lawyer. He would see to it that she would have an immigration attorney and that meanwhile he could guarantee she wouldn't be deported any time soon. She was a material witness. Kowalski also told her he would see to it that she would have some place to stay.

'It won't be like before,' he said, patting her

arm as the translator spoke those words in Spanish. 'I promise.'

There were more questions. Cross was impatient now. He stood, went to the little table offering soft drinks and sandwiches and popped open a Coke. The truth was sitting right there. He could taste the exoneration. But it was tainted with the notion that people like Taupin walked the earth, took what they wanted, discarded what they didn't. Yet the authorities treated him like royalty.

'I'm going out,' Cross said.

'Where?' Kowalski asked, looking worried. Cross had never seen him look worried.

'To do something foolish,' Cross said.

'I figured. What?'

'I need to talk to Sarah Taupin.'

'The daughter.'

'Yes.'

'She's either guilty, in serious danger or about to have the shock of her life.'

TWENTY-SIX

Shanahan tried to sleep, but kept waking up. It was nearing 3 a.m. when he decided to see if they were still serving at the bar downstairs. There were a few hangers-on, most of them in the throes of melancholy. He ordered a Chang beer because it had elephants on the label. He would tell no one that fact.

'I thought you closed at one, that's what the sign says,' Shanahan asked the rough-hewn Thai behind the bar.

'That's the law.' He smiled. 'There are many laws.'

Here's a guy, Shanahan thought, who was a lion tamer, keeping the belligerent locals, irrational criminals, and an assortment of crazy or clueless tourists from killing each other on the premises. It took a special kind of personality and a special kind of knowledge to do that. The other thing that wandered through Shanahan's mind was that the world was a small place. There were bars like this everywhere, places where outsiders, people off the grid, people who had nothing in common with the folks with regular jobs and reality show addictions, gathered.

The old detective was a long way from that glowing moment that drinkers feel, that 'lit' period before caring slips away. He had no trouble identifying Channarong standing at the entrance to the bar, looking around. When he saw Shanahan he jumped a bit, then waved and headed toward the old detective's table.

'I didn't expect you to be awake,' he said, a tired smile on his face. 'I'm glad.'

'I'm not. Didn't expect to see you. A drink?'

'No, thank you.' He sat. 'I came down because I was concerned. I couldn't locate the real Billy the Kid and from what you told me, I suspect there's something wrong.'

Shanahan nodded.

'I take responsibility for my recommendations,' he said.

'Thank you.'

'You're not hurt?' he asked.

'No. The maid died.'

Channarong shook his head. 'Have you located your brother?'

'Not really,' Shanahan said, equivocating on purpose. 'Maybe you can help.'

'Sure.'

Shanahan took a hit of his beer. 'How'd you find me?'

'You weren't where you were supposed to be. The owner told me the story. So close, you know, we never know, do we?' He looked at Shanahan. 'Anyway you're becoming a legend

286

around here now. And people talk about such things.'

'It's not a big place, is it?'

'Yet it appears people can get lost if they want to.'

'You have something specific?' Shanahan asked.

'Just wanted to let you know I was here. That I'm willing to help. Breakfast maybe?'

'Sure.'

'Coffee Shop at the Expat Hotel at nine?'

'OK.'

The Expat, on Pee Road, was cheery – another of those places that could be anywhere, but it was in Phuket and inland a bit from the beach on a dead-end *soi*. Shanahan thought Channarong picked the coffee shop for its western-accommodating breakfast menu. Making Shanahan feel 'at home' was unnecessary but considerate, he thought. The inside was dominated by red, a kind of American wholesome country look tempered by the Thai mind. He arrived early intentionally and had finished his first cup of coffee and got through the newspaper before Channarong got there at the agreed-upon time.

'Decided on a little vacation?' Shanahan asked as Channarong, looking fresh and pressed, slid into the other side of the booth.

'Why not enjoy my work,' he said.

'Anything new in Bangkok?' A moment of

puzzlement crossed Channarong's face. 'Any new word on Fritz?'

He shook his head 'no.' 'And Maureen, where is your beautiful friend?'

'Back home,' Shanahan said. 'Work. Clients. She was feeling guilty.'

Channarong didn't buy it but he didn't argue. 'Do you have any idea who is trying to kill you?'

'I don't know. Someone who doesn't want me to find Fritz.'

Channarong nodded.

The charming waitress came. Channarong ordered tea and something called *johk*. Shanahan ordered scrambled eggs and toast.

The *johk* turned out to be some sort of porridge with an egg floating on top.

'I couldn't call you,' Channarong said. 'I was worried that somehow I wasn't living up to our agreement.'

'And that agreement?'

'To help you find your brother.'

'You're off the hook, Channarong. You've done all you can do. I can reimburse you for your trip, but cannot continue to pay for services.'

'It appears you are in danger.'

'All the more reason to end the relationship.'

He nodded, more in the sense that he understood, not that he agreed.

The two of them talked very little and when they were done with breakfast, they shook hands. Channarong refused any money to pay for his trip down. It wasn't part of the agreement, he said. He couldn't take anything. As he turned to go, Shanahan stopped him.

'Why are you here, Channarong?'

Channarong smiled, put his hands together in that prayerful way, and left.

TWENTY-SEVEN

As was often the case, Cross acted in opposition to the little voice inside him that said, 'Don't do this.' The little voice also called Cross 'stupid' and deserving of the horrible things that would happen to him.

He drove to Woodruff Place, Center Drive. He believed that Sarah Taupin would go there, not to Fishers to be with her father and certainly not to the lake. He believed that she, at least intuitively, knew her father was capable of cold and calculating acts to get what he wanted. With her mother gone, he believed she would be more comfortable on her own.

Standing on the porch, looking through the screen door, and seeing her packing boxes, he realized he was not completely right, merely right enough. She was there, but she had no plans to stay.

He knocked lightly on the wood frame of the door. It rattled a bit. She jumped. She had been lost in her own thoughts and she looked toward the doorway as if she expected a tiger.

Sarah flicked on the porch light. She didn't

recognize Cross.

'Yes?'

'My name is Cross. I'm a private investigator.'

She may not have recognized his face, but she did his name. She froze.

'I believe your life may be in danger.'

He had no more than uttered those words than he saw Raymond Taupin enter the living room from the hall. He held a cell phone to his ear.

'Come away from the door,' he said to Sarah and then apparently interrupted by an operator, said, 'Hello, yes, my name is Raymond Taupin.' After telling them that the man who murdered his wife was at the door, he provided the Woodruff Place address.

Cross wasn't sure, but he thought he saw a small, grim smile cross Taupin's poker face. It didn't matter.

'Your father killed your mother,' Cross said.

Sarah didn't move.

'Come away from the door,' Raymond said, flipping his cell phone shut. 'The police will deal with him.'

'I know you don't want to believe me, but I have a witness. And you, like your mother, are a detail that needs taken care of. You need the protection of the police.'

'He's a lunatic, Sarah. Four bodies. Your mother, for Christ's sake. Come away from the door.' He moved toward her. 'Shut the door and lock it now.'

'Sarah, I'm not sure why your father killed them, but he did. I think you should come outside, get away from him. Please, for your own safety.'

Taupin reached what appeared to be a zombie Sarah. He shut the inner door without even glancing at the detective. Cross could hear the locks click into place. He moved to the three steps on the porch and sat facing the street, waiting. There were streetlamps on the broad grassy median that ran the length of Middle Drive. It was so quiet now. He shut his eyes and listened to the night, hoping to hear approaching sirens, but heard only the faint sound of traffic on Tenth Street, blocks away.

He pulled out his cell and punched in the number for Lieutenant Collins.

He knew full well that Taupin was capable of killing his daughter – and that he now had Cross's visit as cover. 'Yes,' Taupin would say, 'that man killed my entire family.'

Collins's rings ended with a voice telling him to leave a message.

'Taupin is with his daughter. I have reason to believe he might kill her.'

There were sirens now. Getting louder.

A black Ford Victoria and several patrol cars pulled up. But Cross was deeply disappointed. It was Swann, not Collins who approached him, ordering the uniforms to get inside the house with whatever means necessary.

'I thought this was Collins's case,' Cross said.

'There's "was" and there's "is."'

'I see.'

Swann was unlike either Collins or Rafferty, but like most cops. His suit was just a little wrinkled and too tight, bought no doubt a few years earlier, before he put on the inevitable few pounds a decade. His tie had been pulled away from his neck and the top button of his shirt was no longer buttoned. However lax about his dress, Swann was wound pretty tight by the rules. Cross would have bet his life that Swann had never taken a bribe, never looked the other way. He was by the book and in that way also contrasted both Collins and Rafferty. That it was Swann who responded was an indication that Saddler's long leash had been replaced with a short chain and a choker ordered from higher up.

'What are you doing here?' Swann asked, one foot on the second step.

'I came to warn Sarah that her life was in danger.'

He shook his head, looked at the sky. Not getting an answer from above he leaned down, putting his face inches from Cross's. 'You are accused of killing his wife, his son-in-law, two of his staffers and an unknown woman...'

'The maid from the lake house. A Colombian woman.'

'You're coming in,' he said, but his train of thought was hijacked by the discussions inside the house.

293

Cross used the moment to call Kowalski.

'Going downtown,' Cross said.

'You know,' Kowalski said, 'we don't have an uptown, do we? Some places have an uptown as well as a downtown.'

'Swann seems to be in charge.'

'Shit,' Kowalski said.

'Haven't you given Saddler the tape?'

'To her office, I did. I'm not sure she's had a chance to hear it.'

'Can we move this along a little bit?'

'I'll meet you downtown. What's going on at Woodruff Place?'

'Taupin's here to protect his daughter.'

'Dad of the year.'

This time there was no conference room. They were in an interrogation room – the size of a closet. Kowalski leaned back in the corner of the dingy little room. Swann's jacket was off and the tail of his white shirt had escaped from his waist. He either didn't notice or didn't care.

'You say Taupin pulled all of this off,' he said, 'but Taupin's passport indicates he was in Mexico City before, after and during the first two murders.'

'He's the type to have it done,' Kowalski said.

'Let Cross do the talking, OK.'

'He's the type to have it done,' Cross said. 'Lieutenant please, talk to your colleagues. We've got a recorded statement from Taupin's maid that says she saw me taped to the chair

294

when Mrs Taupin was murdered.'

'So you say. But your only witness is your attorney, remember? And now you've got some third-world, illegal immigrant testifying in Spanish about something you probably told her to say. Is that about right?' Swann didn't wait for an answer. 'We have you with both sets of bodies and God knows what went on with Edelman. I count five deaths and you look good for all of them.'

'So what's with Saddler and Collins?' Kowalski asked.

'Yesterday's news,' Swann said. 'Why don't you make it easier on all of us and just tell us what happened? What is it you've got against Taupin?'

'Didn't even know who Taupin was until I was set up with the corpses.'

'DA says it's you,' Swann said. 'Arraignment tomorrow.'

'News at eleven,' Kowalski said.

'What?'

'Play the tape on the news.'

'I can get a gag order in three seconds,' said a skinny man in a dark suit, slipping in the door.

'The DA himself,' Kowalski said.

'Hi Kowalski.'

'Hello professor.'

'Cross here is trying to tell me that Raymond Taupin has guns for hire,' Swann said to the DA.

'You've been watching too many movies,

295

Cross,' the DA said.

'And Mrs Taupin?' Cross asked.

'At the lake. Have phone calls, the timing of which would not allow for Mrs Taupin to be in Indianapolis at the time of death.'

The knock on the door was a surprise. Collins walked in, all dressed for an evening out. With him was Sarah Taupin, looking like she wanted to crawl in a hole.

'Getting kind of crowded in here,' Swann said. 'What's going on?'

The door had yet to be closed and it wasn't until Lauren Saddler came in, looking like the cat who swallowed the canary.

'This game is usually played in a phone booth or a Volkswagen,' Swann said. 'What's going on?'

'You want to tell them, Sarah?' Saddler asked. She glanced at Cross.

'My mother shot my husband and Alejandra Perez.'

'Why?' Swann asked.

'It was inevitable. Marshall was very devoted to human rights and my mother thought only certain people had them. They fought over it many times. This time was too much. She slapped Alejandra. And Marshall said he was going to report her and that he'd see to it that she and my father would do time.'

'She walked into the den and got her shotgun,' Sarah said.

'Hers?' the DA asked.

'Handed down from her father.'

'Yes.' Sarah's voice was small, a little girl's. She was terrified.

'You saw her shoot them?'

'No, but I saw her march them out. It was night. She marched them down to the water.'

'You didn't try to stop her?' Swann asked.

'Smart lady,' Kowalski said. 'She marches the two out into the lake, shoots them while they're waist deep in the water. No blood to clean up at the house. No splatter. Bodies are close to the plane and with the water helping out with gravity are easier to maneuver.'

'Your mother is that cold?' Swann asked.

Sarah just looked at them. 'You don't know them.' She shook her head as if trying to shake sense into it. 'And I thought she was just going to send them away.'

'Why did you come forward now?' the DA asked.

'When Mr Cross came to my door tonight and I saw him and I knew he was going to be punished for it. And then when he said my father killed my mother, I had to think about that. I had to consider what would happen. It was too much. It was really too much. And I knew he did it. Why would this man,' she pointed to Cross, 'kill my family? And what would happen to me if my father found out that I knew? And it was a matter of time before he would know that I knew.'

'We have a call placed from your lake

landline phone to a person who acknowledges she received a call from Mrs Taupin at that time.'

'The plane,' Cross said.

'Mrs Taupin has a pilot's license. It's her plane that's tied up on Lake Wawasee. She can bring the bodies down and return in a very short time,' Kowalski said.

'You'll probably find a call from Raymond to Edelman that night.'

'Why would Edelman play this game?' Swann asked.

'Taupin held Edelman's paper. Edelman lost his wife already and Taupin could take his business any time he wanted,' Cross said. 'Get a forensic accountant to look at his books. There's a safe behind the big fish. Poor Edelman probably did kill himself. He had nothing to live for.'

Swann threw up his hands.

The DA was conspicuous by his silence.

'Why did Taupin kill his wife?'

'She got him into this mess and that act would hang over Raymond for as long she was around to tell the story,' Cross said, looking at Sarah Taupin. 'I'm sorry.'

She shrugged. 'It's not much of a family.'

'If Mrs Taupin went down as the murderer, he was done in the community,' Cross continued. 'All his moral high handedness was a pose anyway, but it couldn't withstand this kind of scandal – murder, illegal immigrants, abuse.

But if she were murdered then he'd have the sympathy of the community. He simply cleaned up all the details. Except for Carolina. And he would have killed her if he could have found her that day. If Kowalski hadn't come along, I'd be dead too, unable to tell tales, and blamed for all of the deaths. He'd be completely in the clear.'

'Where is Taupin?' the DA asked.

'Sitting out front, thinking everything is all right,' Collins said. Cross was glad Sarah could not see the lieutenant's grin.

'Sarah needs protection,' Kowalski said.

'Yes, we know,' Saddler said. 'She'll remain here with Lieutenant Swann as we exit. Once we have Taupin in custody, Sarah will be released. Then it depends on the judge in the morning. Right?' She looked at the DA.

He nodded agreement before shaking his head in frustration. Unpleasant work remained in front of him.

'Free to go?' Cross asked.

Saddler nodded. 'Behave yourself.'

Cross and Kowalski exited the crowded little room and went out. A uniformed officer stood a few feet away from Raymond Taupin who sat in the guest chair at an empty desk.

'You want to catch something to eat at the Slippery Noodle?' Kowalski asked Cross.

'Good idea.' He stopped by Taupin and moved in front of the man. 'Bring you back anything? Hamburger maybe.'

Taupin blinked a few times and glanced away. But, Cross thought, the man had to know that something had just gone terribly wrong. A reptile to the end.

The place was crowded. Serious drinkers in the front room, music lovers in a large back room, down the long hallway. Blues sounds found their way toward them, heavily filtered through the loud conversations and sounds of dining clatter.

Settled in, Kowalski took a deep breath. 'You know, this whole fucking thing came about because Taupin was too cheap to pay a living wage to his help.'

'I doubt if his connection to Colombia was just a couple of apparently expendable maids.'

'Let's eat, drink and be merry,' Kowalski said.

TWENTY-EIGHT

Shanahan had a sense that this was going to be an odd day. It started with the surprise visit from Channarong. After calling to make sure Maureen made it back all right and he had found some less colorful clothing, he made it back to his quarters around noon. The Germans occupied their usual table but paid no attention to Shanahan's arrival. Their conversation was quiet, intimate, conspiratorial. Even as Shanahan sat through his first two beers of the day, the usually obnoxious group was restrained.

He called Maureen.

Kowalski had picked her up from the airport, had Einstein and Casey with him, which was odd enough because they had been put in Cross's care; but Kowalski seemed distracted and somewhat evasive, she said. The animals seemed fine.

'He's a lawyer,' Shanahan told her.

She was tired, jet-lagged she told him and he held on to that as the explanation for the lack of real personal connection. He didn't like the alternative.

The overhead fans in the bar recycled the heat

but at least suggested movement. The beach was without combers, the street between beach and bar without motorbikes and tuk-tuks. The bar would have to make its rent with just the two tables of customers. Shanahan decided to make it harder on the owners. He went upstairs, locked the door. He checked his revolver to make sure it was loaded and put it on the table beside the bed. He looked out the window, which overlooked the back of the bar. It would be difficult for anyone to get to the second floor.

He took off his shoes and crawled on to the bed. He had little sleep last night, getting up early for his breakfast meeting. And he thought little was done for good or evil during the big heat of the day. He wanted to be sharp for later, sharp as he could anyway.

Though Shanahan slept for several hours, it would be hours before darkness. When he awoke he was covered with sweat. He had been many places like this in his lifetime, places so hot and humid you worked up a sweat without even moving. He'd been to worse places, he thought. He remembered one island assignment where the flies wouldn't fly. He showered, dressed.

When he came down, there were a few people taking refuge in the bar. The Germans had gone. Shanahan didn't want to eat at the bar. He found a tuk-tuk driver and had the young man drive him back over to Patong Beach so he could be among people and have a broader choice of dining options.

Once in the heart of the beach business district Shanahan *was* with people. A crush of tourists, mostly, *farang*, sat outside in various places, but these places weren't the little French or Italian cafes Shanahan remembered in his travels. The atmosphere was more like a German beer garden. And if that weren't enough, the sound of German being spoken – loudly – was all too common.

In the swirl of people entering and leaving the confines of the particular restaurant's domain Shanahan had chosen, he saw the cat paw man – the character who, in impatience or duress, splayed his fingers as cats sometimes do with their claws.

He'd only glimpsed the man, impatient to get by a couple of corpulent Caucasians. Instead of an elegant suit as before, he wore denim more in keeping with bargain-seeking tourists. Eventually the man broke free. If Shanahan had been willing to knock over a few tourists, he might have been able to follow him. He also hadn't known what that would do for him other than satisfy a little curiosity.

While he ate, he couldn't help but think that the man's presence was simply part of a gathering of interested parties. The German foursome was around somewhere. Channarong had returned. Now the man with the odd and obsessive tic had returned. Who was who? Were the Bangkok police involved? Mr White, the nightclub owner? Why had Channarong come down? Was he honor-bound to do so?

Conclusion: Shanahan didn't know who they were or precisely what they were doing here. He knew both imprecisely. At least some of them were there for the ruby. And they probably knew more about it than he did. All Shanahan knew was that his brother disappeared into the night and that the presence of all these folks meant that whatever was going to happen would be happening soon.

In the heat, Shanahan preferred the lighter Thai beer to his usual choice. He would have preferred Japanese beer to the Thai brew, but he was happy enough as the cool liquid slid down his throat. He had nearly finished when the kid who rented him the revolver appeared at the table.

'Your brother says to meet him where you last saw him.'

'Where is that?'

'He didn't tell me that.'

'Why should I believe you? You're not who you pretended to be.'

The kid reached in his pocket, pulled out a scrap of paper, on which was written:

I know you followed me down to the beach. Meet me tonight as the sun sets. Remember when we used to go swimming in the moonlight and you were afraid to get in the water?

Shanahan nodded. Fritz knew Shanahan would want verification. The kid waited. Shanahan gave him a couple hundred baht. The kid left.

The sun was falling. It wouldn't be long before it would be gone. He settled the check and went down to the beach. The tourists would be disappointed, he thought. The sky was gunmetal gray and darker shades of navy. The tropical Pacific sunset looked more like the coming of a cold Atlantic night. Shanahan feigned an accidental dropping of the gun-toting bag he carried so that he could look back without being obvious. He saw no one, but knew it didn't necessarily mean he was alone.

Eventually, Shanahan began to see a human shape form in the half-light. Walking in the sand was slow work and he occasionally had to step away from the tide that rolled in a dark, shiny mirror of the sky on the stretch of sand. For just a moment, he allowed himself to think that he was making footprints on the sky.

Though he knew he could be walking to his and to his brother's death – this was, in fact, serious, serious business – he felt a surprising lightness. One way or another all of this, he believed, was about to end. And if he survived it, he'd be on his way home, back to Maureen.

He was closing in on the dark figure ahead. And it appeared the dark figure was moving toward him. Shanahan slipped the revolver out of the bag and held it behind him as he walked.

'Come quickly,' Fritz said. 'I have no time to waste. None.' He motioned impatiently with his arms and Shanahan picked up the pace.

The gap between them narrowed.

'Why did you want me to come?' Shanahan asked.

'To say goodbye.' Fritz looked around.

It seemed like a good idea to see if there were others on the beach with them. Shanahan checked all directions.

'You have the ruby?'

'Of course.' He pulled a small leather pouch from his jacket pocket, plucked out a rough stone. Showed it almost dramatically. 'I'm going out now and I won't be back.' He put the ruby in his coat pocket, without the pouch. 'My ship is coming in Dietrich, literally and figuratively. I meet it out there...'

Fritz came to his older brother, hugged him briefly.

'Take care, my brother. Thanks for seeking me out.' He saw the revolver. 'That's not meant to...'

'No. Things have been dangerous, lately.'

Fritz nodded, still looking around. He looked up at the sky and then out into the bay. He went to his black rubber raft and pulled it out. In the water he pulled the small motor out of the rubber so that it was mounted on the back. He pulled the string and it started.

Four people came down from the dune, running and falling and yelling in German. Fritz had the boat in the water and was heading out by the time they hit the beach. The Germans rushed in the water after him, but as they went deeper, the water slowed them. The raft was moving too fast. One, gun hand outstretched, fired. Shanahan shot him. The other three turned and froze in place. Only one gun among them. That was the good news of the moment. The bad is that Shanahan noticed two other boats, one large and one small, heading toward Fritz's motorized raft.

Fritz stood, wobbled a bit and fell in the boat, arms and legs flailing.

Was he shot? Shanahan hadn't heard any other shots. The boats closed in. Fritz's raft started moving in circles. Shanahan couldn't recognize who they were, but the men on the two boats shouted at each other angrily and at Fritz. The boats came closer to each other. Shanahan could see the flash from the muzzle of a pistol and the man on the larger boat dropped on the deck. The boat kept going, perhaps without anyone to steer her.

The shooter brought his tug-like craft close to Fritz's. He dropped anchor and boarded the raft and tried to subdue Fritz who, during what appeared to be some form of modern dance, fell into the water.

The man did not follow Fritz into the deep. He stayed on Fritz's raft. In the quiet night it was clear that the man was trying to start the small outboard engine and couldn't.

Shanahan kicked off his shoes and ran into the water, swimming as forcefully as he could. The very flailing that caused his brother to fall in the water was now, apparently, keeping him choking but afloat. The tide cooperated by bringing him in.

Even so, it took every bit of Shanahan's strength to get to him, leaving none to get back. It was not easy swimming and trying to hold on to someone mid-seizure. Shanahan could no longer keep track of anything other than to hold his brother, do a version of the side stroke and dog paddle, and keep the shoreline in mind.

He knew he wasn't going to make it. And the question was would he dump his brother and try to make it back or almost guarantee both their deaths by trying to go ashore. It was a decision he ended up not having to make. The motorized raft came up beside them. The man told Shanahan to grab hold of the side. Fritz's body suddenly went limp. The epileptic seizure was over. Fritz was either dead or in a deep sleep.

Eventually they made it to shore. Shanahan recognized the man who operated the raft. It was the man with the cat-paw hands. As the raft was pulled up on the beach and Fritz collapsed like a huge bag of rice, the Cat-paw man pulled a gun from his long, loose raincoat. Shanahan pressed a finger against his brother's neck, searching for a pulse. He looked around. The Germans had left, leaving their leader's body behind. There was a pulse. It was surprisingly strong. From what his brother had described, the sleep was part of the sequence of the seizure. He would shake out of control, sleep, awake in a fugue – a dull confused state of consciousness – and then to consciousness with no memory of anything after the onset of the seizure.

Cat-paw man motioned in the dimmest of light for Shanahan to move back away from his brother. The man began searching Fritz's pockets, while looking at Shanahan, who had just witnessed Cat-paw kill a man. The search became more hurried as he was running out of places to look, then frantic. Fritz was nearly naked and he had been inspected from mouth to shoes by the time Cat-paw concluded the ruby wasn't there.

Shanahan's revolver, which he had dropped on the beach when he went into the water, was gone or buried. He spotted three shapes coming toward them. The Germans coming back with weapons? The police?

It was becoming more and more difficult to see. But the Cat-paw man had gone over to the raft and began feeling around inside. He had lost interest in anything other than the search.

Shanahan recognized Channarong first and then Billy the Kid, the same young man Channarong had once described as some sort of imposter. One of the Germans was with them.

'You have it,' the Cat-paw man said loudly, turning around, surprised by the sudden appearance of additional company. Billy the Kid pulled up a shot gun from his side and aimed it at the Catpaw man.

'I'm going to search you, Mr Shanahan,' Channarong said. 'Please relax and there will be no trouble.'

Shanahan raised his tired arms in a gesture that said, 'be my guest.' And Channarong began.

'You sure he had it?' Channarong asked the German.

'Yes. He held it up. He had it in his hands. We saw it through the night goggles.'

'OK, nothing here.' He took the shotgun from Billy and told Billy to search the Cat-paw man. And Channarong himself searched Fritz who continued in his heavy slumber. From there, Channarong searched the raft.

All efforts were fruitless. Channarong looked out into the bay. He shook his head.

He raised the shotgun and shot the Cat-paw man. It was quick and cold. He looked at Shanahan.

The German ran. It looked for a moment that Channarong was going to shoot him too. But he slowly lowered his rifle.

'He won't go to the police and his little gang is all busted up. Not a worry. As for you, Mr Shanahan,' Channarong said, 'go home.'

'Why did you shoot him?'

'He wouldn't have stopped. One day he would have me killed.'

'I thought you were working for me,' Shanahan said.

'I was.'

'You're working for someone else too.'

'I contracted with you to help you find your brother. I did. That's why you go free. I don't kill clients. I contracted with someone else to locate the ruby. That,' he said, 'I'm still working on. And I will find it.'

'And Fritz?'

'Fritz is no threat now. He's not in control of the ruby nor does he have ... what do you say ... a constituency. Nor do you. I'm not an evil man.' He shook his head.

'And the police?' Shanahan asked.

'You don't want to wait around. If you get them involved, I guarantee you that you won't fare well. You don't know the system. You've killed a man. You'd spend years here sorting this all out.'

Channarong had his boy Billy help Shanahan get Fritz up to Shanahan's room, where he slept for a few more hours. Shanahan had gone downstairs and got an early start on a cold beer. Technically, for him, it wasn't morning, it was night extended because he had yet to sleep.

Two of the remaining Germans, including the one from last night, sat at the table usually occupied by the four of them. They were subdued. There were a few others as well.

At one p.m. there was a tremendous howl

coming from upstairs. Shanahan started toward the stairway only to see his brother half-naked with the hair of a madman coming down the stairs with the ferocity of a charging rhinoceros.

'Where is my ruby?' he shouted. He grabbed Shanahan by the collar. 'Where is my ruby?'

'You lost it.'

'Lost it? Lost it? You took my ruby. Give it to me. Now.'

'If I had it and wanted to keep it, I wouldn't be here, Fritz.'

Fritz's blue eyes seemed to burn. He grew dangerously silent, dangerously white. Suddenly he flipped over a table, then another. That's when he saw the Germans and he charged them. Another table went flying and chairs were overturned. The Germans scattered.

He turned back to Shanahan. 'Who has it?'

'The sea,' Shanahan said.

Fritz fell back into a chair, head in hands. 'It's over. There's nothing left.'

Shanahan helped the bartender straighten up the place as Fritz walked like a robot back up the steps.

'Sorry,' Shanahan said to the bartender.

'I understand,' the man said. 'He wanted it too much.'

'So you know what happened?'

'Everybody on the island knows what happened.'

TWENTY-NINE

Cross spent two weeks with his parents and Maya. After a hard but welcome rain and the coming of September, the weather was perfect and he was able to complete the roof. It felt good to do physical work and to see something tangible at the end of the project. Next project, before winter, was to get the windows fixed, rip off and replace the bad wood and paint the house. The barn, never in great shape, would no doubt slip into complete decrepitude in a decade. And that simply was the way it was. It was already too far gone to fix.

Breakfasts were wonderful and lunch was, as the farmers have always done, really dinner – the big meal of the day. Supper, the evening meal, was light. He was pulled back into the city a couple of times over the Taupin affair. In spite of the abundance of food, the physical work had worked wonders. He had renewed energy and the little paunch that worried him more than he would ever admit, had diminished. He enjoyed his time with Maya and she seemed to like having him around, though that was something she'd never admit.

He'd had lunch twice with Lauren Saddler, the first time at Shapiro's, a busy, brightly-lit deli. The second time was at a dark, little bar downtown.

Taupin would plea, she suggested. She also suggested Cross get a new mattress.

He left Eaton reluctantly, but it was important to drum up some business. He had been busy, but he was his only client and that's no way to run a successful enterprise.

Shanahan's trip was now at a comfortable distance in his mind. His time was being taken up by morning coffee, newspaper reading and gardening. He also took long afternoon walks with Casey usually down to Ellenberger Park. With no business of his own, he kind of enjoyed getting dinner ready on the weekdays when they weren't dining out. He and Maureen discovered a couple of new restaurants – a great Cajun place, Papa Roux, on the far eastside, and R. Bistro on Massachusetts Avenue. Life had settled back in. On the other hand, there were changes: Harry had definitely decided to close his place on December 31 and didn't renew his ad in the Yellow Pages.

One Tuesday afternoon, Maureen came home from work and brought the mail in, looking long and hard at one of the envelopes.

'Who do you know in Sydney, Australia?' she asked as Shanahan chopped up some garlic.

'No one.'

314

'For you,' she said, handing him the envelope. There was no return address.

Dear Dietrich,

Don't try to track me down just yet. This letter was sent to a friend who then mailed it on to you.

Once you arrived and we had a chance to talk, I knew what kind of man you are. I'm so proud to have you as a brother and I knew also that you would be there for me. You were. I couldn't have done it without you, though there was so much pain putting it where sun don't shine – and then getting it out again. I wish I could have included you in the plan; but if my take on you is correct, you might have had a moral issue with me taking the ruby, not to mention the theatricality of the undertaking. Wasn't sure you were Academy Award material. So I counted on you being loyal and honest and tough. And you were.

In a couple of years, if we're both still alive, I'll get in touch. I've got a wonderful place for you to visit for as long as you'd like. The only thing that would make that better is if you bring your beautiful girlfriend.

As soon as the heat is off...
Fritz

After he read it, he handed the letter to Maureen. She began reading. Shanahan went back to the garlic. When she was done reading, she smiled big. She folded the letter and stuffed it back into the envelope.

'I got played,' Shanahan said.

'Well it took a Shanahan to fool a Shanahan,' Maureen said. 'I think that says a lot.'

'He trusted a seventy-year-old out-of-shape man to swim out into the sea and save him, but he didn't trust me to be part of the charade.'

'For someone who hadn't seen you in sixty years,' Maureen said, 'I'd say he knows you pretty well.'

'That was supposed to sound like a compliment, but it wasn't, was it?'

'I love you just like you are. What's for dinner?'

'Minced chicken, some hot green peppers and fish sauce.'

'Do you miss it?'

'Thailand? Oddly yes.'

'A little adventure is good for the soul,' she said. 'Where are we going next?'

'That little table over there, where we'll have a pleasant dinner at home.'

'I have one question about the little beach party you had on Phuket.'

'OK.'

'Who were all of those people shooting at each other?'

Shanahan shook his head, 'Fritz cleared that up for me. Channarong was working with people in the police department – not to recover the ruby for the rightful owner, but to share in the profits. The Germans had connections with a guy who owned a nightclub, basically, a pimp who had had dealings with Fritz before in the ruby business. The guy with the strange flaying or stretching his fingers worked for the Burmese government who had been denied their share of any transactions in rubies.'

'So, Fritz was playing with fire.'

'He was.'

'So are you,' Maureen said with a thin, knowing grin.

'Runs in the family apparently.'

THIRTY

Harry was behind the bar making Maureen a second rum and tonic. Rafferty and Collins sat at the bar, on stools close to the booth occupied by Shanahan, Maureen, Kowalski and Cross. The four in the booth were tossing around some cards in a game called Euchre. There were at least ten customers seated at the bar besides the two cops. Old customers who, after tonight, had no reason to leave their small apartments or dilapidated rooms in the collapsing neighborhood.

That's when Lauren Saddler walked in.

'I heard you were here,' she said to Cross. The big-screen TV was on, showing fireworks from places in the world that brought in the New Year before it came to Indiana. But all eyes were on Cross. His face showed amused confusion.

'You won't have to testify at Raymond Taupin's trial,' she said.

'He plead out?' Kowalski asked.

'Bled out,' Lauren said.

'He was allowed to attend his father's funeral. Crossing the street to the church a big, black,

318

mean-looking Chrysler came from nowhere and ran him down.'

Cross looked at Kowalski. Neither spoke.

'Tinted windows. Didn't see who was driving,' she said.

'You want a drink?' he asked.

'Yeah I could do with one. Martini.'

'A Martini, Harry.' Cross shouted.

'There's isn't an olive for miles,' Harry shouted back.

'I'm a simple girl,' Lauren said. 'A twist of lemon, maybe.'

Harry turned and for the first time saw Lauren.

'Not on your life,' Cross told her.

Rafferty put a dollar bill in the jukebox.

'If I'd known it was for you,' Harry said to Lauren, 'I would have turned myself into an olive tree.'

It was Etta James' voice that filled Harry's dim, down-on-its luck bar. 'At last,' she sang.

'I see Harry has thrown me over for a younger woman,' Maureen said.

'The man has no taste,' Shanahan said.

'So how about a last dance before the new year begins?' she asked.

The two of them found a little space down at the end of the bar, by the door, and danced by the shadowy figures of old guys who had occupied those same stools for the last couple of decades.

'You want to join them on the dance floor?'

Cross asked Lauren Saddler.

She looked at him, started to say something, but stopped. She tried to repress a smile. 'Yeah let's dance.'

'Gotta go. Getting too weird in here.' Collins said. 'Speaking of weird, you coming with me Rafferty? This isn't your style, I suspect.'

Rafferty said nothing. Kowalski joined Harry at the bar.

One of the old guys, a silhouette on a stool yelled out: 'What's a guy gotta do to getta drink around here?'